# FUTURE PERFECT

# FUTURE PERFECT

## SIX STORIES OF GENETIC ENGINEERING

# NANCY KRESS

*an imprint of*

ARC
**MANOR**
Rockville, Maryland

ISBN:     978-1-61242-063-9

**www.PhoenixPick.com**
**Great Science Fiction & Fantasy**
**Free Ebook every month**

THE FLOWERS OF AULIT PRISON © Nancy Kress, 1996. First appeared in *ASIMOV'S SCIENCE FICTION*, October/November 1996

FIRST RITES © Nancy Kress, 2008. First appeared in *JIM BAEN'S UNIVERSE*, October 2008

TRINITY © Nancy Kress, 1984. First appeared in *ISAAC ASIMOV'S SCIENCE FICTION MAGAZINE*, October 1984

MARGIN OF ERROR © Nancy Kress, 1994. First appeared in *OMNI*, October 1994

DANCING ON AIR © Nancy Kress, 1993. First appeared in *ASIMOV'S SCIENCE FICTION*, July 1993

AND NO SUCH THINGS GROW HERE © Nancy Kress, 2001. First appeared in *ASIMOV'S SCIENCE FICTION*, June 2001

Published by Phoenix Pick
*an imprint of Arc Manor*
P. O. Box 10339
Rockville, MD 20849-0339
www.ArcManor.com

# CONTENTS

# THE FLOWERS OF AULIT PRISON

MY SISTER LIES SWEETLY on the bed across the room from mine. She lies on her back, fingers lightly curled, her legs stretched straight as elindel trees. Her pert little nose, much prettier than my own, pokes delicately into the air. Her skin glows like a fresh flower. But not with health. She is, of course, dead.

I slip out of my bed and stand swaying a moment, with morning dizziness. A Terran healer once told me my blood pressure was too low, which is the sort of nonsensical thing Terrans will sometimes say—like announcing the air is too moist. The air is what it is, and so am I.

What I am is a murderer.

I kneel in front of my sister's glass coffin. My mouth has that awful morning taste, even though last night I drank nothing stronger than water. Almost I yawn, but at the last moment I turn it into a narrow-lipped ringing in my ears that somehow leaves my mouth tasting worse than ever. But at least I haven't disrespected Ano. She was my only sibling and closest friend, until I replaced her with illusion.

"Two more years, Ano," I say, "less forty-two days. Then you will be free. And so will I."

Ano, of course, says nothing. There is no need. She knows as well as I the time until her burial, when she can be released from the chemicals and glass that bind her dead body and can rejoin our ancestors. Others I have known whose relatives were under atonement bondage said the bodies complained and recriminated, especially in dreams, making the house a misery. Ano is more considerate. Her corpse never troubles me at all. I do that to myself.

I finish the morning prayers, leap up, and stagger dizzily to the piss closet. I may not have drunk pel last night, but my bladder is nonetheless bursting.

At noon a messenger rides into my yard on a Terran bicycle. The bicycle is an attractive design, sloping, with interesting curves. Adapted for our market, undoubtedly. The messenger is less attractive, a surly boy probably in his first year of government service. When I smile at him, he looks away. He would rather be someplace else. Well, if he doesn't perform his messenger duties with more courteous cheer, he will be.

"Letter for Uli Pek Bengarin."

"I am Uli Pek Bengarin."

Scowling, he hands me the letter and pedals away. I don't take the scowl personally. The boy does not, of course, know what I am, any more than my neighbors do. That would defeat the whole point. I am supposed to pass as fully real, until I can earn the right to resume being so.

The letter is shaped into a utilitarian circle, very business-like, with a generic government seal. It could have come from the Tax Section, or Community Relief, or Processions and Rituals. But of course it hasn't; none of those sections would write to me until I am real again. The sealed letter is from Reality and Atonement. It's a summons; they have a job for me.

And about time. I have been home nearly six weeks since the last job, shaping my flowerbeds and polishing dishes and trying to paint a skyscape of last month's synchrony, when all six moons were visible at once. I paint badly. It is time for another job.

I pack my shoulder sack, kiss the glass of my sister's coffin, and lock the house. Then I wheel my bicycle—not, alas, as interestingly curved as the messenger's—out of its shed and pedal down the dusty road toward the city.

Frablit Pek Brimmidin is nervous. This interests me; Pek Brimmidin is usually a calm, controlled man, the sort who never replaces reality with illusion. He's given me my previous jobs with no fuss. But now he actually can't sit still; he fidgets back and forth across his small office, which is cluttered with papers, stone sculptures in an exaggerated style I don't like at all, and plates of half-eaten food. I don't comment on either the food or the pacing. I am fond of Pek Brimmidin, quite apart from my gratitude to him, which is profound. He was the official in R&A who voted to give me a chance to become real again. The other two judges voted for perpetual death, no chance of atonement. I'm not supposed to know this much detail about my own case, but I do. Pek Brimmidin is middle-aged, a stocky man whose neck fur has just begun to yellow. His eyes are gray, and kind.

"Pek Bengarin," he says, finally, and then stops.

"I stand ready to serve," I say softly, so as not to make him even more nervous. But something is growing heavy in my stomach. This does not look good.

"Pek Bengarin." Another pause. "You are an informer."

"I stand ready to serve our shared reality," I repeat, despite my astonishment. Of course I'm an informer. I've been an informer for two years and eighty-two days. I killed my sister, and I will be an informer until my atonement is over, I can be fully real again, and Ano can be released from death to join our ancestors. Pek Brimmidin knows this. He's assigned me every one of my previous informing jobs, from the first easy one in currency counterfeiting right through the last one, in baby stealing. I'm a very good informer, as Pek Brimmidin also knows. What's wrong with the man?

Suddenly Pek Brimmidin straightens. But he doesn't look me in the eye. "You are an informer, and the Section for Reality and Atonement has an informing job for you. In Aulit Prison."

So that's it. I go still. Aulit Prison holds criminals. Not just those who have tried to get away with stealing or cheating or child-snatching, which are, after all, normal. Aulit Prison holds those who are unreal, who have succumbed to the illusion that they are not part of shared common reality and so may do violence to the most concrete reality of others: their physical bodies. Maimers. Rapists. Murderers.

Like me.

I feel my left hand tremble, and I strive to control it and to not show how hurt I am. I thought Pek Brimmidin thought better of me. There is of course no such thing as partial atonement—one is either real or one is not—but a part of my mind nonetheless thought that Pek Brimmidin had recognized two years and eighty-two days of effort in regaining my reality. I have worked so hard.

He must see some of this on my face because he says quickly, "I am sorry to assign this job to you, Pek. I wish I had a better one. But you've been requested specifically by Rafkit Sarloe." Requested by the capital; my spirits lift slightly. "They've added a note to the request. I am authorized to tell you the informant job carries additional compensation. If you succeed, your debt will be considered immediately paid, and you can be restored at once to reality."

Restored at once to reality. I would again be a full member of World, without shame. Entitled to live in the real world of shared humanity, and to hold my head up with pride. And Ano could be buried, the artificial chemicals washed from her body, so that it could return to World and her sweet spirit could join our ancestors. Ano, too, would be restored to reality.

"I'll do it," I tell Pek Brimmidin. And then, formally, "I stand ready to serve our shared reality."

"One more thing, before you agree, Pek Bengarin." Pek Brimmidin is fidgeting again. "The suspect is a Terran."

I have never before informed on a Terran. Aulit Prison, of course, holds those aliens who have been judged unreal: Terrans, Fallers, the weird little Huhuhubs. The problem is that even after thirty years of ships coming to World, there is still considerable debate about whether *any* aliens are real at all. Clearly their bodies exist; after all, here they are. But their thinking is so disordered they might almost qualify as all being unable to recognize shared social reality, and so just as unreal as those poor empty children who never attain reason and must be destroyed.

Usually we on World just leave the aliens alone, except of course for trading with them. The Terrans in particular offer interesting objects, such as bicycles, and ask in return worthless items, mostly perfectly obvious information. But do any of the aliens have souls, capable of recognizing and honoring a shared reality with the souls of others? At the universities, the argument goes on. Also in market squares and pel shops, which is where I hear it. Personally, I think aliens may well be real. I try not to be a bigot.

I say to Pek Brimmidin, "I am willing to inform on a Terran."

He wiggles his hand in pleasure. "Good, good. You will enter Aulit Prison a Capmonth before the suspect is brought there. You will use your primary cover, please."

I nod, although Pek Brimmidin knows this is not easy for me. My primary cover is the truth: I killed my sister Ano Pek Bengarin two years and eighty-two days ago and was judged unreal enough for perpetual death, never able to join my ancestors. The only un-true part of the cover is that I escaped and have been hiding from the Section police ever since.

"You have just been captured," Pek Brimmidin continues, "and assigned to the first part of your death in Aulit. The Section re-cords will show this."

Again I nod, not looking at him. The first part of my death in Aulit, the second, when the time came, in the kind of chemical bondage that holds Ano. And never ever to be freed—*ever*. What if it were true? I should go mad. Many do.

"The suspect is named 'Carryl Walters.' He is a Terran healer. He murdered a World child, in an experiment to discover how real people's brains function. His sentence is perpetual death. But the Section believes that Carryl Walters was working with a group of World people in these experiments. That somewhere on World there is a group that's so lost its hold on reality that it would mur-der children to investigate science."

For a moment the room wavers, including the exaggerated swooping curves of Pek Brimmidin's ugly sculptures. But then I get hold of myself. I am an informer, and a good one. I can do this. I am redeeming myself, and releasing Ano. I am an informer.

"I'll find out who this group is," I say. "And what they're doing, and where they are."

Pek Brimmidin smiles at me. "Good." His trust is a dose of shared reality: two people acknowledging their common percep-tions together, without lies or violence. I need this dose. It is prob-ably the last one I will have for a long time.

How do people manage in perpetual death, fed on only solitary illusion?

Aulit Prison must be full of the mad.

Traveling to Aulit takes two days of hard riding. Somewhere my bicycle loses a bolt and I wheel it to the next village. The woman who runs the bicycle shop is competent but mean, the sort who gazes at shared reality mostly to pick out the ugly parts.

"At least it's not a *Terran* bicycle."

"At least," I say, but she is incapable of recognizing sarcasm.

"Sneaky soulless criminals, taking us over bit by bit. We should never have allowed them in. And the government is supposed to protect us from unreal slime, ha, what a joke. Your bolt is a non-standard size."

"Is it?" I say.

"Yes. Costs you extra."

I nod. Behind the open rear door of the shop, two little girls play in a thick stand of moonweed.

"We should kill all the aliens," the repairer says. "No shame in destroying them before they corrupt us."

"Eurummmn," I say. Informers are not supposed to make themselves conspicuous with political debate. Above the two children's heads, the moonweed bends gracefully in the wind. One of the little girls has long brown neck fur, very pretty. The other does not.

"There, that bolt will hold fine. Where you from?"

"Rafkit Sarloe." Informers never name their villages.

She gives an exaggerated shudder. "I would never visit the capital. Too many aliens. They destroy *our* participation in shared reality without a moment's thought! Three and eight, please."

I want to say *No one but you can destroy your own participation in shared reality*, but I don't. Silently I pay her the money.

She glares at me, at the world. "You don't believe me about the Terrans. But I know what I know!"

I ride away, through the flowered countryside. In the sky, only Cap is visible, rising on the horizon opposite the sun. Cap glows with a clear white smoothness, like Ano's skin.

The Terrans, I am told, have only one moon. Shared reality on their world is, perhaps, skimpier than ours: less curved, less rich, less warm.

Are they ever jealous?

Aulit prison sits on a flat plain inland from the South Coast. I know that other islands on World have their own prisons, just as they have their own governments, but only Aulit is used for the alien unreal, as well as our own. A special agreement among the governments of World makes this possible. The alien governments protest, but of course it does them no good. The unreal is the unreal, and far too painful and dangerous to have running around loose. Besides, the alien governments are far away on other stars.

Aulit is huge and ugly, a straight-lined monolith of dull red stone, with no curves anywhere. An official from R&A meets me and turns me over to two prison guards. We enter through a barred gate, my bicycle chained to the guards', and I to my bicycle. I am led across a wide dusty yard toward a stone wall. The guards of course don't speak to me; I am unreal.

My cell is square, twice my length on a side. There is a bed, a piss pot, a table, and a single chair. The door is without a window, and all the other doors in the row of cells are closed.

"When will the prisoners be allowed to be all together?" I ask, but of course the guard doesn't answer me. I am not real.

I sit in my chair and wait. Without a clock, it's difficult to judge time, but I think a few hours pass totally without event. Then a gong sounds and my door slides up into the ceiling. Ropes and pulleys, controlled from above, inaccessible from inside the cell.

The corridor fills with illusionary people. Men and women, some with yellowed neck fur and sunken eyes, walking with the shuffle of old age. Some young, striding along with that dangerous mixture of anger and desperation. And the aliens.

I have seen aliens before, but not so many together. Fallers, about our size but very dark, as if burned crisp by their distant star. They wear their neck fur very long and dye it strange bright colors, although not in prison. Terrans, who don't even have neck fur but instead fur on their heads, which they sometimes cut into fanciful curves—rather pretty. Terrans are a little intimidating because of their size. They move slowly. Ano, who had one year at the university before I killed her, once told me that the Terrans' world makes them feel lighter than ours does. I don't understand this, but Ano was very intelligent and so it's probably true. She also explained that Fallers, Terrans, and World people are somehow related far back in time, but this is harder to believe. Perhaps Ano was mistaken.

Nobody ever thinks Huhuhubs could be related to us. Tiny, scuttling, ugly, dangerous, they walk on all fours. They're covered with warts. They smell bad. I was glad to see only a few of them, sticking close together, in the corridor at Aulit.

We all move toward a large room filled with rough tables and chairs and, in the corner, a trough for the Huhuhubs. The food is already on the tables. Cereal, flatbread, elindel fruit—very basic, but nutritious. What surprises me most is the total absence of guards. Apparently prisoners are allowed to do whatever they wish to the food, the room, or each other, without interference. Well, why not? We aren't real.

I need protection, quickly.

I choose a group of two women and three men. They sit at a table with their backs to the wall, and others have left a respectful distance around them. From the way they group themselves, the oldest woman is the leader. I plant myself in front of her and look directly into her face. A long scar ridges her left cheek to disappear into grizzled neck fur.

"I am Uli Pek Bengarin," I say, my voice even but too low to be heard beyond this group. "In Aulit for the murder of my sister. I can be useful to you."

She doesn't speak, and her flat dark eyes don't waver, but I have her attention. Other prisoners watch furtively.

"I know an informer among the guards. He knows I know. He brings things into Aulit for me, in return for not sharing his name."

Still her eyes don't waver. But I see she believes me; the sheer outrage of my statement has convinced her. A guard who had already forfeited reality by informing—by violating shared reality—might easily turn it to less pernicious material advantage. Once reality is torn, the rents grow. For the same reason, she easily believes that I might violate my supposed agreement with the guard.

"What sort of things?" she says, carelessly. Her voice is raspy and thick, like some hairy root.

"Letters. Candy. Pel." Intoxicants are forbidden in prison; they promote shared conviviality, to which the unreal have no right.

"Weapons?"

"Perhaps," I say.

"And why shouldn't I beat this guard's name out of you and set up my own arrangement with him?"

"He will not. He is my cousin." This is the trickiest part of the cover provided to me by R&A Section; it requires that my would-be protector believe in a person who has kept enough sense of reality to honor family ties but will nonetheless violate a larger shared reality. I told Pek Brimmidin that I doubted that such a twisted state of mind would be very stable, and so a seasoned prisoner would not believe in it. But Pek Brimmidin was right and I was wrong. The woman nods.

"All right. Sit down."

She does not ask what I wish in return for the favors of my supposed cousin. She knows. I sit beside her, and from now on I am physically safe in Aulit Prison from all but her.

Next, I must somehow befriend a Terran.

This proves harder than I expect. The Terrans keep to themselves, and so do we. They are just as violent toward their own as all the mad doomed souls in Aulit; the place is every horror whispered by children trying to shock each other. Within a tenday I see two World men hold down and rape a woman. No one interferes. I see a Terran gang beat a Faller. I see a World woman knife another woman, who bleeds to death on the stone floor. This is the only time guards appear, heavily armored. A priest is with them. He wheels in a coffin of chemicals and immediately immerses the body so that it cannot decay to release the prisoner from her sentence of perpetual death.

At night, isolated in my cell, I dream that Frablit Pek Brimmidin appears and rescinds my provisional reality. The knifed, doomed corpse becomes Ano; her attacker becomes me. I wake from the dream moaning and weeping. The tears are not grief but terror. My life, and Ano's, hang from the splintery branch of a criminal alien I have not yet even met.

I know who he is, though. I skulk as close as I dare to the Terran groups, listening. I don't speak their language, of course, but Pek Brimmidin taught me to recognize the cadences of "Carryl Walters" in several of their dialects. Carryl Walters is an old Terran, with gray head fur cut in boring straight lines, wrinkled brownish skin, and sunken eyes. But his ten fingers—how do they keep the extra ones from tangling them up?—are long and quick.

It takes me only a day to realize that Carryl Walters's own people leave him alone, surrounding him with the same nonviolent respect that my protector gets. It takes me much longer to figure out why. Carryl Walters is not dangerous, neither a protector nor a punisher. I don't think he has any private shared realities with the guards. I don't understand until the World woman is knifed.

It happens in the courtyard, on a cool day in which I am gazing hungrily at the one patch of bright sky overhead. The knifed woman screams. The murderer pulls the knife from her belly and blood shoots out. In seconds the ground is drenched. The woman doubles over. Everyone looks the other way except me. And Carryl Walters runs over with his old-man stagger and kneels over the body, trying uselessly to save the life of a woman already dead anyway.

Of course. He is a healer. The Terrans don't bother him because they know that, next time, it might be they who have need of him.

I feel stupid for not realizing this right away. I am supposed to be *good* at informing. Now I'll have to make it up by immediate action. The problem, of course, is that no one will attack me while I'm under Afa Pek Fakar's protection, and provoking Pek Fakar herself is far too dangerous.

I can see only one way to do this.

I wait a few days. Outside in the courtyard, I sit quietly against the prison wall and breathe shallowly. After a few minutes I leap up. The dizziness takes me; I worsen it by holding my breath. Then I ram as hard as I can into the rough stone wall and slide down it.

Pain tears through my arm and forehead. One of Pek Fakar's men shouts something.

Pek Fakar is there in a minute. I hear her—hear all of them— through a curtain of dizziness and pain.

"—just *ran* into the wall, I saw it—"

"—told me she gets these dizzy attacks—"

"—head broken in—"

I gasp, through sudden real nausea, "The healer. The Terran—"

"The Terran?" Pek Fakar's voice, hard with sudden suspicion. But I gasp out more words, "...disease...a Terran told me...since childhood...without help I..." My vomit, unplanned but useful, spews over her boots.

"Get the Terran," Pek Fakar rasps to somebody. "And a towel!"

Then Carryl Walters bends over me. I clutch his arm, try to smile, and pass out.

When I come to, I am lying inside, on the floor of the eating hall, the Terran cross-legged beside me. A few World people hover near the far wall, scowling. Carryl Walters says, "How many fingers you see?"

"Four. Aren't you supposed to have five?"

He unbends the fifth from behind his palm and says, "You fine."

"No, I'm not," I say. He speaks childishly, and with a odd accent, but he's understandable. "I have a disease. Another Terran healer told me so."

"Who?"

"Her name was Anna Pek Rakov."

"What disease?"

"I don't remember. Something in the head. I get spells."

"What spells? You fall, flop on floor?"

"No. Yes. Sometimes. Sometimes it takes me differently." I look directly into his eyes. Strange eyes, smaller than mine, and that improbable blue. "Pek Rakov told me I could die during a spell, without help."

He does not react to the lie. Or maybe he does, and I don't know how to read it. I have never informed on a Terran before.

Instead he says something grossly obscene, even for Aulit Prison: "Why you unreal? What you do?"

I move my gaze from his. "I murdered my sister." If he asks for details, I will cry. My head aches too hard.

He says, "I sorry."

Is he sorry that he asked, or that I killed Ano? Pek Rakov was not like this; she had some manners. I say, "The other Terran healer said I should be watched carefully by someone who knows what to do if I get a spell. Do you know what to do, Pek Walters?"

"Yes."

"Will you watch me?"

"Yes." He is, in fact, watching me closely now. I touch my head; there is a cloth tied around it where I bashed myself. The headache is worse. My hand comes away sticky with blood.

I say, "In return for what?"

"What you give Pek Fakar for protection?"

He is smarter than I thought. "Nothing I can also share with you." She would punish me hard.

"Then I watch you, you give me information about World."

I nod; this is what Terrans usually request. And where information is given, it can also be extracted. "I will explain your presence to Pek Fakar," I say, before the pain in my head swamps me without warning, and everything in the dining hall blurs and sears together.

Pek Fakar doesn't like it. But I have just given her a gun, smuggled in by my "cousin." I leave notes for the prison administration in my cell, under my bed. While the prisoners are in the courtyard—which we are every day, no matter what the weather—the notes are replaced by whatever I ask for. Pek Fakar had demanded a "weapon"; neither of us expected a Terran gun. She is the only person in the prison to have such a thing. It is to me a stark reminder that no one would care if all we unreal killed each other off completely. There is no one else to shoot; we never see anyone not already in perpetual death.

"Without Pek Walters, I might have another spell and die," I say to the scowling Pek Fakar. "He knows a special Terran method of flexing the brain to bring me out of a spell."

"He can teach this special method to me."

"So far, no World person has been able to learn it. Their brains are different from ours."

She glares at me. But no one, even those lost to reality, can deny that alien brains are weird. And my injuries are certainly real: bloody head cloth, left eye closed from swelling, skin scraped raw the length of my left cheek, bruised arm. She strokes the Terran gun, a boringly straight-lined cylinder of dull metal. "All right. You may keep the Terran near you—if he agrees. Why should he?"

I smile at her slowly. Pek Fakar never shows a response to flattery; to do so would be to show weakness. But she understands. Or thinks she does. I have threatened the Terran with her power, and the whole prison now knows that her power extends among the aliens as well as her own people. She goes on glaring, but she is not displeased. In her hand the gun gleams.

And so begin my conversations with a Terran.

Talking with Carryl Pek Walters is embarrassing and frustrating. He sits beside me in the eating hall or the courtyard and publicly scratches his head. When he is cheerful, he makes shrill horrible whistling noises between his teeth. He mentions topics that belong only among kin: the state of his skin (which has odd brown lumps on it) and his lungs (clogged with fluid, apparently). He does not know enough to begin conversations with ritual comments on flowers. It is like talking to a child, but a child who suddenly begins discussing bicycle engineering or university law.

"You think individual means very little, group means everything," he says.

We are sitting in the courtyard, against a stone wall, a little apart from the other prisoners. Some watch us furtively, some openly. I am angry. I am often angry with Pek Walters. This is not going as I'd planned.

"How can you say that? The individual is very important on World! We care for each other so that no individual is left out of our common reality, except by his own acts!"

"Exactly," Pek Walters says. He has just learned this word from me. "You care for others so no one left alone. Alone is bad. Act alone is bad. Only together is real."

"Of course," I say. Could he be stupid after all? "Reality is always shared. Is a star really there if only one eye can perceive its light?"

He smiles and says something in his own language, which makes no sense to me. He repeats it in real words. "When tree falls in forest, is sound if no person hears?"

"But—do you mean to say that on your star, people believe they…" What? I can't find the words.

He says, "People believe they always real, alone or together. Real even when other people say they dead. Real even when they do something very bad. Even when they murder."

"But they're not real! How could they be? They've violated shared reality! If I don't acknowledge you, the reality of your soul, if I send you to your ancestors without your consent, that is proof that I don't understand reality and so am not seeing it! Only the unreal could do that!"

"Baby not see shared reality. Is baby unreal?"

"Of course. Until the age when children attain reason, they are unreal."

"Then when I kill baby, is all right, because I not kill real person?"

"Of course it's not all right! When one kills a baby, one kills its chance to become real, before it could even join its ancestors! And also all the chances of the babies to which it might become ancestor. No one would kill a baby on World, not even these dead souls in Aulit! Are you saying that on Terra, people would kill babies?"

He looks at something I cannot see. "Yes."

My chance has arrived, although not in a form I relish. Still, I have a job to do. I say, "I have heard that Terrans will kill people for science. Even babies. To find out the kinds of things that Anna Pek Rakov knew about my brain. Is that true?"

"Yes and no."

"How can it be yes *and* no? Are children ever used for science experiments?"

"Yes."

"What kinds of experiments?"

"You should ask, what kind children? Dying children. Children not born yet. Children born…wrong. With no brain, or broken brain."

I struggle with all this. Dying children…he must mean not children who are really dead, but those in the transition to join their ancestors. Well, that would not be so bad, provided the bodies were then allowed to decay properly and release the souls. Children without brains or with broken brains…not bad, either. Such poor unreal things would be destroyed anyway. But children not born yet…In or out of the mother's womb? I push this away, to discuss another time. I am on a different path.

"And you never use living, real children for science?"

He gives me a look I cannot read. So much of Terran expression is still strange. "Yes. We use. In some experiments. Experiments who not hurt children."

"Like what?" I say. We are staring directly at each other now. Suddenly I wonder if this old Terran suspects that I am an informer seeking information, and that is why he accepted my skimpy story about having spells. That would not necessarily be bad. There are ways to bargain with the unreal once everyone admits that bargaining is what is taking place. But I'm not sure whether Pek Walters knows that.

He says, "Experiments who study how brain work. Such as, how memory work. Including shared memory."

"Memory? Memory doesn't 'work.' It just is."

"No. Memory work. By memory-building pro-teenz." He uses a Terran word, then adds, "Tiny little pieces of food," which makes no sense. What does food have to do with memory? You don't eat memories, or obtain them from food. But I am further down the path, and I use his words to go further still.

"Does memory in World people work with the same…'pro-teenz' as Terran memory?"

"Yes and no. Some same or almost same. Some different." He is watching me very closely.

"How do you know that memory works the same or different in World people? Have Terrans done brain experiments on World?"

"Yes."

"With World children?"

"Yes."

I watch a group of Huhuhubs across the courtyard. The smelly little aliens are clustered together in some kind of ritual or game. "And have you, personally, participated in these science experiments on children, Pek Walters?"

He doesn't answer me. Instead he smiles, and if I didn't know better, I'd swear the smile was sad. He says, "Pek Bengarin, why you kill your sister?"

The unexpectedness of it—now, so close to almost learning something useful—outrages me. Not even Pek Fakar has asked me that. I stare at him angrily. He says, "I know, I not should ask. Wrong for ask. But I tell you much, and answer is important—"

"But the question is obscene. You should not ask. World people are not so cruel to each other."

"Even people damned in Aulit Prison?" he says, and even though I don't know one of the words he uses, I see that yes, he recognizes that I am an informer. And that I have been seeking information. All right, so much the better. But I need time to set my questions on a different path.

To gain time, I repeat my previous point. "World people are not so cruel."

"Then you—"

The air suddenly sizzles, smelling of burning. People shout. I look up. Aka Pek Fakar stands in the middle of the courtyard with the Terran gun, firing it at the Huhuhubs. One by one they drop as the beam of light hits them and makes a sizzling hole. The aliens pass into the second stage of their perpetual death.

I stand and tug on Pek Walters's arm. "Come on. We must clear the area immediately or the guards will release poison gas."

"Why?"

"So they can get the bodies into bondage chemicals, of course!" Does this alien think the prison officials would let the unreal get even a little bit decayed? I thought that after our several conversations, Pek Walters understood more than that.

He rises slowly, haltingly, to his feet. Pek Fakar, laughing, strolls toward the door, the gun still in her hand.

Pek Walters says, "World people not cruel?"

Behind us, the bodies of the Huhuhubs lie sprawled across each other, smoking.

The next time we are herded from our cells into the dining hall and then the courtyard, the Huhuhub corpses are of course gone. Pek Walters has developed a cough. He walks more slowly, and once, on the way to our usual spot against the far wall, he puts a hand on my arm to steady himself.

"Are you sick, Pek?"

"Exactly," he says.

"But you are a healer. Make the cough disappear."

He smiles, and sinks gratefully against the wall. " 'Healer, heal own self.' "

"What?"

"Nothing. So you are informer, Pek Bengarin, and you hope I tell you something about science experiments on children on World."

I take a deep breath. Pek Fakar passes us, carrying her gun. Two of her own people now stay close beside her at all times, in case another prisoner tries to take the gun away from her. I cannot believe anyone would try, but maybe I'm wrong. There's no telling what the unreal will do. Pek Walters watches her pass, and his smile is gone. Yesterday Pek Fakar shot another person, this time not even an alien. There is a note under my bed requesting more guns.

I say, "*You* say I am an informer. I do not say it."

"Exactly," Pek Walters says. He has another coughing spell, then closes his eyes wearily. "I have not an-tee-by-otics."

Another Terran word. Carefully I repeat it. " 'An-tee-by-otics'?"

"Pro-teenz for heal."

Again that word for very small bits of food. I make use of it. "Tell me about the pro-teenz in the science experiments."

"I tell you everything about experiments. But only if you answer questions first."

He will ask about my sister. For no reason other than rudeness and cruelty. I feel my face turn to stone.

He says, "Tell me why steal baby not so bad for make person unreal always."

I blink. Isn't this obvious? "To steal a baby doesn't damage the baby's reality. It just grows up somewhere else, with some other people. But all real people of World share the same reality, and anyway after the transition, the child will rejoin its blood ancestors. Baby stealing is wrong, of course, but it isn't a really serious crime."

"And make false coins?"

"The same. False, true—coins are still shared."

He coughs again, this time much harder. I wait. Finally he says, "So when I steal your bicycle, I not violate shared reality too much, because bicycle still somewhere with people of World."

"Of course."

"But when I steal bicycle, I violate shared reality a little?"

"Yes." After a minute I add, "Because the bicycle is, after all, *mine*. You…made my reality shift a little without sharing the decision with me." I peer at him; how can all this not be obvious to such an intelligent man?

He says, "You are too trusting for be informer, Pek Bengarin."

I feel my throat swell with indignation. I am a *very good* informer. Haven't I just bound this Terran to me with a private shared reality in order to create an exchange of information? I am about to demand his share of the bargain when he says abruptly, "So why you kill your sister?"

Two of Pek Fakar's people swagger past. They carry the new guns. Across the courtyard a Faller turns slowly to look at them, and even I can read fear on that alien face.

I say, as evenly as I can manage, "I fell prey to an illusion. I thought that Ano was copulating with my lover. She was younger, more intelligent, prettier. I am not very pretty, as you can see. I didn't share the reality with her, or him, and my illusion grew. Finally it exploded in my head, and I…did it." I am breathing hard, and Pek Fakar's people look blurry.

"You remember clear Ano's murder?"

I turn to him in astonishment. "How could I forget it?"

"You cannot. You cannot because of memory-building pro-teenz. Memory is strong in your brain. Memory-building pro-teenz are strong in your brain. Scientific research on World children for discover what is structure of pro-teenz, where is pro-teenz, how pro-teenz work. But we discover different thing instead."

"What different thing?" I say, but Pek Walters only shakes his head and begins coughing again. I wonder if the coughing spell is an excuse to violate our bargain. He is, after all, unreal.

Pek Fakar's people have gone inside the prison. The Faller slumps against the far wall. They have not shot him. For this moment, at least, he is not entering the second stage of his perpetual death.

But beside me, Pek Walters coughs blood.

He is dying. I am sure of it, although of course no World healer comes to him. He is dead anyway. Also, his fellow Terrans keep away, looking fearful, which makes me wonder if his disease is catching. This leaves only me. I walk him to his cell, and then wonder why I can't just stay when the door closes. No one will check. Or, if they do, will care. And this may be my last chance to gain the needed information, before either Pek Walters is coffined or Pek Fakar orders me away from him because he is too weak to watch over my supposed blood sickness.

His body has become very hot. During the long night he tosses on his bunk, muttering in his own language, and sometimes those strange alien eyes roll in their sockets. But other times he is clearer, and he looks at me as if he recognizes who I am. Those times, I question him. But the lucid times and unlucid ones blur together. His mind is no longer his own.

"Pek Walters. Where are the memory experiments being conducted? In what place?"

"Memory...memories..." More in his own language. It has the cadences of poetry.

"Pek Walters. In what place are the memory experiments being done?"

"At Rafkit Sarloe," he says, which makes no sense. Rafkit Sarloe is the government center, where no one lives. It is not large. People flow in every day, running the Sections, and out to their villages again at night. There is no square measure of Rafkit Sarloe that is not constantly shared physical reality.

He coughs, more bloody spume, and his eyes roll in his head. I make him sip some water. "Pek Walters. In what place are the memory experiments being done?"

"At Rafkit Sarloe. In the Cloud. At Aulit Prison."

It goes on and on like that. And in the early morning, Pek Walters dies.

There is one moment of greater clarity, somewhere near the end. He looks at me, out of his old, ravaged face gone gaunt with his transition. The disturbing look is back in his eyes, sad and kind, not a look for the unreal to wear. It is too much sharing. He says, so low I must bend over him to hear, "Sick brain talks to itself. You not kill your sister."

"Hush, don't try to talk..."

"Find...Brifjis. Maldon Pek Brifjis, in Rafkit Haddon. Find..." He relapses again into fever.

A few moments after he dies, the armored guards enter the cell, wheeling the coffin full of bondage chemicals. With them is the priest. I want to say, *Wait, he is a good man, he doesn't deserve perpetual death*—but of course I do not. I am astonished at myself for even thinking it. A guard edges me into the corridor and the door closes.

That same day, I am sent away from Aulit Prison.

"Tell me again. Everything," Pek Brimmidin says.

Pek Brimmidin is just the same: stocky, yellowing, slightly stooped. His cluttered office is just the same. Food dishes, papers, overelaborated sculptures. I stare hungrily at the ugly things. I hadn't realized how much I'd longed, in prison, for the natural sight of curves. I keep my eyes on the sculptures, partly to hold back my question until the proper time to ask it.

"Pek Walters said he would tell me everything about the experiments that are, yes, going on with World children. In the name of science. But all he had time to tell me was that the experiments involve 'memory-building pro-teenz,' which are tiny pieces of food from which the brain constructs memory. He also said the experiments were going on in Rafkit Sarloe and Aulit Prison."

"And that is all, Pek Bengarin?"

"That is all."

Pek Brimmidin nods curtly. He is trying to appear dangerous, to scare out of me any piece of information I might have forgotten. But Frablit Pek Brimmidin can't appear dangerous to me. I have seen the real thing.

Pek Brimmidin has not changed. But I have.

I ask my question. "I have brought to you all the information I could obtain before the Terran died. Is it sufficient to release me and Ano?"

He runs a hand through his neck fur. "I'm sorry I can't answer that, Pek. I will need to consult my superiors. But I promise to send you word as soon as I can."

"Thank you," I say, and lower my eyes. *You are too trusting for be informer, Pek Bengarin.*

Why didn't I tell Frablit Pek Brimmidin the rest of it, about 'Maldon Pek Brifjis' and 'Rafkit Haddon' and not really killing my sister? Because it is most likely nonsense, the ravings of a fevered brain. Because this 'Maldon Pek Brifjis' might be an innocent World man, who does not deserve trouble brought to him by an unreal alien. Because Pek Walters's words were personal, addressed to me alone, on his deathbed. Because I do not want to discuss Ano with Pek Brimmidin's superiors one more useless painful time.

Because, despite myself, I trust Carryl Pek Walters.

"You may go," Pek Brimmidin says, and I ride my bicycle along the dusty road home.

I make a bargain with Ano's corpse, still lying in curled-finger grace on the bed across from mine. Her beautiful brown hair floats in the chemicals of the coffin. I used to covet that hair desperately, when we were very young. Once I even cut it all off while she slept. But other times I would weave it for her, or braid it with flowers. She was so pretty. At one point, when she was still a child, she wore eight bid rings, one on each finger. Two of the bids were in negotiation between the boys' fathers and ours. Although older, I have never had a single bid.

Did I murder her?

My bargain with her corpse is this: If the Reality & Atonement Section releases me and Ano because of my work in Aulit Prison, I will seek no further. Ano will be free to join our ancestors; I will be fully real. It will no longer matter whether or not I killed my sister, because both of us will again be sharing in the same reality as if I had not. But if Reality & Atonement holds me unreal still longer, after all I have given them, I will try to find this "Maldon Pek Brifjis."

I say none of this aloud. The guards at Aulit Prison knew immediately when Pek Walters died, inside a closed and windowless room. They could be watching me here, now. World has no devices to do this, but how did Pek Walters know so much about a World man working with a Terran science experiment? Somewhere there are World people and Terrans in partnership. Terrans, as everyone knows, have all sorts of listening devices we do not.

I kiss Ano's coffin. I don't say it aloud, but I hope desperately that Reality & Atonement releases us. I want to return to shared reality, to the daily warmth and sweetness of belonging, now and forever, to the living and dead of World. I do not want to be an informer anymore.

Not for anyone, even myself.

The message comes three days later. The afternoon is warm and I sit outside on my stone bench, watching my neighbor's milkbeasts eye her sturdily fenced flowerbeds. She has new flowers that I don't recognize, with blooms that are entrancing but somehow foreign—could they be Terran? It doesn't seem likely. During my time in Aulit Prison, more people seem to have made up their minds that the Terrans are unreal. I have heard more mutterings, more anger against those who buy from alien traders.

Frablit Pek Brimmidin himself brings the letter from Reality and Atonement, laboring up the road on his ancient bicycle. He has removed his uniform, so as not to embarrass me in front of my neighbors. I watch him ride up, his neck fur damp with unaccustomed exertion, his gray eyes abashed, and I know already what the sealed message must say. Pek Brimmidin is too kind for his job.

That is why he is only a low-level messenger boy all the time, not just today.

These are things I never saw before.

*You are too trusting for be informer, Pek Bengarin.*

"Thank you, Pek Brimmidin," I say. "Would you like a glass of water? Or pel?"

"No, thank you, Pek," he says. He does not meet my eyes. He waves to my other neighbor, fetching water from the village well, and fumbles meaninglessly with the handle of his bicycle. "I can't stay."

"Then ride safely," I say, and go back in my house. I stand beside Ano and break the seal on the government letter. After I read it, I gaze at her a long time. So beautiful, so sweet-natured. So loved.

Then I start to clean. I scrub every inch of my house, for hours and hours, climbing on a ladder to wash the ceiling, sloshing thick soapsuds in the cracks, scrubbing every surface of every object and carrying the more intricately-shaped outside into the sun to dry. Despite my most intense scrutiny, I find nothing that I can imagine being a listening device. Nothing that looks alien, nothing unreal.

But I no longer know what is real.

Only Bata is up; the other moons have not risen. The sky is clear and starry, the air cool. I wheel my bicycle inside and try to remember everything I need.

Whatever kind of glass Ano's coffin is made of, it is very tough. I have to swing my garden shovel three times, each time with all my strength, before I can break it. On the third blow the glass cracks, then falls leisurely apart into large pieces that bounce slightly when they hit the floor. Chemicals cascade off the bed, a waterfall of clear liquid that smells only slightly acrid.

In my high boots I wade close to the bed and throw containers of water over Ano to wash off chemical residue. The containers are waiting in a neat row by the wall, everything from my largest wash basin to the kitchen bowls. Ano smiles sweetly.

I reach onto the soggy bed and lift her clear.

In the kitchen, I lay her body—limp, soft-limbed—on the floor and strip off her chemical-soaked clothing. I dry her, move her to the waiting blanket, take a last look, and wrap her tightly. The bundle of her and the shovel balances across the handles of my bicycle. I pull off my boots and open the door.

The night smells of my neighbor's foreign flowers. Ano seems weightless. I feel as if I can ride for hours. And I do.

I bury her, weighted with stones, in marshy ground well off a deserted road. The wet dirt will speed the decay, and it is easy to cover the grave with reeds and toglif branches. When I've finished, I bury my clothes and dress in clean ones in my pack. Another few hours of riding and I can find an inn to sleep in. Or a field, if need be.

The morning dawns pearly, with three moons in the sky. Everywhere I ride are flowers, first wild and then cultivated. Although exhausted, I sing softly to the curving blooms, to the sky, to the pale moonlit road. Ano is real, and free.

Go sweetly, sweet sister, to our waiting ancestors.

Two days later I reach Rafkit Haddon.


It is an old city, sloping down the side of a mountain to the sea. The homes of the rich either stand on the shore or perch on the mountain, looking in both cases like rounded great white birds. In between lie a jumble of houses, market squares, government buildings, inns, pel shops, slums and parks, the latter with magnificent old trees and shabby old shrines. The manufacturing shops and warehouses lie to the north, with the docks.

I have experience in finding people. I start with Rituals & Processions. The clerk behind the counter, a pre-initiate of the priesthood, is young and eager to help. "Yes?"

"I am Ajma Pek Goranalit, attached to the household of Menanlin. I have been sent to inquire about the ritual activity of a citizen, Maldon Pek Brifjis. Can you help me?"

"Of course," she beams. An inquiry about ritual activity is never written; discretion is necessary when a great house is considering honoring a citizen by allowing him to honor their ancestors. A person so chosen gains great prestige—and considerable material wealth. I picked the name "Menanlin" after an hour's judicious listening in a crowded pel shop. The family is old, numerous, and discreet.

"Let me see," she says, browsing among her public records. "Brifjis...Brifjis...it's a common name, of course...which citizen, Pek?"

"Maldon."

"Oh, yes...here. He paid for two musical tributes to his ancestors last year, made a donation to the Rafkit Haddon Priest House...Oh! And he was chosen to honor the ancestors of the house of Choulalait!"

She sounds awe-struck. I nod. "We know about that, of course. But is there anything else?"

"No, I don't think so...wait. He paid for a charity tribute for the ancestors of his clu merchant, Lam Pek Flanoe, a poor man. Quite a lavish tribute, too. Music, and three priests."

"Kind," I said.

"Very! Three priests!" Her young eyes shine. "Isn't it wonderful how many truly kind people share reality?"

"Yes," I say. "It is."

I find the clu merchant by the simple method of asking for him in several market squares. Sales of all fuels are of course slow in the summer; the young relatives left in charge of the clu stalls are happy to chat with strangers. Lam Pek Flanoe lives in a run-down neighborhood just behind the great houses by the sea. The neighborhood is home to servants and merchants who provide for the rich. Four more glasses of pel in three more pel shops, and I know that Maldon Pek Brifjis is currently a guest in the home of a rich widow. I know the widow's address. I know that that Pek Brifjis is a healer.

A healer.

*Sick brain talks to itself. You not kill your sister.*

I am dizzy from four glasses of pel. Enough. I find an inn, the kind where no one asks questions, and sleep without the shared reality of dreams.

\* \* \*

It takes me a day, disguised as a street cleaner, to decide which of the men coming and going from the rich widow's house is Pek Brifjis. Then I spend three days following him, in various guises. He goes a lot of places and talks to a lot of people, but none of them seem unusual for a rich healer with a personal pleasure in collecting antique water carafes. On the fourth day I look for a good opportunity to approach him, but this turns out to be unnecessary.

"Pek," a man says to me as I loiter, dressed as a vendor of sweet flatbreads, outside the baths on Elindel Street. I have stolen the sweets before dawn from the open kitchen of a bake shop. I know at once that the man approaching me is a bodyguard, and that he is very good. It's in the way he walks, looks at me, places his hand on my arm. He is also very handsome, but that thought barely registers. Handsome men are never for such as me. They are for Ano.

Were for Ano.

"Come with me, please," the bodyguard says, and I don't argue. He leads me to the back of the baths, through a private entrance, to a small room apparently used for private grooming of some sort. The only furniture is two small stone tables. He checks me, expertly but gently, for weapons, looking even in my mouth. Satisfied, he indicates where I am to stand, and opens a second door.

Maldon Pek Brifjis enters, wrapped in a bathing robe of rich imported cloth. He is younger than Carryl Walters, a vigorous man in a vigorous prime. His eyes are striking, a deep purple with long gold lines radiating from their centers. He says immediately, "Why have you been following me for three days?"

"Someone told me to," I say. I have nothing to lose by an honest shared reality, although I still don't fully believe I have anything to gain.

"Who? You may say anything in front of my guard."

"Carryl Pek Walters."

The purple eyes deepen even more. "Pek Walters is dead."

"Yes," I say. "Perpetually. I was with him when he entered the second stage of death."

"And where was that?" He is testing me.

"In Aulit Prison. His last words instructed me to find you. To... ask you something."

"What do you wish to ask me?"

"Not what I thought I would ask," I say, and realize that I have made the decision to tell him everything. Until I saw him up close, I wasn't completely sure what I would do. I can no longer share reality with World, not even if I went to Frablit Pek Brimmidin with exactly the knowledge he wants about the scientific experiments on children. That would not atone for releasing Ano before the Section agreed. And Pek Brimmidin is only a messenger, anyway. No, less than a messenger: a tool, like a garden shovel, or a bicycle. He does not share the reality of his users. He only thinks he does.

As I had thought I did.

I say, "I want to know if I killed my sister. Pek Walters said I did not. He said 'sick brain talks to itself,' and that I had not killed Ano. And to ask *you*. Did I kill my sister?"

Pek Brifjis sits down on one of the stone tables. "I don't know," he says, and I see his neck fur quiver. "Perhaps you did. Perhaps you did not."

"How can I discover which?"

"You cannot."

"Ever?"

"Ever." And then, "I am sorry."

Dizziness takes me. The "low blood pressure." The next thing I know, I lie on the floor of the small room, with Pek Brifjis's fingers on my elbow pulse. I struggle to sit up.

"No, wait," he says. "Wait a moment. Have you eaten today?"

"Yes."

"Well, wait a moment anyway. I need to think."

He does, the purple eyes turning inward, his fingers absently pressing the inside of my elbow. Finally he says, "You are an informer. That's why you were released from Aulit Prison after Pek Walters died. You inform for the government."

I don't answer. It no longer matters.

"But you have left informing. Because of what Pek Walters told you. Because he told you that the skits-oh-free-nia experiments might have...No. It can't be."

He too has used a word I don't know. It sounds Terran. Again I struggle to sit up, to leave. There is no hope for me here. This healer can tell me nothing.

He pushes me back down on the floor and says swiftly, "When did your sister die?" His eyes have changed once again; the long golden flecks are brighter, radiating from the center like glowing spokes. "Please, Pek, this is immensely important. To both of us."

"Two years ago, and 152 days."

"Where? In what city?"

"Village. Our village. Gofkit Ilo."

"Yes," he says. "*Yes*. Tell me everything you remember of her death. Everything."

This time I push him aside and sit up. Blood rushes from my head, but anger overcomes the dizziness. "I will tell you nothing. Who do you people think you are, ancestors? To tell me I killed Ano, then tell me I didn't, then say you don't know—to destroy the hope of atonement I had as an informer, then to tell me there is no other hope—no, there might be hope—no, there's not—how can you live with yourself? How can you twist people's brains away from shared reality and offer *nothing to replace it*!" I am screaming. The bodyguard glances at the door. I don't care; I go on screaming.

"You are doing experiments on children, wrecking their reality as you have wrecked mine! You are a murderer—" But I don't get to scream all that. Maybe I don't get to scream any of it. For a needle slides into my elbow, at the inner pulse where Maldon Brifjis has been holding it, and the room slides away as easily as Ano into her grave.

A bed, soft and silky, beneath me. Rich wall hangings. The room is very warm. A scented breeze whispers across my bare stomach. Bare? I sit up and discover I am dressed in the gauzy skirt, skimpy bandeau, and flirting veil of a prostitute.

At my first movement, Pek Brifjis crosses from the fireplace to my bed. "Pek. This room does not allow sound to escape. Do not resume screaming. Do you understand?"

I nod. His bodyguard stands across the room. I pull the flirting veil from my face.

"I am sorry about that," Pek Brifjis says. "It was necessary to dress you in a way that accounts for a bodyguard carrying a drugged woman into a private home without raising questions."

A private home. I guess that this is the rich widow's house by the sea. A room that does not allow sound to escape. A needle unlike ours: sharp and sure. Brain experiments. "Skits-oh-free-nia."

I say, "You work with the Terrans."

"No," he says. "I do not."

"But Pek Walters..." It doesn't matter. "What are you going to do with me?"

He says, "I am going to offer you a trade."

"What sort of trade?"

"Information in return for your freedom."

And he says he does not work with Terrans. I say, "What use is freedom to me?" although of course I don't expect him to understand that. I can never be free.

"Not that kind of freedom," he says. "I won't just let you go from this room. I will let you rejoin your ancestors, and Ano."

I gape at him.

"Yes, Pek. I will kill you and bury you myself, where your body can decay."

"You would violate shared reality like that? For *me*?"

His purple eyes deepen again. For a moment, something in those eyes looks almost like Pek Walters's blue ones. "Please understand. I think there is a strong chance you did not kill Ano. Your village was one where...subjects were used for experimentation. I think that is the true shared reality here."

I say nothing. A little of his assurance disappears. "Or so I believe. Will you agree to the trade?"

"Perhaps," I say. Will he actually do what he promises? I can't be sure. But there is no other way for me. I cannot hide from the government all the years until I die. I am too young. And when they find me, they will send me back to Aulit, and when I die there they will put me in a coffin of preservative chemicals...

I would never see Ano again.

The healer watches me closely. Again I see the Pek Walters look in his eyes: sadness and pity.

"Perhaps I will agree to the trade," I say, and wait for him to speak again about the night Ano died. But instead he says, "I want to show you something."

He nods at the bodyguard who leaves the room, returning a few moments later. By the hand he leads a child, a little girl, clean and well-dressed. One look makes my neck fur bristle. The girl's eyes are flat and unseeing. She mutters to herself. I offer a quick appeal for protection to my ancestors. The girl is unreal, without the capacity to perceive shared reality, even though she is well over the age of reason. She is not human. She should have been destroyed.

"This is Ori," Pek Brifjis says. The girl suddenly laughs, a wild demented laugh, and peers at something only she can see.

"Why is it here?" I listen to the harshness in my own voice.

"Ori was born real. She was made this way by the scientific brain experiments of the government."

"Of the government! That is a lie!"

"Is it? Do you still, Pek, have such trust in your government?"

"No, but..." To make me continue to earn Ano's freedom, even after I had met their terms...to lie to Pek Brimmidin...those offenses against shared reality are one thing. The destruction of a real person's physical body, as I had done with Ano's (had I?) is another, far far worse. To destroy a *mind*, the instrument of perceiving shared reality...Pek Brifjis lies.

He says, "Pek, tell me about the night Ano died."

"Tell me about this...thing!"

"All right." He sits down in a chair beside my luxurious bed. The thing wanders around the room, muttering. It seems unable to stay still.

"She was born Ori Malfisit, in a small village in the far north—"

"What village?" I need desperately to see if he falters on details.

He does not. "Gofkit Ramloe. Of real parents, simple people, an old and established family. At six years old, Ori was playing in the forest with some other children when she disappeared. The other children said they heard something thrashing toward the marshes. The family decided she had been carried off by a wild kilfreit—there are still some left, you know, that far north—and held a procession in honor of Ori's joining their ancestors.

"But that's not what happened to Ori. She was stolen by two men, unreal prisoners promised atonement and restoration to full reality, just as you were. Ori was carried off to Rafkit Sarloe, with eight other children from all over World. There they were given to the Terrans, who were told that they were orphans who could be used for experiment. The experiments were ones that would not hurt or damage the children in any way."

I look at Ori, now tearing a table scarf into shreds and muttering. Her empty eyes turn to mine, and I have to look away.

"This part is difficult," Pek Brifjis says. "Listen hard, Pek. The Terrans truly did not hurt the children. They put ee-lek-trodes on their heads…you don't know what that means. They found ways to see which parts of their brains worked the same as Terran brains and which did not. They used a number of tests and machines and drugs. None of it hurt the children, who lived at the Terran scientific compound and were cared for by World childwatchers. At first the children missed their parents, but they were young, and after a while they were happy."

I glance again at Ori. The unreal, not sharing in common reality, are isolated and therefore dangerous. A person with no world in common with others will violate those others as easily as cutting flowers. Under such conditions, pleasure is possible, but not happiness.

Pek Brifjis runs his hand through his neck fur. "The Terrans worked with World healers, of course, teaching them. It was the usual trade, only this time we received the information and they the physical reality: children and watchers. There was no other way World could permit Terrans to handle our children. Our healers were there every moment."

He looks at me. I say, "Yes," just because something must be said.

"Do you know, Pek, what it is like to realize you have lived your whole life according to beliefs that are not true?"

"No!" I say, so loudly that Ori looks up with her mad, unreal gaze. She smiles. I don't know why I spoke so loud. What Pek Brifjis said has nothing to do with me. Nothing at all.

"Well, Pek Walters knew. He realized that the experiments he participated in, harmless to the subjects and in aid of biological understanding of species differences, were being used for something else. The roots of skits-oh-free-nia, misfiring brain sir-kits—" He is off on a long explanation that means nothing to me. Too many Terran words, too much strangeness. Pek Brifjis is no longer talking to me. He is talking to himself, in some sort of pain I don't understand.

Suddenly the purple eyes snap back to mine. "What all that means, Pek, is that a few of the healers—our own healers, from World—found out how to manipulate the Terran science. They took it and used it to put into minds memories that did not happen."

"Not possible!"

"It is possible. The brain is made very excited, with Terran devices, while the false memory is recited over and over. Then different parts of the brain are made to…to recirculate memories and emotions over and over. Like water recirculated through mill races. The water gets all scrambled together…No. Think of it this way: different parts of the brain send signals to each other. The signals are forced to loop together, and every loop makes the unreal memories stronger. It is apparently in common use on Terra, although tightly controlled."

*Sick brain talks to itself.*

"But—"

"There are no objections possible, Pek. It is real. It happened. It happened to Ori. The World scientists made her brain remember things that had not happened. Small things, at first. That worked. When they tried larger memories, something went wrong. It left her like this. They were still learning; that was five years ago. They got better, much better. Good enough to experiment on adult subjects who could then be returned to shared reality."

"One can't plant memories like flowers, or uproot them like weeds!"

"These people could. And did."

"But—*why?*"

"Because the World healers who did this—and they were only a few—saw a different reality."

"I don't—"

"They saw the Terrans able to do everything. Make better machines than we can, from windmills to bicycles. Fly to the stars. Cure disease. Control nature. Many World people are afraid of Terrans, Pek. And of Fallers and Huhuhubs. Because their reality is superior to ours."

"There is only one common reality," I said. "The Terrans just know more about it than we do!"

"Perhaps. But Terran knowledge makes people uneasy. And afraid. And jealous."

*Jealous. Ano saying to me in the kitchen, with Bata and Cap bright at the window, "I will too go out tonight to see him! You can't stop me! You're just jealous, a jealous ugly shriveled thing that not even your lover wants, so you don't wish me to have any—" And the red flood swamping my brain, the kitchen knife, the blood—*

"Pek?" the healer says. "Pek?"

"I'm...all right. The jealous healers, they hurt their own people, World people, for revenge on the Terrans—that makes no sense!"

"The healers acted with great sorrow. They knew what they were doing to people. But they needed to perfect the technique of inducing controlled skits-oh-free-nia...they *needed* to do it. To make people angry at Terrans. Angry enough to forget the attractive trade goods and rise up against the aliens. To cause war. The healers are mistaken, Pek. We have not had a war on World in a thousand years; our people cannot understand how hard the Terrans would strike back. But you must understand: the outlaw scientists thought they were doing the right thing. They thought they were creating anger in order to save World.

"And another thing—with the help of the government, they were careful not to make any World man or woman permanently unreal. The adults manipulated into murder were all offered atonement as informers. The children are all cared for. The mistakes, like Ori, will be allowed to decay someday, to return to her ancestors. I will see to that myself."

Ori tears the last of the scarf into pieces, smiling horribly, her flat eyes empty. What unreal memories fill her head?

I say bitterly, "Doing the right thing…letting me believe I killed my sister!"

"When you rejoin your ancestors, you will find it isn't so. And the means of rejoining them was made available to you: the completion of your informing atonement."

But now that atonement never will be completed. I stole Ano and buried her without Section consent. Maldon Brifjis, of course, does not know this.

Through my pain and anger I blurt, "And what of *you*, Pek Brifjis? You work with these criminal healers, aiding them in emptying children like Ori of reality—"

"I don't work with them. I thought you smarter, Pek. I work against them. And so did Carryl Walters, which is why he died in Aulit Prison."

"Against them?"

"Many of us do. Carryl Walters among them. He was an informer. And my friend."

Neither of us says anything. Pek Brifjis stares into the fire. I stare at Ori, who has begun to grimace horribly. She squats on an intricately woven curved rug which looks very old. A reek suddenly fills the room. Ori does not share with the rest of us the reality of piss closets. She throws back her head and laughs, a horrible sound like splintering metal.

"Take her away," Pek Brifjis says wearily to the guard, who looks unhappy. "I'll clean up here." To me he adds, "We can't allow any servants in here with you."

The guard leads away the grimacing child. Pek Brifjis kneels and scrubs at the rug with chimney rags dipped in water from my carafe. I remember that he collects antique water carafes. What a long way that must seem from scrubbing shit, from Ori, from Carryl Walters coughing out his lungs in Aulit Prison, among aliens.

"Pek Brifjis—did I kill my sister?"

He looks up. There is shit on his hands. "There is no way to be absolutely sure. It is possible you were one of the experiment subjects from your village. You would have been drugged in your house, to awake with your sister murdered and your mind altered."

40

I say, more quietly than I have said anything else in this room, "You will really kill me, let me decay, and enable me to rejoin my ancestors?"

Pek Brifjis stands and wipes the shit from his hands. "I will."

"But what will you do if I refuse? If instead I ask to return home?"

"If you do that, the government will arrest you and once more promise you atonement—if you inform on those of us working to oppose them."

"Not if I go first to whatever part of the government is truly working to end the experiments. Surely you aren't saying the *entire* government is doing this…thing."

"Of course not. But do you know for certain which Sections, and which officials in those Sections, wish for war with the Terrans, and which do not? *We* can't be sure. How can you?"

Frablit Pek Brimmidin is innocent, I think. But the thought is useless. Pek Brimmidin is innocent, but powerless.

It tears my soul to think that the two might be the same thing.

Pek Brifjis rubs at the damp carpet with the toe of his boot. He puts the rags in a lidded jar and washes his hands at the washstand. A faint stench still hangs in the air. He comes to stand beside my bed.

"Is that what you want, Uli Pek Bengarin? That I let you leave this house, not knowing what you will do, whom you will inform on? That I endanger everything we have done in order to convince you of its truth?"

"Or you can kill me and let me rejoin my ancestors. Which is what you think I will choose, isn't it? That choice would let you keep faith with the reality you have decided is true, and still keep yourself secret from the criminals. Killing me would be easiest for you. But only if I consent to my murder. Otherwise, you will violate even the reality you have decided to perceive."

He stares down at me, a muscular man with beautiful purple eyes. A healer who would kill. A patriot defying his government to prevent a violent war. A sinner who does all he can to minimize his sin and keep it from denying him the chance to rejoin his own ancestors. A believer in shared reality who is trying to bend the reality without breaking the belief.

I keep quiet. The silence stretches on. Finally it is Pek Brifjis that breaks it. "I wish Carryl Walters had never sent you to me."

"But he did. And I choose to return to my village. Will you let me go, or keep me prisoner here, or murder me without my consent?"

"Damn you," he says, and I recognize the word as one Carryl Walters used, about the unreal souls in Aulit Prison.

"Exactly," I say. "What will you do, Pek? Which of your supposed multiple realities will you choose now?"

It is a hot night, and I cannot sleep.

I lie in my tent on the wide empty plain and listen to the night noises. Rude laughter from the pel tent, where a group of miners drinks far too late at night for men who must bore into hard rock at dawn. Snoring from the tent to my right. Muffled lovemaking from a tent farther down the row, I'm not sure whose. The woman giggles, high and sweet.

I have been a miner for half a year now. After I left the northern village of Gofkit Ramloe, Ori's village, I just kept heading north. Here on the equator, where World harvests its tin and diamonds and pel berries and salt, life is both simpler and less organized. Papers are not necessary. Many of the miners are young, evading their government service for one reason or another. Reasons that must seem valid to them. Here government sections rule weakly, compared to the rule of the mining and farming companies. There are no messengers on Terran bicycles. There is no Terran science. There are no Terrans.

There are shrines, of course, and rituals and processions, and tributes to one's ancestors. But these things actually receive less attention than in the cities, because they are more taken for granted. Do you pay attention to air?

The woman giggles again, and this time I recognize the sound. Awi Pek Crafmal, the young runaway from another island. She is a pretty thing, and a hard worker. Sometimes she reminds me of Ano.

I asked a great many questions in Gofkit Ramloe. *Ori Malfisit,* Pek Brifjis said her name was. *An old and established family.* But I asked and asked, and no such family had ever lived in Gofkit Ram-loe. Wherever Ori came from, and however she had been made into that unreal and empty vessel shitting on a rich carpet, she had not started her poor little life in Gofkit Ramloe.

Did Maldon Brifjis know I would discover that, when he released me from the rich widow's house overlooking the sea? He must have. Or maybe, despite knowing I was an informer, he didn't understand that I would actually go to Gofkit Ramloe and check. You can't understand everything.

Sometimes, in the darkest part of the night, I wish I had taken Pek Brifjis's offer to return me to my ancestors.

I work on the rock piles of the mine during the day, among miners who lift sledges and shatter solid stone. They talk, and curse, and revile the Terrans, although few miners have as much as seen one. After work the miners sit in camp and drink pel, lifting huge mugs with dirty hands, and laugh at obscene jokes. They all share the same reality, and it binds them together, in simple and happy strength.

I have strength, too. I have the strength to swing my sledge with the other women, many of whom have the same rough plain looks as I, and who are happy to accept me as one of them. I had the strength to shatter Ano's coffin, and to bury her even when I thought the price to me was perpetual death. I had the strength to follow Carryl Walters's words about the brain experiments and seek Maldon Brifjis. I had the strength to twist Pek Brifjis's divided mind to make him let me go.

But do I have the strength to go where all of that leads me? Do I have the strength to look at Frablit Pek Brimmidin's reality, and Carryl Walters's reality, and Ano's, and Maldon Brifjis's, and Ori's—and try to find the places that match and the places that don't? Do I have the strength to live on, never knowing if I killed my sister, or if I did not? Do I have the strength to doubt everything, and live with doubt, and sort through the millions of separate realities on World, searching for the true pieces of each—assuming that I can even recognize them?

Should anyone have to live like that? In uncertainty, in doubt, in loneliness. Alone in one's mind, in an isolated and unshared reality.

I would like to return to the days when Ano was alive. Or even to the days when I was an informer. To the days when I shared in World's reality, and knew it to be solid beneath me, like the ground itself. To the days when I knew what to think, and so did not have to.

To the days before I became—unwillingly—as terrifyingly real as I am now.

# FIRST RITES

## —1: Haihong—

She sat rigid on the narrow seat of the plane, as if her slightest movement might bring the Boeing 777 down over the Pacific. No one noticed. Pregnant women often sat still, and this one was very pregnant. Only the flight attendant, motherly and inquisitive, bent over the motionless figure.

"Can I bring you anything, ma'am?"

The girl's head jerked up as if shot. "No...no." And then, in nearly unaccented English, "Wait. Yes. A Scotch and soda."

The flight attendant's mouth narrowed, but she brought the drink. These girls today—you'd think this one would know better. Although maybe she came from some backward area of China without prenatal care. In her plain brown maternity smock and sandals, it was hard to tell. The girl wasn't pretty and wore no wedding ring. Well, maybe that was why the poor thing was so nervous. An uneducated provincial going home to face the music. Still, she shouldn't drink. In fact, at this late stage, she shouldn't even be flying. What if she went into labor on the plane?

Deng Haihong, one chapter short of her Ph.D. thesis at U.C. San Diego, gulped the Scotch and closed her eyes, waiting for its warmth to reach her brain. Another three hours to Shanghai, two-and-a-half to Chengdu, and perhaps two hours on the bus to Auntie's. If no one questioned her at the airports. If she wasn't yet on any official radar. If she could find Auntie.

*If...*

Eyes still closed, Haihong laid both hands on her bulging belly, and shuddered.

Shuangliu Airport in Chengdu had changed in four years. When Haihong had left, it had been the glossy, bustling gateway to the prosperous southwest and then on to Tibet, and Chengdu had been China's fifth largest city. Now, since half of Sichuan province had been under quarantine, only seven people deplaned from an aircraft so old that it had no live TV-feed. Five of the seven already wore pathogen masks. Haihong pulled on hers, not because she thought any deadly pathogens from the war still lingered here—she knew better—but because it made her more inconspicuous. Her stomach roiled as she approached Immigration.

*Let it be just one more bored official…*

It was not. "Passport and Declaration Card?"

Haihong handed them over, inserted her finger into the reader, and tried to smile. The woman took forever to scrutinize her papers and biological results. The screen at her elbow scrolled but Haihong couldn't see what it said…For a long terrible moment she thought she might faint.

Then the woman smiled. "Welcome home. You have come home to have your child here, in the province of your ancestors?"

"Yes," Haihong managed.

"Congratulations."

"Thank you." Emily's curious American phrase jumped into her mind: *I would give my soul for a drink right now.*

Too bad Haihong had already sold her soul.

Chengdu had finished the Metro just before the quarantine, and it was still operating. Everyone wore the useless paper pathogen masks. In California, Emily had laughed at the idea that the flimsy things would protect against any pathogens that had mutated around their terminator genes, and she and Haihong had had their one and only fight. "The people are just trying to survive!" Haihong had yelled, and Emily had gone all round-eyed and as red as only those blonde Americans could, and said apologetically, "I suppose that whatever makes them feel better…" Haihong had stormed out of the crummy apartment she shared with Emily and Tess only because it saved money.

It had been Emily who told her about the clinic in the first place.

As Haihong pulled her rolling suitcase toward Customs, her belly lurched hard. She stopped, terror washing through her: *Not here, not here!* But after that one hard kick, the baby calmed down. Haihong made it though Customs, the pills intact in the lining of her dress. She made it onto the Metro, off at the bus station.

The terror abated. Not departed—it would never do that, she realized bleakly. But at least the chance of detection was over. In the bus station, crowded as Shuangliu had not been, she was just one more Chinese girl in inexpensive cotton clothing that had probably been made in Guangdong province before being exported to the U.S. Only the poorest Chinese remained in Sichuan; everyone who could afford to had gone through bio-decon and fled. Chengdu had been the place that North Korea chose to bio-attack to bring the huge Chinese dragon to its knees. Sichuan had been the sacrifice, and rather than have the attack continued on Guangdong's export factories or Beijing's government or Shanghai's soaring foreign tourism, China had not retaliated toward its ancient enemy, at least not with weapons. Politics had been more effective, aided by the world's outrage. Now North Korea was castrated, full of U.N. peace-keeping forces and bio-inspectors and very angry Chinese administrators. Both of Haihong's parents had died in the brief war.

"Be careful, Little Sister." An ancient man, gnarled as an old tree, took Haihong's elbow to help her onto the bus. The small kindness nearly made her cry. Pregnant women cried so easily. The trip had been so long, so draining…she wanted a drink.

"*Shie-shie,*" she said, and watched his face to see if he frowned at her accent. She had spoken only English for so long. But his expression didn't change.

The bus, nearly as ancient as the kind grandfather, smelled of unwashed bodies and urine. Haihong fell asleep, mercifully without dreams. When she woke, it was night in the mountains and the baby was kicking hard. Her stomach growled with hunger. A different passenger sat beside her, a boy of maybe six or seven, with his mother snoring across the aisle. He ducked his head and said shyly, "Do you wish for a boy or a girl?"

The baby was a boy. Ben, shaken, had analyzed with Haihong the entire genome from amnio tissue. Haihong knew the baby's eye and hair color, prospective height, blood type, probable IQ, degree of far future baldness. She knew the father was Mexican. She knew the fetus's polymorphic alleles.

She smiled at the boy and said softly, "Whatever Heaven sends."

Haihong's screams shattered the night. The midwife, back in prominence after the doctor left and the village clinic closed, murmured gently from her position beside the squatting Haihong. The smell of burning incense didn't mask the earthy odor of her spilt waters. Auntie held a kerosene lamp above the midwife's waiting hands. Auntie's face had not unclenched, not once, since Haihong had finally found her living in a hut at the edge of a vast vineyard in which she, like everyone else, toiled endlessly. The workers' huts had running water but no electricity. Outside, more women had gathered to wait.

Haihong cried, "I will die!"

"You will not die," the midwife soothed. Through the haze of pain, Haihong realized that the woman thought she feared death. If only it were that simple...But Haihong had done all she could. Had explained to Auntie, who was not her aunt but her old amah and therefore much harder to trace directly to Haihong, about the pills. She had explained, but would the old woman understand? O, to have come this far and not succeed, not save her son...

Her body split in two, and the child was born. His wail filled the hut. Haihong, battered from within, gasped, "Give...me!"

They laid the bloody infant in her arms. Auntie remembered what had been rehearsed, drilled into her, for the past nine days. Her obedience had made her an ideal amah when Haihong had been young. Her obedience, and her instinctive love. Her eyes never left the crying baby, but wordlessly she held out to Haihong the prepared dish holding pulverized green powder.

With the last of her strength, Haihong transferred three grains of powder to her fingertip and touched the baby's tongue. The grains dissolved. The baby went on wailing and all at once Haihong was sick of him, sick of the chance she had taken and the sacrifice she had made, sick of it all, necessary as it had been. She said, "Take him," and Auntie greedily grabbed the baby from her arms. Haihong tried to shut her ears against his crying. She wanted nothing now but sleep. Sleep, and the drink that, surrounded as they were by vineyards, would be possible soon, today, tomorrow, all the days left in her utterly ruined life.

## —2: Cixin—

DENG CIXIN WAS IN LOVE with the mountains. Unlike anything else, they made him feel calm inside, like still water.

"Sit still, *bow bei'r*," Auntie said many times each day. "Be calm!" But Cixin could not sit still. He raced out the door, scattering the chickens, through the neat rows of grapes tied to their stakes, into the village. He scooped up handfuls of pebbles and hurled them at the other children, provoking cries of, "*Fen noon an hi!*" *Angry boy.* He was always angry, never knowing at what, always running, always wanting to be someplace else. Except when he was in the mountains.

His mother took him there once every week. She put him into his seat on her bicycle, sometimes pedaling hard with sweat coming out in interesting little globes on the back of her neck, and sometimes walking the bicycle. They covered several miles. After he turned four, Cixin walked part of the way. He liked to run in circles around his mother until he got too tired and she scooped him back onto the bicycle seat. The ride back down was thrilling, too: a headlong dash like the wind. Cixin urged her on: *Faster! Faster!* If he could just go fast enough, they might leave the ground forever and he would never have to go back to the village.

The best part, however, was in the mountains. Mama brought a *picnic*—that was a word from the secret language, the one he and his mother always used when not even Auntie was around.

Nobody else knew about the secret language. It was for the two of them alone. The picnic had all the things Cixin liked best: congee with chicken and sweetened bean curd and orange juice. Although the orange juice was only for him; Mama had wine or beer.

As they ascended higher and higher, Cixin would feel his shoulders and knees and stomach loosen. He didn't run around up here; he didn't *have* to run around. The air grew sharp and clean. The mountains stood, firm and tall and strong—and how long they stood there! Millions of years, Mama said. Cixin liked thinking about that. You couldn't be angry at something so strong and old. You could rest in it.

"Tell me again," Cixin would say, sitting on the edge of Mama's blanket. "Where do the mountains go?"

"All the way to Tibet, *bow bei'r*."

"And Tibet is the highest place in the world."

"The very highest."

After a while Mama would fall asleep, thin and pale on her blanket, her short dark hair flopping sideways. Even then Cixin didn't feel the need to run around. He sat and looked at the mountains, and his mind seemed to drift among the clouds, until sometimes he couldn't tell which was clouds and which was himself. Sometimes a small animal or bird would sit on the ground only meters away, and Cixin would let it rest, too.

When Mama awoke, it was time for the *once-a-week*. That was a word from the secret language, too.

The once-a-week was tiny little green specks that Mama counted carefully. They melted on Cixin's tongue and tasted faintly sour. Mama always said the same words, every time, and he had to answer the same words, every time.

"You must swallow the once-a-week, Cixin."

"I must swallow the once-a-week."

"*Every* week."

"Every week."

"If you do not swallow it, you will die."

"I will die." Dead birds, dead rats, a mangy dog dead in the road. Cixin could picture himself like that. The picture terrified him.

"And you must not tell anyone except Auntie about the once-a-week. Ever."

"I must not tell anyone except Auntie about the once-a-week ever."

"Promise me, *bow bei'r*."

"I promise." And then, for the first time, "Where does the once-a-week come from?"

"Ah." Mama looked sad. "From very far away."

"From Tibet?"

"No. Not Tibet."

"Where?" He had a sudden idea, fueled by the stories Auntie told him of dragons and ghost warriors. "From a land of magic?"

"There is no magic." Mama's voice sounded even sadder. "Only science."

"Is science a kind of magic?"

She laughed, but it was not a happy sound. "Yes, I suppose it is. Black magic, sometimes. Now fold the blanket; we must go back."

Cixin forgot about science and magic and the once-a-week at the exciting thought of the wild bicycle dash down the mountain.

Twice a year Mama took the bus to Chengdu, another far away land of black magic. For days before she left, Auntie spent extra time kneeling at the household shrine. Cixin, five, eight, nine years old, raced around even more than usual. Mama snapped at him.

"Sit still!"

"Ah, he's wild today, that one," Auntie said, but unlike Mama, she was smiling. Auntie was very old. She didn't work in the vineyards any more, but Mama did. Some nights Mama didn't come home. Some nights she came home very late, falling down and either giggling or crying. Then she and Auntie argued when they thought Cixin could not hear.

"I said sit still!" Mama slapped him.

Cixin raced out the door, tried to kick the neighbor's dog, did not connect. He kept running in circles until he was exhausted and his heart was too tired to hurt so much and he saw Xiao sitting by the irrigation ditch with her ancient iPod. Cixin, panting, dropped down beside her.

"Let me see, Xiao."

She handed over the iPod. A year younger than Cixin and the daughter of the vineyard foreman, Xiao had possessions that the other village children could only dream of. Sweet-natured and docile, she always shared.

Cixin put the iPod to his ear but was too restless to listen to the music. But instead of hurling it into the ditch, as he might have done with anybody else, he handed it carefully back to Xiao. With her, he always tried to be careful.

"My mother is going to a magic land. To Chengdu."

Xiao laughed. She was the only person that Cixin allowed to laugh at him. Her laugh reminded him of flowers. She said, "Chengdu isn't a magic land. It's a city. I went there."

"You *went* there? When?"

"Last year. My father took me on the bus. Look, there's your mother waiting for the bus. She—" Xiao dropped her eyes.

Cixin spat. "She's drunk."

"I know." Xiao was always truthful.

"I don't care!" Cixin shouted. He wanted to leap up and race around again, he wanted to sit beside Xiao and ask about Chengdu, he didn't know what he wanted. The bus stopped and Mama lurched on. "I hope she never comes back!"

"You don't mean that," Xiao said. She took his hand. Cixin jerked his whole body to face her.

"Kiss me!"

"No!" Shocked, she dropped his hand and got to her feet.

He jumped up. "Don't go, Xiao! You don't have to kiss me!" Just saying the words desolated him. "You don't ever have to kiss me. Nobody ever has to kiss me."

She studied him from her beautiful dark eyes. "You're very strange, Cixin."

"I am not." But he knew he was.

A band of boys emerged from between the rows of grapes. When they saw Cixin, they began to yell. "*Fen noon an hi! Ben dan!*"

Cixin knew he was an angry boy but not a stupid one. He grabbed a rock from the irrigation ditch and hurled it at the boys.

It fell short but they swarmed around him, careful not to touch Xiao.

Cixin broke free and raced off. They shouted after him: "Half breed! Son of a whore!" He was faster than all of them, even among the trees that began on the other side of the village, even when the ground began to slope upward toward the mountains. He and his mother never went there anymore. So now Cixin would go by himself. He would run higher and higher, all the way to Tibet, and maybe he would go live with the monks and maybe he would die on the way and it didn't matter which. No one would care. His mother was a drunk and a whore, his Auntie was old and would die soon anyway, Xiao was so rich and she had an iPod and she would never ever kiss him.

He leaned against a tree until his breath was strong again. Then he again started up the mountain, walking to Tibet.

## —3: Ben—

Ben Malloy brought his coffee to the farthest booth of the San Diego cybershop and closed the door. The booth smelled of urine and semen. Public booths, used only by the desperately poor or desperately criminal or deeply paranoid, were always unsavory. He shouldn't have brought coffee but he'd been up all night, working when the lab was quiet and deserted, and he needed the caffeine.

He accessed the untraceable account, encrypted through remixers in Finland and God-knew-where-else, and her email was there.

> B—
> Your package arrived. Thank you. Still no breakthrough. Symptoms unchanged. I suspect elevated CRF and cortisol, serotonin fluctuations, maybe neuron damage. Akathesia, short REM latency. Sichuan quarantine may lift soon—rumors.
> H
> I cannot do this anymore. I just cannot.

Akathesia. Short REM latency. Ben had taught her those terms, so far from her own field. Haihong had always been a quick study.

He closed his eyes and let the guilt wash over him. She'd made the choices—both of them—so why was the guilt his? All he'd done was break several laws and risk his professional future to try to save her.

The guilt was because he'd failed.

Also because he'd misunderstood so much. He had thought of Haihong as an American. Taking her California Ph.D. in English literature, going out for hamburgers at Burger King and dancing to pellet rock and loving strappy high-heeled shoes. A girl with more brains than sense, to whom he'd attributed American attitudes and expediencies. And he'd been wrong. Underneath the California-casual-cum-grad-student-intensity-cum-sexually-liberated woman, Haihong had been foreign to him in ways he had not understood. Ben Jinkang Molloy's grandmother and father had both married Americans; his father and Ben himself had been born here. He didn't even speak Chinese.

His father had called him, all those years ago, from Florida. "Ben, your second cousin is coming from China to study in San Diego."

"My second cousin? What second cousin?"

"Her name is Deng Haihong. She's my cousin Deng Song's daughter, from near Chengdu. You need to look out for her."

Ben, busy with his first post-doc, had been faintly irritated with this intrusion into his life. "Does she even speak English?"

"Well, I should hope so. She's studying for a doctorate in English literature. Listen, buddy, she's an orphan. Both parents were casualties of that stupid savagery in Sichuan. She has nobody."

His father knew how to push Ben's buttons. Solitary by nature, Ben was nonetheless a sucker for stray kittens, homeless beggars, lost causes. He could picture his father, tanned and relaxed in the retirement condo in West Palm Beach, counting on this trait in Ben.

He said resignedly, "When does she arrive?"

"Tuesday. You'll meet her plane, won't you?"

"Yes," Ben had said, not realizing that the single syllable would commit him to four years of mentorship, of playing big brother, of pleasure and exasperation, all culminating in the disastrous conversation that had been the beginning of the end.

He and Haihong had sat across from each other in a dark booth at a favorite campus bar, Fillion's.

"I'm pregnant," Haihong said abruptly. "No beer for me tonight."

He had stiffened. Oh God, that arrogant bastard Scott, he'd warned her the guy was no good, *why* did women always go for the bad-boy jerks...

Haihong laughed. "No, it's not Scott's. You're always so suspicious, Ben."

"Then who—"

"It's nobody's. I'm a surrogate."

He peered at her, struggling to take it in, and saw the bravado behind her smile. She was defiant, and scared, and determined, all at once. Haihong's determination could crack granite. It had to be, for her to have come this far from where she'd been born. He said stupidly, "A surrogate?"

Again that brittle laugh. "You sound as if you never heard the word before. What kind of geneticist are you?"

"Haihong, if you needed money..."

"It's not that. I just want to help some infertile couple."

She was lying, and not well. Haihong, he'd learned, lied often, usually to cover up what she perceived as her own inadequacies. And she was fiercely proud. Look at the way she always leapt to the defense of her two friends and roommates, slutty Tess and brainless Emily. If Ben castigated Haihong now, if he was anything other than supportive, she would never trust him again.

But something here didn't smell right.

He said carefully, "I know another woman who acted as a surrogate, and it took a year for her to complete the medical surveillance and background checks. Have you been planning this for a whole year?"

"No, this is different. The clinic is in Mexico. American restrictions don't apply."

Alarms sounded in Ben's head. Haihong, despite her intelligence, could be very naïve. She'd grown up in some backwater village that was decades behind the gloss and snap of Shanghai or Beijing. Ben was not naïve. His post-doc had been at a cutting-edge big-pharm; he was now a promising researcher at the San Diego Neuroscience Institute. A lot of companies found it convenient to have easy access to Mexico for drug testing. FDA approval required endless and elaborate clinical trials, but the starving Mexican provinces allowed a lot more latitude as long as there was "full disclosure to all participants." As if an ignorant and desperate day laborer could, or would, understand the medical jargon thrown at him in return for use of his body. Congress had been conducting hearings on the issue for years, with no effect whatsoever. Any procedure or drug experimented with in Mexico would, of course, then have to be re-tested in the U.S. But ninety percent of all new drugs failed. Mexico made a cheap winnowing ground.

And, of course, there were always rumors of totally banned procedures available there for a price. But no big pharm or rogue genetics outfit would actually use a legitimate fertility clinic for experimentation…would they?

"Haihong, what's the name of the clinic?"

"Why?"

Their drinks came, Dos Equis for him and Diet Coke for her. After the waitress left, Ben said casually, "I may be able to find out stuff for you. Their usual pay rate for surrogates, for instance. Make sure you're not getting ripped off." Unlike Haihong, Ben was a good liar.

Haihong nodded. So it was the money. "Okay. The clinic is called Dispensario de las Colinas Verdes."

He'd never heard of it. "How did you learn about this place?"

"Emily." She was watching him warily now, ready to resent any criticism of her friend. He said only, "Okay, I'll get on it. How did your meeting with your thesis advisor go yesterday?"

He saw her relax. She launched into a technical discussion of semiotics that he didn't even try to follow. Instead he tried to find traces of his family's faces in hers. Around the eyes, maybe, and the nose…but he and his brothers stood six feet, his hair was red, and he had the spare tire of most sedentary Americans. She was tiny, fragilely made. And fragile in other ways, too, capable of an hysterical emotionalism kept in check only by her relentless drive to accomplishment. Ben had seen her drunk once, it was not pretty, and she'd never let him see her that way again. Haihong was a mass of contradictions, this cousin of his, and he groped through his emotions to find one that fit how he felt about her. He didn't find it.

Abruptly he said, interrupting something about F. Scott Fitzgerald, "Is the egg yours or a donor's?"

Anger darkened her delicate features. "None of your business!"

So the egg was hers, and she was more uneasy about the whole business than she pretended. All at once he remembered a stray statistic: Twenty-one percent of surrogate mothers changed their mind about giving up their babies.

"Sorry," he said. "Now what was that again about Fitzgerald?"


She was eight months along before he cracked Dispensario de las Colinas Verdes.

His work at the Neuroscience Institute was with genetically modified proteins that packaged different monoamines into secretory vesicles, the biological storage and delivery system for signal molecules. Ben specialized in brain neurotransmitters. This allowed him access to work-in-progress by the Institute's commercial and academic partners. Colinas Verdes was not among them.

However, months of digging—most of it not within the scope of his grant and some of it blatant favor-trading—finally turned up that one of the Institute's partners had a partner. That small company, which had already been fined twice by the FDA, had buried in its restricted on-line sites a single reference to the Mexican clinic. It was enough. Ben was good at follow-through.

Haihong was huge. She waddled around campus, looking as if she'd swallowed a basketball, her stick legs in their little sandals looking unable to support her belly. The final chapter of her dissertation had been approved in draft form by her advisor. The date for her oral defense had been set. She beamed at strangers; she fell into periods of vegetable lassitude; she snapped at friends; she applied feverishly for teaching posts. Sometimes she cried and then, ten minutes later, laughed hysterically. Ben watched her take her vitamins, do her exercises, resolutely avoid alcohol. He couldn't bring himself to tell her anything.

The day in her fourth month that she said to him, awe in her voice, "Right now he's growing eyelashes," Ben was sure. She was going to keep the baby.

Twenty-one percent.

He went himself to Mexico, presenting his passport at the border, driving his Saab through the dusty countryside. Two hours from Tijuana he reached the windowless brick building that was not the bright and convenient clinic Haihong had gone to. This was the clinic's research headquarters, its controlling brain. Ben went in armed with the names and forged references of the partner company, with his formidable knowledge of cutting-edge genetics, with pretty good Spanish, with American status and bluster. He spent an hour with the Mexican researchers on site, and left before he was exposed. He obtained names and then checked them out in the closed deebees at the Institute. Previous publications, conference appearances, chatter on the e-lists that post-docs, in self-defense, create to swap information that might impact their collective futures. It took all his knowledge to fill in the gaps, complete the big picture.

Then he sat with his head in his hands, anxiety battering him in waves, and wondered how he was ever going to tell Haihong.

He waited another week, working eighteen hours a day, sleeping in his lab on a cot, neglecting the job he was paid to do and cutting off both his technicians and his superiors. The latter decided to indulge him; they all thought he was brilliant. Every few hours Ben picked up the phone to call the FBI, the FDA, the USBP, anyone in the alphabet soup of law enforcement who could have shut it all down. But each time he put down the phone. Not until he had the inhibitor, which no one would have permitted him to cobble together had they known. Let alone permit giving it to Haihong.

A lot had been known about neurotransmitters for over seventy years, ever since the first classes of antidepressants. Only the link with genetics was new, and in the last five years, that field—Ben's field—had exploded. He had the fetus's genome. The genetics were new, but the countermeasures for the manifested behaviors were not. Ben knew enough about brain chemistry and cerebral structures.

What he hadn't known enough about was Haihong.

"An inhibitor," she said at the end of his long, lurching explanation, and her calm should have alerted him. An eerie, dangerous calm, like the absence of ocean sucked away from the beach just before the tsunami rolls in. He should have recognized it. But he'd been awake for twenty-two hours straight. He was so tired.

"Yes, an inhibitor," he echoed. "And it will work."

"You're sure."

Nothing like this was ever sure, but he said, "Yes. As sure as I can be." He tried to put an arm around her but she pushed him away.

"An inhibitor calibrated to body weight."

"Yes. Increasing in direct proportion."

"For his entire life."

"Yes. I think so. Haihong—"

"Side effects?" Still that eerie calm.

Ben ran his hand through his red hair, making it all stand up. "I don't know. How can I know?" He wanted to be reassuring, but the brain contained a hundred billion neurons, each with a thousand or so branches. That was ten-to-the-hundred-trillionth power of possible neural connections. He was pretty sure what neurotransmitters the genemods on the baby would increase production of, and pretty sure he could inhibit it. But the side effects? Anybody's guess. Even aspirin affected different people differently.

Haihong said, "A six-month shelf life and a one-week half-life in the body."

She echoed his terminology perfectly, still in that quiet, mechanical voice. Ben put out his hand to touch her again, drew it back. "Yes. Haihong, we need to call the FDA, now that I have something to use as an emergency drug, and let them take over the—"

"Give me the first batch."

He did. This was why he'd made it, because he'd known months ago what she had never told him in words. Twenty-one percent.

He agreed to put off calling the authorities for one more day. "Just give me time to assimilate it all, Ben. A little time. Okay?"

He'd agreed. It was her life, her child. Not his.

The next day she'd been gone.

In the foul public cyberbooth, nine years later, Ben deleted Haihong's email. *Rumors*, she'd written, *Sichuan quarantine may lift soon.* Interred in her remote village, which the most modern of technologies had forced back into the near primitive, she hadn't even heard the news. The quarantine had always been as much political as anything else, or it wouldn't have been in force so long. It was to be lifted today and even now, right there in Chengdu from which she must have sent her email, she still seemed oblivious. *I cannot do this anymore. I just cannot.*

What exactly did that mean?

He left his coffee untouched in the filthy booth. Outside, in the fresh air under California's blue sky, he pulled out his handheld and booked a flight to China.

—4: Haihong—

She left the People's Internet Building at dusk. Usually she spent several hours on-line, as long as she could afford, in an orgy of catching up on news, on the academic world, on anything outside the quarantine. She only had the opportunity every six months.

This time, she left as soon as she'd emailed Ben, uploading onto him her bi-annual report, her gratitude, her despair. Unfair, of course, but how could it matter? Ben, in California, had everything; he could add a little despair to his riches. To Haihong nothing mattered any longer, nothing except Cixin, the unruly child who did not love her and for whom she'd given her future. A fruitless sacrifice, since Cixin had no future, either. Everything barren, everything a waste.

She clutched the package in her hand, the precious six-month supply of inhibitor of proteins in the posterior superior parietal lobes. The pills were sewn inside a gift for Cixin, a stuffed toy he was too old for. Ben had not done any further work on the side-effects. Maybe he had no way to measure them, eight thousand miles away from his research subject. Maybe he had lost interest. So Cixin would go on being irritable, restless, underweight, over-stressed. He would—

Outside, Haihong blinked. The sparse and rotting skeleton left of Chengdu seemed to have gone mad! Gongs sounded, sirens blared, people poured out of the dilapidated buildings, more people than she had known were left in the city. They were shouting something, something about the quarantine...

Starting forward, she didn't even see the pedicab speeding around the corner, racing along the nearly trafficless street. The driver, a strong and large man, saw her too late. He yelled and braked, but Haihong had already gone flying. Her tiny and mal-nourished body struck the ground head first. Bleeding from her mouth, unable to feel any of her body below the neck, her last thought was a wordless prayer for her son.

## —5: Cixin—

BY AFTERNOON CIXIN WAS EXHAUSTED from walking away from the village, up into the mountains. His legs ached and his empty stomach moaned. Worse, he was afraid he was lost.

He had been careful to follow the path where Mama used to ride her bicycle, and it had led him to their old picnic place. Cixin had stopped and rested there, but the usual calm had not come over him. Should he try to worship, like Auntie did when she bowed in front of her little shrine? Mama said, in the secret language, that worship was nonsense. But nothing Mama said could be trusted. She was a drunk and a whore.

Cixin swiped a tear from his dusty cheek. It was stupid to cry. And he wasn't really lost. After the picnic place, the path had be-come narrower and harder to see, and maybe—*maybe*—he had lost it, but he was still climbing uphill. Tibet was uphill, at the top of the mountains. He was all right.

But so thirsty! If he just had some water...

An hour later he came to a stream. It was shallow and muddy, but he lay on his belly and lapped at the water. That helped a little. Cixin staggered up on his aching legs and resumed climbing.

An hour after that, it began to get dark.

Now fear took him. He'd been sure he would reach Tibet before nightfall…after all, look how far he'd come! There should be monks coming out to greet him, taking him into a warm place with water and bean curd and congee…Nothing was right.

"Stupid monks!" he screamed as loud as he could, but then stopped because what if the monks were on their way to get him and they heard him and turned back? So he yelled, "I didn't mean it!"

But still no monks came.

Darkness fell swiftly. Cixin huddled at the base of a pine tree, arms wrapped around his body and legs drawn up for warmth. It didn't help. He didn't want to race around, not on his hurting legs and not in the dark, and yet it was hard to sit still and do nothing. Every noise terrified him—what if a tiger came? Mama said the tigers were all gone from China but Mama was a drunk and a whore.

Shivering, he eventually slept.

In the morning the sun returned, warming him, but everything else was even worse. His belly ached more than his legs. Somehow his tongue had swollen so that it seemed to fill his entire dry mouth. Should he go back to the place where the water had been? But he didn't remember how to get there. All the pine trees, all the larches, all the gray boulders, looked the same.

Cixin whimpered and started climbing. Surely Tibet couldn't be much farther. There'd been a map of China in the village school he'd attended until his inability to sit still made him leave, and on the map Tibet looked very close to Sichuan. He was almost there.

The second nightfall found him no longer able to move. He collapsed beside a boulder, too exhausted even to cry. The picture of the dead dog in the road filled his mind, filled his fitful dreams. When he woke, he was covered with small, stinging bites from something. His cry came out as a hoarse, frustrated whimper. The rising sun filled his eyes, blinding him, and he turned away and tried to sit up.

Then it happened.

Cixin *knew.*

He was lifted out of his body. Thirst and hunger and insect bites vanished. He was not Cixin, and everything—the whole universe— was Cixin. He was woven into the universe, breathed with it, was one with it, and it spoke to him wordlessly and sang to him without music. Everything was him, and he was everything. He was the gray boulder and the yellow sun rising and the rustling pine trees and the hard ground. He was *them* and he felt them, it, all, and the mountains reverberated with surprise and with his name: *Cixin.*

*Come.*

*Cixin.*

The child sat on the parched ground, expressionless, and was still and calm.


"Cixin!"

A sour, familiar taste melting on his tongue, a big hand in his mouth. Then, after a measureless time that was not time, water forced down his throat.

"Cixin!"

Cixin blinked. Then he cried out and would have toppled over had not the big man—how big he was! How pale!—steadied him. More water touched Cixin's lips.

"Not too much, buddy, not at first," the big man said, and he spoke the secret language that only Cixin and Mama knew. How could that be? All at once everything on Cixin hurt, his belly and neck and swollen legs and most of all his head. And the big man had red hair standing up all over his head like an attacking rooster. Cixin started to cry.

The big man lifted him in his arms and put him over his shoulder. Cixin just glimpsed the two other men, one from his village and one a stranger, their faces rigid with something that Cixin didn't understand. Then he fainted.

When he came to, he lay on his bed at Auntie's house. The big man was there, and the stranger, but the village man was not. The big man was saying, very slowly, some words in the secret language to the stranger, and he was repeating them in real words to Auntie. Cixin tried to say something—he didn't even know what—but only a croak came out.

Auntie rushed over to him. She had been crying. Auntie never cried, and fear of this made Cixin wail. Something terrible had happened, and it had happened to Mama. How did Cixin know this? He knew.

And underneath: that other knowing, half memory and half dream, already faded and yet somehow more real even than Auntie's tears or the big man's strange red hair:

*Cixin. Come. Cixin.*

The big man was Cousin Benjamin Jinkang Molloy. Cixin tasted the ridiculous name on his tongue. Despite the red hair, Cousin Ben sometimes looked Chinese, but mostly he did not. That made no sense, but then neither did anything else.

Auntie didn't like Cousin Ben. She didn't say so, but she wouldn't look at him, didn't offer him tea, frowned when his back was turned and she wasn't crying or at her shrine. Ben visited every day, at first with his "translator" and then, when he saw how well Cixin spoke the secret language, alone. He paid money to Xiao's father to sleep at Xiao's house. Xiao was not allowed to visit Cixin at his bed.

He said, "Why can you talk Mama's secret words?"

"It's English. Where I live, everybody speaks English."

"Do you live in Tibet?" That would be exciting!

"No. I live in America."

Cixin considered this. America might be exciting, too—Xiao's iPod came from there. Sudden tears pricked Cixin's eyes. He wanted to see Xiao. He wanted Mama, who was as dead as the dog in the road. He wanted an iPod. He wanted to get out of bed and race around but his body hurt and anyway Auntie wouldn't let him get up.

Ben said carefully, "Cixin, what happened to you up on the mountain?"

"I got lost."

"I know. I found you, remember? But what happened before that?"

"Nothing." Cixin closed his lips tight. He didn't actually remember what had happened on the mountain, only that something had.

But whatever it was, he wasn't going to share it with some strange red-headed cousin who wasn't even from Tibet. It was *his*. Maybe if Mama hadn't got dead…

The tears came then and Cixin, ashamed, turned his face toward the wall. Gently Ben turned it back.

"I know you miss your mother, buddy. But my time here is short and I need you to pay attention."

That was just stupid. People needed food and water and clothes and iPods—they didn't "need" Cixin's attention. He scowled.

Ben said, "Listen to me. It's very important that you go on taking the pills your mother was giving you."

"You mean the once-a-week?"

"Yes. I'm going to show you exactly how much to take, and you must do it *every single week*."

"I know. Or I will die."

Ben shut his eyes, then opened them again. "Is that what she told you?"

"Yes." Something inside him trembled, like a tremor deep in the earth. "Is it true?"

"Yes. It's true. In a very important way."

"Okay." All at once Cixin liked speaking the secret language again. It made Mama seem closer, and it made Cixin special. Suddenly he had a thought that made him jerk upright in bed, rattling his head. "Are you really from America?"

"Yes."

"And Mama was, too?"

"She lived there for a while, yes."

"She liked it there?"

"Yes, I think she did."

"Take me to America with you!"

Ben didn't look surprised—why not? Cixin himself was surprised by his thought: surprised, delighted, frightened. In America he would be away from the village boys, away from the school that threw him out. In America he could have an iPod. "Please, Cousin Ben, please please please!"

"Cixin, I can't. Auntie is your closest relative and she—"

"She's not really my Auntie! She was Mama's amah, is all! You're my elder cousin!"

Ben said gently, "She loves you."

Cixin fell back on his bed, hurting his head even more. *Love.* Mama loved him and she died and left him. Auntie loved him and she was keeping him from going to America. Cousin Ben didn't love him or he would take him away from this evil village. Love was terrible and ugly. Cixin glared savagely at this horrible cousin. "Then after you go I won't take my once-a-week and I will die!"

Ben stood. "I will not be blackmailed by a nine-year-old."

Cixin didn't know what "blackmail" was, but it sounded evil. Everywhere he was surrounded by evil. Better to die. Again he turned his face to the wall.

Later, he would always think that had made the difference. His silence, his turning away. If he had fought back, Ben would have said more about blackmail and gone away, angry. But instead he ran his hand through his red hair until it stood up like bristly grass—Cixin could just see this out of the corner of his eye—and then put his hand over his face.

"All right, Cixin. I'll take you to America. But I warn you, it may take a long, long time to arrange."

## —6: BEN—

It took nearly two years.

If Ben hadn't had family contacts at the State Department, it would have been even longer, might have been impossible. The Chinese were discouraging foreign adoptions; Cixin was from within formerly-quarantined Sichuan; the death certificate for Haihong needed to be obtained from a glacially slow bureaucracy and presented in triplicate. But on the other hand, Chinese-American relations were in a positive phase. Ben could prove Haihong had been his second cousin. Ben had received a Citizens' Commendation from the FBI for exposing the surrogate-ring of American girls exploited by a sleazy Mexican fertility clinic. And Uncle James was on the State desk for East Asia.

During those two years, Ben sent Auntie money and Cixin presents. An iPod, which seemed to be a critical object. Jeans and sneakers. Later, a laptop, to be used at the vineyard foreman's house to communicate with Ben. They exchanged email, and Cixin's troubled Ben. Fluent in spoken English, Cixin was barely literate in any language, and he didn't seem to be learning much from the school software Ben supplied.

> Cuzin Ben this is Cixin. Wen r yu comin 4 me. Anty is sik agen. Evrybuddy hates me. I hate it hear. Com soon or I wil die.   Cixin.

> Cixin—I am making plans to bring you here as fast as I can. Please be patient.

Could Cixin read that word? Maybe not. The backward connection at the foreman's house didn't permit even such a basic tool as a camlink.

> Please wait without fuss.

*Haihong saying during her pregnancy, "Ben, please don't fuss at me!"*

> Take your once-a-week, use your school software, and be good.

What else? How did you write to a child you'd barely met?

> You will like America. Soon, I hope.   Ben.

*Soon, I hope.* But did he? Cixin would be an enormous responsibility, and Ben would bear it mostly alone. His parents, old when Ben had been born, lived in failing health in Florida, his sisters in Des Moines and Buffalo. Ben worked long hours in his lab. What was he going to do with a illegally genemod, barely literate, ADH adolescent who shared less than three percent of Ben's genetic heritage and nothing of his cultural one?

And then, because complications always attracted more complications, he met Renata.

A group from his department at the Institute went out for Friday Happy Hour. Ordinarily Ben avoided these gatherings.

People drank too much, barriers were lowered that might better have stayed raised, flirtations started that proved embarrassing on Monday morning. But Ben knew he was getting a reputation as standoffish, if not downright snobbish, and he had to work with these people. So he went to Happy Hour.

They settled into a long table, scientists and technicians and secretaries. Dan Silverstein, a capable researcher fifteen years Ben's senior, talked about his work with envelope proteins. Susie, the intern whom somebody really should do something about, shot Ben smoldering glances across the table. Ben spotted Renata at the bar.

She sat alone. Tall, a mop of dirty blonde curls, glasses. Pretty enough but nothing remarkable about her except the intensity with which she was both consuming beer and marking on a sheaf of papers. At Grogan's during a Friday Happy Hour? Then she looked up, pure delight on her face, and laughed out loud at something on the papers.

Ben excused himself to go to the men's room. Taking the long way back, he peered over her shoulders. School tests of some kind—

"Do I know you?" She'd caught him. Her tone was cool but not belligerent, looking for neither a fight nor a connection. Self-sufficient.

"No, we've never met." And then, because she was turning back to her papers, dismissing him, "Are you a teacher? What was so funny?"

She turned back, considering. The set of her mouth said, *This better not be a stupid pick-up line,* but there was a small smile in her eyes. "I teach physics at a community college."

"And physics is funny?"

"Are you at all familiar with John Wheeler's experiments?"

She flung the question at him like a challenge, and all at once Ben was enjoying himself. "The 1980 delayed-choice experiment?"

The smile reached her mouth, giving him full marks. "Yes. Listen to this. The question is, *'Describe what Wheeler found when he used particle detectors with photon beams.'* And the answer should be…" She looked at Ben, the challenge more friendly now.

"That the presence or absence of a detector, no matter how far down the photon's path, and even if the detector is switched on *after* the photon passes the beam splitter, affects the outcome. The detector's presence or absence determines whether the photon registers as a wave or a particle."

"Correct. This kid wrote, 'Wheeler's particles and his detectors acted weird. I think both were actually broken. Either that or it was a miracle.'" She laughed again.

"And it's funny when your students don't learn anything?"

"Oh, he's learned something. He's learned that when you haven't got the vaguest idea, give it a stab anyway." She looked fondly at the paper. "I like this kid. I'm going to fail him, but I like him."

Something turned over in Ben's chest. It was her laugh, or her cheerful pragmatism, or… He didn't know what. He stuck out his hand. "I'm Ben Molloy. I work at the Neuroscience Institute."

"Renata Williams." She shook hands, her head tipped slightly to one side, the bar light glinting on her glasses. "I've always had a thing for scientists. All that arcane knowledge."

"Not so arcane."

"Says you. Sit down, Ben."

They talked until long after his department had left Grogan's. Ben found himself telling her things he'd never told anyone else, incidents from his childhood that were scary or funny or puzzling, dreams from his adolescence. She listened intently, her glasses on top of her head, her chin tilted to one side. Renata was more reticent about her own past ("Not much to tell—I was a goody-goody grind"), but she loved teaching and became enthusiastic about her students. They were carrying out some elaborate science project involving the data from solar flares; this was an active sunspot year. Renata pulled out her students' sunspot charts and explained them in the dim light from the bar. Eventually the weary bartender stopped shooting them meaningful glances and flatly told them, "Leave, already!"

Ben drove to her apartment. They left her car in the parking lot of the bar until the next day. In bed she was different: more vulnerable, less sure of herself. Softer. She slept with one hand all night on Ben's hip, as if to make sure he was still actually there. Ben lay awake and felt, irrationally but definitely, that he had come home.

Renata worked long hours, teaching five courses ("Community colleges are the sweatshops of academe"), but with a difference.

When she wasn't working, she had a life. She saw friends, she kick-boxed, she played in a chess league, she went to movies. Ben, who did none of these things, felt both envious and left-out. Renata just laughed at him.

"If you really wanted to kick-box, you'd take a class in it. People generally end up doing what they want to do, if they can. My hermit." She kissed him on the nose.

*If they can.* Ben didn't tell Renata about Cixin. The first month, he assured himself, they were just getting to know each other. (A lie: he'd known her, *recognized* her, that first night at Grogan's.) Then, as each month passed—three, four, six—it got harder to explain why he'd delayed. How would Renata react? She was kind but she was also honest, valuing openness and sincerity, and she had a temper.

*I'm adopting a Chinese boy for whom I've broken several laws that could still send me to jail, including practicing medicine without a license and administering untested drugs that induce socially disabling side-effects.* Perfect. Nothing added to romance like felony charges. Unless it was medical experimentation on a child.

Sometimes Ben looked at Renata, sleepy after sex or squinting at her computer, glasses on top of her curly head, and thought, *It will be all right.* Renata would understand. She came from a large family, and although she didn't want kids herself, she would accept Cixin. Look at how much effort she put into her students, how many endless extra hours working with them on the sunspot project. And Cixin was eleven; in seven more years he'd be off onto his own life.

Other times he knew that he'd lied to Renata, that Cixin was not an easy-to-accept or lovable child, and that his arrival would make Ben's world fall apart. At such times, his desperation made him moody. Renata usually laughed him out of it. But still he didn't tell her.

Then, in August, Uncle James called from Washington. His voice was jubilant.

"I just got the final approval, Ben. You can go get your cousin any time now. You're a daddy! And send me a big cigar—it's a boy!"

Ben clutched his cell so tight that all blood left his fingers. "Thanks," he said.

"Tell me how it works," Renata said. They were the first words she'd spoken in fifteen long minutes, all of which Ben had spent talking. Her dangerous calm reminded him of Haihong, all those years ago.

They were in his apartment, which had effectively if not officially become hers as well. His half-packed suitcase lay open on the bed. Ben stood helplessly beside the suitcase, a pair of rolled-up socks in his hand. Renata sat in a green brocade chair that had been a gift from his mother and Ben knew that if he approached that chair, she would explode.

He took refuge in science. "It's an alteration in the genes that create functional transporter proteins. Those are the amines that get neurotransmitters across synapses to the appropriate brain-cell receptors. The mechanisms are well understood—in fact, there are polymorphic alleles. If you have one gene, your body makes more transporters; with the other version, you get less."

"What difference does that make?"

"It affects mood and behavior. Less serotonin, for example, is connected to depression, irritability, aggression, inflexibility."

"And this alleged genemod in your cousin gave him less serotonin?"

"No." *Alleged genemod*. Ben dragged his hand through his hair. "He probably does have less serotonin, but that's a side effect. The genemod affected other proteins that in turn affected others…it's a cascade. Everything's interconnected in the brain. But the functional result in Cixin would be a flood of transporters and neurotransmitters in two brain regions, the superior parietal lobes and the temporoparietal region."

"I don't want jargon, Ben. I want explanations."

"I'm trying to give them to you. I'm doing the best I can to—"

"Then do better! Six months we've been together and you never mention that you're adopting a child…what is the *effect* of the extra transporters on those parts of the brain?"

"Without the inhibiting drug I designed for him, near-total catatonia."

"That doesn't make sense! Nobody would deliberately design genes to do that!"

"They didn't." Suddenly tired, he sat on the edge of the bed. His flight to Shanghai left in six hours. "Those brain areas orient the body in space and differentiate between self and others. The research company was trying to develop heightened awareness, perception of others' movements, and reactions to muscular shifting."

She got it. "Better fighting machines."

"Yes."

"Then why—"

"They were rogue geneticists, Renata. They didn't have access to all the most recent research. They screwed up. They're all in jail now."

"And the Neuroscience Institute—"

His patience gave way. "Of course the Institute wasn't involved! I told you—we helped shut the whole thing down."

"Except for your little part in supplying this kid with home-made inhibitors. His other problems you mentioned, the restlessness and aggression—"

"Most likely side-effects of the inhibitor," Ben said wearily. "You can't alter the ratio of neurotransmitters in the brain without a lot of side effects. Cixin's body is under huge stress and his behavior is consistent with fluctuating neurotransmitters and high concentrations of cortisol and other stress hormones."

She said nothing.

"Renata, I promise you—"

"Yeah, well, I've seen what your words are worth." She got up from the green chair and walked around him, toward the door. He knew better than to try to stop her. "If you'd told me about Cixin from the beginning—even only that he was coming here to live with you—that would be one thing. I could have accepted it. I mean—that poor kid. It's not his fault, and I understand family ties as well as you Chinese, or part-Chinese, or whatever you're calling yourself now. But, Ben, I *asked* you. I said after our first week or so, 'Do you see yourself ever wanting children in your life?' And you said no. And now you tell me—" She broke off.

All this time he'd been holding the socks. Carefully, as if they were made of glass, he laid them into his suitcase. A small part of his chaotic mind registered that, like most socks nowadays, they had probably been exported from China. He said, "Will you still be here when I get back?"

"I don't know."

They looked at each other.

"I don't know, Ben," she repeated. "I don't know who you really are."

It was the rainy season in Sichuan and over ninety degrees. Ben's clothing stuck to his body as he waited in the bus station in Chengdu; Cixin's village still had no maglev service. The station looked cleaner and more prosperous than when he'd come to China two years ago. Children in blue-and-white school uniforms marched past, carrying pictures of giant pandas. Ben had emailed Cixin to ask Auntie to bring him to Chengdu, but Cixin got off the bus alone.

He hadn't grown much. At eleven—almost twelve—he was a small, weedy boy with suspicious dark eyes, thin cheeks, and an unruly shock of black hair falling over his forehead. A large green-ish bruise on one cheek. He carried a small backpack, nothing else. He didn't smile.

Ben locked his knees against a tide of conflicting emotions. Apprehension. Pity. Resentment. Longing for Renata. But he tried. He said, "Hey, buddy" and put a hand on Cixin's shoulder. Cixin flinched and Ben removed the hand.

He tried again. "Hello, Cixin. It's good to see you. Now let's go to America."

## —7: Cixin—

HE DIDN'T KNOW who he really was.

Not now, in these strange and bewildering places. Cixin had never been out of his village. He'd assumed the videos on his laptop had been made-up lies, like Mama telling him about Tibet. But here was Chengdu, full of cars and pedicabs and scooters and huge buildings like mountains and buildings partly fallen down and signs that sprang up from the ground but dissolved when you walked through them and flashing lights and millions of people and men with big guns.... Cixin, who just last week had beaten up three village boys at once and thought of himself secretly as "The Tiger," clutched Ben's hand and didn't know what this world was, what he himself was anymore.

"It's all right, buddy," Ben said and Cixin glared at him and dropped the hand, angry because Ben wasn't afraid.

They sat together in the back of the plane to Shanghai. For a while Cixin was content to stare out the window as the ground fell away and they rose into clouds—up into *clouds*! But eventually he couldn't stay still.

"I'm getting up," he told Ben.

"Toilet's just behind us," Ben said.

Cixin didn't need a toilet, he needed to run. Space between the rows of seats was narrow but he barreled down it, waving his arms. A boy a few years older walked in the opposite direction—on Cixin's aisle! The boy didn't step aside. Cixin shoved him away and kept running. The boy staggered up and started after Cixin but was stopped by a shout in Chinese from a man seated nearby. Cixin ran the length of the aisle, cut across the plane, ran back down a different aisle, where Ben grabbed him by the arm.

"Sit, Cixin. *Sit.* You can't run in here."

"Why? Will they throw me off?" This was funny—they were on a plane!—and Cixin laughed. Once he started, he couldn't seem to stop. A man in a blue uniform moved purposefully toward them. Cixin stopped laughing—what if it was a soldier with a hidden gun? He cowered into his seat and tried to make himself very small.

The maybe-soldier and Cousin Ben talked softly. Ben sat down and shook a yellow pill from a plastic bottle. "Take this with your bottled water."

"That's not my once-a-week!" The once-a-week, for reasons Cixin didn't understand, had to be left behind at Auntie's. *Too risky for Customs*, Ben said, *especially for me*. Which made no sense be-cause Ben didn't take the once-a-week, only Cixin did.

"No, it's not your once-a-week," Ben said, "but take it anyway. Now!"

Cixin recognized anger. Ben might have a gun, too. In the videos, all Americans had guns. He took the pill, tapped on the window, kicked the back of the seat until the woman in it turned around and said something sharply in Chinese.

Cixin wasn't clear on what it was. A slow languor had fallen over the plane. Then sleep slid into him as softly as the fog by the river, as calmly as something…something right at the edge of memory…a pine tree and a gray boulder and…

He slept.

Another airport. Stumbling through it half awake. Shouting, people surging, a wait in a locked room…maybe it was a dream. Ben's face tired and white as old snow. Then another plane, or maybe not…yes. Another plane. More sleep. When he woke truly and for real, he lay in a small room with blue walls and red cloth at the windows, four stacked houses up into the sky, in San Diego, America.

Cixin ran. Waves pounded the shore, the wind whistled hard—whoosh! whoosh!—and sand blew against his bare legs, his pump-ing arms, his face. He laughed and swallowed sand. He ran.

Ben waited where the deserted beach met the parking lot, the hood of his jacket pulled up, his face red and angry. "Cixin! Get in the car!"

Cixin, exhausted and dripping and happy—as happy as he ever got here—climbed into the front seat of Ben's Saab. Rain pounded the windshield. Ben shouted, "You ran away from your tutor again!"

Cixin nodded. His tutor was stupid. The man had been telling him that rainstorms like this were rare and due to the Earth get-ting hotter. But with his own body Cixin had experienced many rainstorms, every summer of his life, and they all were hot. So he ran away from the stupid tutor, and from the even stupider girl who was supposed to come take care of him after the tutor left and before Ben came home from work. He ran the seven streets from Ben's house-in-the-sky to the beach because the beach was the only place in America that he liked. And because he wanted to run in the rain.

"You can't just leave the condo by yourself," Ben said. "And I pay that tutor to bring you up to speed before school starts in September, even though—you can't just go down to the beach during a typhoon! And I had to leave the lab in the middle of—"

There was more, but Cixin didn't listen. He'd only been in America ten days but already he knew that Ben wouldn't beat him. Still, Ben was very angry, and Ben was good to him, and Ben had showed him the wonderful beach in the first place. So Cixin hung his head and studied the sand stuck to his knees, but he didn't actually listen. That much was not necessary.

"—adjust your dosage," Ben finished. Cixin said nothing, respectfully. Ben sighed and started the car, his silly red hair stuck to his head.

When they were nearly back at the houses-stacked-in-the-sky, Cixin said, "You look sick, Cousin Ben."

"I'm fine," Ben said shortly.

"You don't eat."

"I eat enough. But, Cixin, you're driving me crazy."

"Yes." It seemed polite to agree. "But you don't eat and you look sick and sad. Are you sad?"

Ben glanced over, rain dripping off his collar. "You surprise me sometimes, buddy."

That was *not* a polite answer. Cixin scowled and stared out the window at the "typhoon" and tapped his sandy sneaker on the sodden floor of the car. He wanted to run again.

And Ben was too sad.

In the "condo," instead of the stupid tutor, a woman sat on the sofa. How did she get in? A robber! Cixin rushed to the phone, shouting, "911! 911!" Ben had taught him that. Robbers—how exciting!

But Ben called, "It's all right, Cixin." His voice sounded so strange that Cixin stopped his mad dash and, curious, looked at him.

"Renata," Ben said thickly.

"I couldn't stay away after all," the woman said, and then they were hugging. Cixin turned away, embarrassed. Chinese people did not behave like that. And the woman was ugly, too tall and too pale, like a slug. Not pretty like Xiao. The way Ben was holding her…Cixin hated the woman already. She was evil. She was not necessary.

He rushed into his room and slammed the door.

But at dinnertime the woman was still there. She tried to talk to Cixin, who refused to talk back.

"Answer Renata," Ben said, his voice dangerously quiet.

"What did you say?" Cixin made his voice high and silly, to insult her.

"I asked if you found any sand dollars on the beach."

He looked at her then. "Dollars made of sand?"

"No. They're the shells of ocean creatures. Here." She put something on the table beside his plate. "I found this one last week. I'll bet you can't find one bigger than this."

"Yes! I can!" Cixin shouted. "I'm going now!"

"No, you're not," Ben said, pulling him back into his chair. But Ben was smiling. "Tomorrow's Saturday. We'll all go."

"And if we go in the evening and if the clouds have lifted, there should be something interesting to see in the sky," Renata said. "But I won't tell you what, Cixin. It's a surprise."

Cixin couldn't wait until Saturday evening. He woke very early. Ben and Renata were still asleep in Ben's bed—she must be a whore even if she wasn't as ugly as he thought at first—and here it was *morning*. A little morning, pale gray in a corner of the sky. The rainstorm was all gone.

He dressed, slipped out of the house-in-the-sky, and ran to the beach. No one was there. The air was calm now and the water had stopped pounding and something strange was happening to the sky over the water. Ribbons of color—green, white, green—waved in the sky like ghosts. Maybe they were ghosts! Frightened, Cixin turned his back, facing the part of the sky where the sun would come up and chase the ghosts away. But then he couldn't see the water. He turned back and ran and ran along the cool sand. To his left, in San Diego, sirens started to sound. Cixin ignored them.

Finally, exhausted, he plopped down. The sun was up now and the sky ghosts gone. Nobody else came out on the beach. Cixin watched the nearest tiny waves kissing the sand.

Something happened.

A soft, calm feeling stole through him, calm as the water. He didn't even want to run any more. He sat cross-legged, half hidden by a sand drift, dreamily watching the ocean, and all at once he *was* the ocean. Was the sand, was the sky, was the whole universe and they were him.

*Cixin. Come. Cixin.*

Voices, everywhere and nowhere, but Cixin didn't have to answer because they already knew the answer. They were him and he was them.

Peace. Belonging. Everything. Time and no time.

And then Ben was forcing open his mouth, putting in something that melted on his tongue, and it all went away.

But this time memory lingered. It had happened. It was real.

# —8: BEN—

"I'D DROPPED THE DOSAGE to try to mitigate the side effects," Ben said. He ran his hand through his filthy hair. Cixin lay asleep in his room, sunburned and exhausted. God only knew how long he'd been gone before Ben found his empty bed.

Renata pulled her eyes from CNN. The solar flare, the largest ever recorded and much more powerful than anticipated, had played havoc with radio communications from Denver to Beijing. Two planes had crashed. The aurora borealis was visible as far south as Cuba. Renata said, "Ben, you can't go on fiddling with his dosage and giving him sleeping pills when you get it wrong. You're not even an M.D., and yet you're playing God with that child's life!"

"And what do you think I should do?" Ben shouted. It was a relief to shout, even as he feared driving her away again. "Should I let him go catatonic? You didn't see him two years ago in China—I did! He'd been in a vegetative state for two days and he would have died if I hadn't found him! Is that what you think should happen?"

"No. You should get him medical help. You wouldn't have to say anything about the genemods or—"

"The hell I wouldn't! What happens when they ask me what meds Cixin takes? If I didn't tell them, he could die. If I do, I go to jail. And how long do you think it would take a medical team to find drug traces in his body? Inhibitors have a long half-life. And even if I explain everything, and if I'm believed, what happens to Cixin then? He's not even on my medical insurance until the adoption is final! So he'd be warehoused, catatonic, in some horrifying state hospital, and I'd be standing trial. Is that what you want?"

"No. Wait. I don't know." She wasn't yelling at him now; her voice held sorrow and compassion. CNN announced that a total of 312 people had died in the two air disasters. "But, sweetheart, the situation as it stands isn't good for you or Cixin, either. What are you going to do?"

"What can I do? He just isn't anything like a normal—Cixin!"

The boy stood in the doorway, his shock of black hair stiff from salt air, his eyes puffy from sleep. He suddenly looked much older.

"Ben—what does the once-a-week do to me?"

Renata drew a long breath.

"It's complicated," Ben said finally.

"I need to know."

Cixin wasn't fidgeting, or yelling, or running. Something had happened on the beach, something besides sunburn and dehydration. Ben's tired mind stabbed around for a way to explain things to a nearly illiterate eleven-year-old. Nothing occurred to him.

Renata switched off the television and said quietly, "Tell him, Ben. Or I will."

"Butt out, Renata!"

"No. And don't you ever try to bully me. You'll lose."

He had already lost. Shooting a single furious glance at her, Ben turned to Cixin. "You have a…a sickness. A rare disease. If you don't take the once-a-week, you will die like your mother said, but first you go all stiff and empty. Like this." Ben, feeling like a fool, sat on the rug and made his body rigid and his face blank.

"Empty?"

"Yes. No thoughts, nothing. No *Cixin*. That's how you were on the beach, like that for a long time, which is why you're so sunburned." And maybe more than sunburned. A big solar flare came with a proton storm, and those could cause long-term biochemical damage. Ben couldn't cope with that just now, not on top of everything else. "Do you understand, Cixin? You went empty. Like a…a Coke can all drunk up."

"Empty," Cixin repeated. All at once he smiled, a smile so enigmatic and complicated that Ben was startled. Then the boy went back into his room and closed the door.

"Spooky," Ben said inadequately. He struggled up from the rug. "How do you think he took it?"

"I don't know." Renata seemed as disconcerted as Ben. "I only know what I would be thinking if I were him."

"What would you be thinking?" All at once he desperately wanted to know.

"I would be wondering who I really was. Wondering where the pills ended and I, Cixin, began."

"He's eleven," Ben said scornfully. Scorn was a relief. "He doesn't have sophisticated thoughts like that."

September. Cixin started school, the oldest kid in the fourth grade. Fortunately, he was small enough to sort of fit in and large enough to not be picked on by his classmates. He could not read at grade level, could not concentrate on his worksheets, could not sit still during lessons. After one week, his teacher called Ben to school for an "instructional team meeting." The team recommended Special Ed.

After two weeks, Cixin had another episode of catatonia. Again Ben found him at the beach, sitting half in the water, motionless amid frolicking children and splashing teens and sunbathing adults. A small boy with a sand pail said conversationally, "That kid dead."

"He's not dead," Ben snapped. Wearily he forced a dose of inhibitor onto Cixin's tongue. It melted, and he came to and stared at Ben from dark, enigmatic eyes that slowly turned resentful.

"Go away, Ben."

"I can't, damn it!"

Cixin said, "You don't understand."

In his khakis and loafers—the school had called him at work to report Cixin's absence—Ben lowered himself to sit on the wet sand. The blue Pacific rolled in, frothy at the whitecaps and serene beyond. The sun shone brightly. Ben said, "Make me understand."

"I can't."

"Try. Why do you do it, Cixin? What happens when you go empty?"

"It's not empty."

"Then what is it?" He willed himself to patience. This was a child, after all.

Cixin took a long time answering. Finally he said, "I see. Everything."

"What kind of everything?"

"*Everything*. And it talks to me."

Ben went as still as Cixin had been. He hadn't even realized…. hadn't even *thought* of that. He'd thought of neurotransmitter ratios, neural architecture plasticity, blood flow changes, synaptic miscues. And somehow he'd missed this. *It talks to me.*

Cixin leapt up. "I'm not going back to special Ed!" he yelled and raced away down the sand, his school papers streaming out of the unzipped backpack flapping on his skinny shoulders.

"Temporal lobe epilepsy?" Renata said doubtfully. "But…he doesn't have seizures?"

"It's not *grand mal*," Ben said. They sat in Grogan's. Ben had drugged Cixin again with Dozarin, hating himself for doing it but needing, beyond all reason, to escape his apartment for a few hours. "With *petit mal*, seizures can go completely unnoticed. And obviously it's not the only aberration going on in his brain, but I think it's a factor."

"But…if he's hearing voices, isn't that more likely to be schizophrenia or something like that?"

"I'm no doctor, as you're constantly telling me, but temporal-lobe epilepsy is a very well documented source of religious transports. Joan of Arc, Hildegaard of Bingen, maybe even Saul on the road to Damascus."

"But why does your inhibitor work on him at all? Isn't epilepsy a thing about electrical firing of—"

"I don't know why it works!" Ben said. He drained his gin and tonic and set the glass, harder than necessary, onto the table between them. "Don't you get it, Renata? I don't know anything except that I'm reaching the end of my rope!"

"I can see that," Renata said. "Have you considered that Cixin might be telling the truth?"

"Of course he's 'telling the truth,' as he experiences it. Temporal-lobe seizures can produce visual and auditory hallucinations that seem completely real."

"That's not what I meant."

"What did you mean?"

Renata fiddled with the rim of her glass. "Maybe the voices Cixin hears *are* real."

Ben stared at her. *You think you know someone…* "Renata, you teach science. Since when do you dabble in mysticism?"

"Since always. I just don't advertise it to everybody."

That hurt. "I'm hardly 'everybody.' Or at least I thought I wasn't."

"You're taking it wrong. I just meant that I haven't closed the door on the possibility of other worlds besides this one, other levels of being. Spirits, aliens, gods and angels, parallel universes that bleed through…I don't know. But there's never been a human society, ever, that didn't believe in some sort of mystery beyond the veil."

He didn't know anymore who she was. Ben motioned to the waiter for another gin and tonic. When his thoughts were at least partly collected, he said, "You can't—"

"What I can or cannot do doesn't matter. The point is, what are *you* going to do now?"

"I'm going to have an implant inserted under Cixin's skin that will deliver the correct dose of inhibitor automatically."

"Really." Her tone was dangerous. "And who will perform this surgery? You?"

"Of course not. It can be done in Mexico."

"Do you know what you're saying, Ben? You're piling one criminal offense on top of another, and you're treating that boy like a lab rat."

"He's sick and I'm trying to make him better!" God, why wouldn't she understand?

"Are you going to at least explain all that to him?"

"No. He wouldn't understand."

She finished her wine, stood, and looked down at him with the fearlessness he both admired and disliked in her. The light from behind the bar glinted on her glasses. "Tell Cixin what you're going to do. Or I will."

"It's none of your business! I'm his guardian!"

"You've made it my business. And even if you were fully his legal guardian—which you're not, yet—you're not being his friend. Not until you can consider his mind as well as his brain."

"There's no difference, Renata,"

"The hell there isn't. Tell him, Ben. Or I will."

He took a day to think about it, a day during which he was furious with Renata, and longed for her, and addressed angry arguments to her in his mind. Then, reluctantly, he left work in the middle of the afternoon (his boss was beginning to grumble about all the absences) to pick up Cixin at school.

Cixin wasn't there.

## —9: Cixin—

THE VOICES CAME TO HIM as he colored a map of the neighborhood around his school. All week they'd been working on maps, which wasn't as stupid as the other schoolwork. Cixin sat at his desk and vigorously wielded crayons. Playground, 7-11, houses, maglev stop, school building. North, west, legend to tell what the little drawings were. Blue, red, green...

*Cixin.*

He froze, his hand holding the green crayon suspended above his desk.

*Cixin.*

The voice was faint—but it was there. He looked wildly around the room. He knew the room was there, the other kids were there, he was there. In this school room, not on the beach, and not in that other place where even the beach disappeared and he could feel the Earth and sky breathe. So how could he be hearing...

*Cix...in...*

"Where are you?" he cried.

"I'm right here," the teacher's aide said. She hurried to Cixin's desk and put a hand on his shoulder.

*Cixin...*

"Come back!" He jumped up, scattering the crayons and knocking away the teacher's hand.

"I haven't gone anywhere," she said soothingly. "I'm right here, dear. What do you need?"

Standing, he could see out the classroom window to the parking lot. Ben's white car pulled in and parked.

Ben was coming for him. Cixin didn't know how he knew that, but he knew. Ben didn't like the voices. Ben was very smart and very American and he knew how to do things, get things, make things happen. Ben was coming for Cixin and Ben was going to make the voices go away forever.

Cixin's mind raced. Ben would have to pass front-door security, go to the school office, get a pass, come down the hall.... Cixin didn't hesitate. He ran.

"Cixin!" his teacher called. The other children began shouting. The aide tried to grab Cixin but he twisted away, ran out of the room and down the hall, zigged left, dashed toward the door to the playground. The school doors were locked from the outside but not the inside; Cixin burst through and kept running. Across the playground, over the fence, behind houses to the street...*run, fen noon nan hi...*

Eventually he had to stop, panting hard, leaning over with his hands on his knees. The houses here were small and didn't go up into the sky like Ben's house. Beyond were stores and eating houses and a gas station. Cixin walked behind a place with the good smell of pizza coming from it. Except for the beach, pizza was the best thing about America. Back here no one in a white car could see him. There was a big metal box with an opening high up.

Climbing on a broken chair, Cixin peered inside the big metal box. Some garbage, not much, and a bad smell, not too bad. He hauled himself up and tumbled inside. The garbage included a lot of pizza boxes, some with half-eaten pizzas inside. And no one could find him.

Many things were clear to him now. Ben saying to Renata, "I'll have to adjust the dosage. He's growing." The way to hear the voices, to go to that other place where he saw everything and breathed with the sky, was by having no once-a-week, and by waiting until the one he took before wasn't in his head anymore. Ben had made him swallow the last once-a-week last Wednesday. This was Tuesday, and already the voices, faint, were there.

He curled up in a corner of the dumpster to wait.

## —10: BEN—

HE LOOKED EVERYWHERE, the beach first. The day was warm and the sands choked with people who didn't have to be at work, as well as teenagers who probably should have been in school, but no Cixin. Ben raced back to the apartment: nothing. He called the school again, which advised him to call the police. Instead he called Renata's cell; she had no classes Tuesday afternoon.

"I'm very worried about—"

"How did you hear so *fast?*" she demanded.

"What?"

"You're inside, aren't you? Was the TV on at the lab? If there's a basement in your building go there but stay away from the power connections and make sure you can get out easily if there's a fire.

We put the bulletin out on campus, but who knows how many won't hear it—twenty minutes! God!"

"What are you talking about?"

"The flare! The solar flare!" And then, "What are *you* talking about?"

"Cixin's missing. He ran away."

"Shit!" And then, very rapidly, "Listen, Ben, another solar flare's been detected, a huge one, I mean *really* huge. Word just came down from the *Hinode*. It's bigger than the 1859 superflare and that one—just *listen*. There's an associated proton storm and nobody knows exactly when it will hit but the one in 2005 accelerated to almost a third of light speed. Best estimate is twenty minutes. There's going to be fires and power outages and communication disruptions but also proton storms that have biological consequences to living tissue that—you can't go down to the beach to look for him now!"

"I've already been. He's not there."

"Then where—"

"I don't know!" Ben shouted. "But I've got to look!"

"Where?" she asked, and her practicality only enraged him more.

"I don't know! But he's out there alone and if there are fires—"

The phone went dead.

He stood holding it, this dead and useless piece of technology, listening to the sirens start outside and mount to a frenzied wail. Where could Cixin have gone? Ben knew no place else to look, no place else that Cixin ever went. Although he had liked that V-R arcade Ben had once taken him to...

He tore out of the apartment, raced down the stairs, and stopped, frozen.

In the bright sunlight, lights were going out. Traffic lights, the neon window sign at Rosella's Café. They sparked in a glowing electrical arc and went dead. Smoke poured from the windows of a gas station a block over. People stopped, stared, and turned to their cell phones. Ben saw their faces when they realized the cells were all dead.

The sirens grew louder, then all at once stopped.

"What is it?" a young Hispanic woman asked him, clutching his arm. She wore shorts and a green halter top and she wheeled a pram with a fat, gurgling baby.

Ben shook off her hand. "A solar flare, get inside and stay away from windows and appliances!" She let out a great cry of horrified non-understanding but he was already gone, running the several blocks to the V-R arcade.

It took him ten minutes. Cixin wasn't there. The doors yawned crazily open, and a machine in one of the cubicles had shorted and begun to burn.

The city couldn't survive this. The country couldn't survive this. Panic, no communications, fires, the grid gone…and the radiation of a proton storm. Ten more minutes.

He found a corner of the arcade farthest from the booths, near the refreshment counter, and crawled under the largest table. It wouldn't help, of course, and it didn't make him feel better. But it was all he could do: wait for the beginning of the end under a wooden picnic table whose underside was stuck with wads of gum from children that might or might not be alive by tomorrow.

## —11: Cixin—

CIXIN.

"I'm here," he said aloud, to the empty pizza boxes in the dumpster. That was kind of funny because the voices didn't speak out loud; they didn't really have words at all. Just a feeling inside his head, and the feeling was him, Cixin. And then a picture:

The whole world, out in space, but covered with such a big gray fog that he couldn't even see the planet. But Cixin knew it was under the fog, and knew too that the voices hadn't known it. Not before. But now they did, because they knew Cixin was here. He was them and they were him and both were everything. It was all the way it should be, and he was calm and safe—he would always be safe now.

*Hi,* he said and it might have been out loud or not, it was all the same thing.

## —12: BEN—

NO OTHER V-R BOOTH SHORTED and caught fire, although the first one was still smoking. Ben crawled out from under the table. He'd been there half an hour—how long did a proton storm last? He had no idea.

In his pocket, his cell rang.

Ben pulled it out and stared at it incredulously. How... After a moment he had the wits to answer.

"Ben! Are you all right?"

Renata. "Yes. No. I don't know, I didn't find Cixin...How come this thing works?"

"I don't know." She sounded bewildered. "Mine came on, so I called you...Some communications are back. Not where the grid is out or the satellites destroyed, of course, but the radio stations that didn't get hit are coming through clear now and—it isn't possible!"

For the first and only time ever, he heard hysteria in her voice. In *Renata's* voice. "The solar radiation. It...it isn't reaching Earth anymore."

"It missed us?"

"No! I mean, yes, apparently...before the *Hinode* burned out, it—that's the Japanese spacecraft designed especially to monitor the sun, I told you about it—the data shows—the coronal mass ejection—"

"Renata, you're not making sense." Perversely, her panic steadied him. "Where are you?"

"I'm home. I have a radio. I'm not—it isn't –"

"Stay there. I'll get to you somehow. How much of the city is on fire?"

"Not enough!" she cried, which made no sense. "Did you find Cixin?"

"No." He'd told her that already. Pain scorched his heart. "Stay where you are. I'll call the cops about Cixin and then come."

"You won't get through to the police," she said, her voice still high with that un-Renata-like hysteria.

"I know," he said.

It took him over an hour to walk to her place. He kept trying the cops on his cell until the battery went dead. He skirted fires, looting, police cars, crying people in knots on the sidewalk, but Renata was right: This was not enough damage compared to what he had seen starting in the first few minutes of the solar storm. What the fuck had happened?

"It was deflected," Renata said when he finally got to her apartment. She'd calmed down. The power was off but bright sunlight poured into the window; the battery-powered radio was turned to the federal emergency station; beside the radio lay a gun that Ben had no idea Renata even owned. He stared at the gun while she said, "Cixin?"

"Still no idea."

She locked the door and put her arms around him. "You're bleeding."

"It's nothing, a fuss with some homeless guy that—what does the radio say?"

"Not much." She let him go and turned the volume lower. "The satellites are mostly knocked out, but not all because a few were in high orbit nightside and didn't get here until it…stopped."

"*What* stopped?"

"All of it," she said simply. "The radiation, including the proton storm, just curved around the Van Allen Belt and was deflected off into space."

He was no physicist. "That's good, right? Isn't that what the Van Allen is supposed to do? Only…only why did the radiation start for a while and *then* stop?"

"Bingo." Abruptly she sat down hard on the sofa. Ben joined her, surprised at how much his legs hurt. "What happened can't happen, Ben. Radiation just doesn't deflect that way by itself. And the magnetic fields contained in the coronal mass ejection were not only really intense, they were in direct opposition with Earth's magnetic field. We should have take a hit like…like nothing ever before. Far, far worse than the superstorm of 1859. And we didn't. In fact, protons should still be entering the atmosphere. And they aren't."

He tried to understand, despite the anxiety swamping him for Cixin. "Why isn't that all happening?"

"Nobody knows."

"Well, what does the radio say?"

She flung out her hands. "Unknown quantum forces. Angels. Aliens. God. Secret government shields. Don't you understand… *nobody knows.* This just can't be happening."

But it was. Ben said wearily, "Where do you think I should look next for Cixin?"

They found him two days later. It took that long for basic city services to begin to resume and for anyone to approach the dumpster. Cixin was catatonic, dehydrated, bitten by rats. He was taken to the overburdened hospital. Ben was called when a nurse discovered Cixin's name and phone number sewn into the waistband of his jeans—Renata's idea. He found Cixin rigid on a gurney parked in a hallway jammed with more patients. He had an IV, a catheter, and multiple bandages. His eyes were empty.

Ben put the inhibitor on Cixin's tongue. Slowly Cixin woke up, his dark eyes over sunken cheeks turning reproachful. Ben yelled for a doctor, but no one came.

"Cixin."

"They…didn't…know," he croaked.

"It's okay, buddy, I'm here now, it's okay… Who didn't know what?"

But painfully Cixin turned his face to the wall and would say no more.

The staff wanted to do a psych evaluation. Ben argued. They turned stubborn. Eventually he said they could get a court order if they wanted to but for right now he was taking his boy home as soon as the treatment for dehydration was completed. The harassed hospital official said several harsh things and promised legal action. A day later Ben signed out Cixin AMA, against medical advice, and drove him home through streets returning to normal much faster than anyone had thought possible.

There was a dreary familiarity to the scene: Cixin asleep in his room, Ben and Renata with drinks in the living room, talking about him. How many times in the last few months had they done this? How many more to come?

Renata had just come from the small bedroom. She'd asked to talk to Cixin alone. "He won't tell you anything," Ben had warned, but she'd gone in anyway. Now she sat, pale and purse-lipped, on Ben's sofa, holding her drink as if it were an alien object.

"Did he tell you anything?" Ben said tiredly. He stood by the window, facing her.

"Yes. No. Just what he told you—'They didn't know' and 'Let me go back.' Plus one other thing."

"What?" Jealousy, perverse and ridiculous, prodded him: Cixin had talked more freely to her than to him.

"He said there was a big explosion, a long time ago."

"A big explosion?"

"A long time ago."

That hardly seemed useful. Ben said, "I don't know what to do. I just don't."

Renata hesitated. "Ben...do you remember when we met? At Grogan's?"

"Yes, of course—why wouldn't I? Why bring that up now?"

"I was correcting papers, remember? My students were supposed to answer questions about Wheeler's two-slit experiments."

Ben stared at her. She was very pale and her expression was strange, both hesitant and wide-eyed, completely unlike Renata. "I remember," he said. "So?"

"The original 1927 two-slit experiment showed that a photon could be seen as both a wave and a particle that—"

"Don't insult my intelligence," Ben snapped, and wondered at whom his nasty tone was aimed. He tried again. "Of course I know that. And your students were writing about Wheeler's demonstration that observation determines the outcome of which one a photon registers as."

"The presence or absence of observation also determines the results of a whole slew of other physics experiments," she said. "All right, you know all that. But *why?*"

"Feynman's probability wave equations—"

"Explain exactly nothing! They describe the phenomena, they quantify it, but they don't explain why *observation*, which essentially means human consciousness, should be so woven into the very fabric of the universe at its most basic level. Until humans observe anything fundamental, in a very real sense it doesn't exist. It's only a smear of unresolved probability. So why does consciousness give form to the entire universe?"

"I don't know. Why?"

"I don't know either. But I think Cixin does."

Ben stared at her.

Renata looked down at the drink in her hand. Her shoulders trembled. "The explosion Cixin said he saw in his mind—he said, 'It made everything.' I think he was talking about the Big Bang. I think he feels a presence of some kind when he's in his catatonic state. That whatever genemods he has, they've somehow opened up parts of his mind that in the rest of us are closed."

Ben put his glass down carefully on the coffee table and sat beside her on the sofa. "Renata, he does feel a presence. He's experiencing decreased blood flow in the posterior superior parietal lobes, which define body borders. He loses those borders when he goes into his trance. And very rapid firing in the temporoparietal region can lead to the sense of an 'other' or presence in the brain. Cixin's consciousness gets caught in neural feedback loops in both those areas—which are, incidentally, the same areas of the brain that SPECT images highlight in Buddhist monks who are meditating. What Cixin feels is real to him—but that doesn't make it real in the cosmos. Doesn't make it a…a…."

"Overmind," she said. "Cosmic consciousness. I don't know what to call it. But I think it's there, and I think it's woven into the universe at some deeply fundamental level, and I think Cixin was accidentally given a heightened ability to be in contact with it."

Ben said, "I don't know what to say."

"Don't say anything. Just think about it. I'm going home now, Ben. I can't take any more tonight."

Neither could he. He was flabbergasted, dismayed, even horrified by what she'd said. How could she believe such mystical bullshit? He didn't know who she was anymore.

It wasn't until hours later that, unable to sleep, he realized that Renata also thought her "cosmic consciousness" had diverted the solar flare radiation away from Earth in order to protect Cixin.

## —13: Cixin—

CIXIN SAT IN HIS BEDROOM, cross-legged on the bed. His iPod lay beside him, but he wasn't listening to it, hadn't listened to it for the past week. Nor had he gone to school, played video games, or sent email to Xiao. He was just waiting.

Xiao—he would miss her. Ben had been very good to him, and so had Renata, but he knew he wouldn't miss them. That was bad, maybe, but it was true.

Maybe Xiao would come one day, too. After all, if the voices were everything, and they were him, then they should be Xiao, too, right? But Xiao couldn't hear them. Ben couldn't hear them. Renata couldn't hear them. Only Cixin could, and probably not until tomorrow. And this time...

The nurse hired to watch him while he was "sick" looked up from her magazine, smiled, and turned another page. Cixin didn't hate her. He was surprised he didn't hate her, but she couldn't help being stupid. Any more than Ben could help it, or Renata, or Xiao. They didn't know.

Cixin knew.

And when he felt the calm steal over him, felt himself expand outward, he knew the voices would be early and that was so good!

*Cixin.*

*Yes*, he said, but only inside his mind, where the nurse couldn't hear.

*Come.*

*Yes*, he thought, because that was right, that was where he belonged. With the voices. But there was something to do first.

He made a picture in his mind, the same picture he'd seen once before, the whole Earth wrapped in a gray fog. He made the sun shining brightly, and a ray gun shooting from the sun to the Earth, the way Renata had described it to him. The picture said POW!! Like a video game. Then he made the ray gun go away.

*Yes*, formed in his mind. *We'll watch over them.*

Cixin sighed happily. Then he became everything and went home, to where he knew, beyond any need to race around or yell at people or be *fen noon nan hi*, who he really was.

He never heard the nurse cry out.


## —14: BEN—


SHE CAME TO HIM through the bright sunshine, hurrying down the cement path, her dirty blond curls hidden by a black hat. The black dress made her look out of place. This was Southern California; people wore black only for gala parties, not for funerals. But Renata, his numb and weary mind irrelevantly remembered, came originally from Ohio.

Ben turned his back on her.

She wasn't fooled. Somehow she knew that he hadn't turned away from not wanting her there, but from wanting her there too much. No one else stood beside the grave. Ben hadn't told his family about Cixin's death, and he'd discouraged his few friends from attending. And they, bewildered to learn only after the death that anti-social Ben had been adopting a child, nodded and murmured empty consolations. And then, of course, there were the sunspots. A second coronal mass ejection had occurred just yesterday, and everyone was jumpy.

"Ben, I just heard and I'm so sorry," Renata said. From her, the words didn't sound so empty. Her eyes held tears, and the hand she put on his arm held a tenderness he badly needed but wouldn't allow himself to take.

"Thank you," he said stiffly. If she even alluded to all that other nonsense....And of course, being Renata, she did. "I know you loved him. And you did the best you could for him—I know that, too. But maybe he's where he wanted to be."

"Can it, Renata."

"All right. Will you come have coffee with me now?"

He looked down. So small a coffin. Two cemetery employees waited, trying not to look impatient, to lower the coffin into its hole, cover it up, and get back inside. To their eyes, this was a non-funeral: no mourners, no minister or priest or rabbi, only this one dour man reading from a book that wasn't even holy.

"Please," Renata said. "You shouldn't stay here, love."

He let himself be led away. Behind him the men began to work with feverish speed.

"They're afraid," he said. "Idiots."

"Not everybody can understand science, Ben." Then, shockingly, she laughed. He knew why, but she clapped one hand over her mouth. "I'm so sorry!"

"Forget it."

Not everybody could understand science, no. In Ben's experience, almost nobody even tried. Half the population still equated evolution with the devil. But the president had made a speech on TV last night and another one this morning: *The new solar flare presents no danger. There will be no repeat of last week's crisis. The radiation is not reaching Earth.* Wisely, she had not tried to say why the radiation was not reaching Earth. Nor why the astronauts on *Hope of Heaven*, the Chinese space shuttle, had not been fried in orbit. *No danger* was as far as the president could go. It was already like crossing into Wonderland.

Ben and Renata walked to his Saab. If she'd parked her own car somewhere in the cemetery, as she must have, she seemed willing to leave it. Gently she took the book from his hands and studied the cover.

"I'm not giving in," he said, too harshly.

"I know."

"If there really were...'more,' were really were something that could be reached, contacted, by more or different brain connec-

95

tions—then what evolutionary gain could have made humanity lose it? Was it too distracting, interfering with survival? Too calming? Too *what*?"

"I don't know."

"It doesn't make sense," Ben said. "And if it really were genetic, really were that the rest of us aren't making enough of some chemicals or connective tissues or…I just can't believe it, Renata."

"I know."

He wished she would stop saying that. She handed back to him James Behren's *Quantum Physics and Consciousness*, but he knew she'd already seen the page he'd dog-eared and underlined. She already knew that over the grave of Cixin, who could barely decipher any language, Ben had read aloud about two-slit and delayed-choice and particle-detector experiments. Renata knew, always, everything.

"Maybe," she said after a long silence, "if they know now that the rest of us possess consciousness, however rudimentary, not just Cixin…if they know that, then maybe someday…"

She could never just leave anything alone. That's who she was. Ben shifted the book to his other hand and put an arm around her.

"No," he said. "Not possible."

This time she didn't answer. But she leaned against him and they walked out of the cemetery together, under the bright blue empty sky.

# TRINITY

*"Lord, I believe; help Thou mine unbelief!"*
—Mark 9:24

AT FIRST I DIDN'T RECOGNIZE Devrie.

Devrie—I didn't recognize *Devrie*. Astonished at myself, I studied the wasted figure standing in the middle of the bare reception room: arms like wires, clavicle sharply outlined, head shaved, dressed in that ugly long tent of light-weight gray. God knew what her legs looked like under it. Then she smiled, and it was Devrie.

"You look like shit."

"Hello, Seena. Come on in."

"I am in."

"Barely. It's not catching, you know."

"Stupidity fortunately isn't," I said and closed the door behind me. The small room was too hot; Devrie would need the heat, of course, with almost no fat left to insulate her bones and organs. Next to her I felt huge, although I am not. Huge, hairy, sloppy-breasted.

"Thank you for not wearing bright colors. They do affect me."

"Anything for a sister," I said, mocking the old childhood formula, the old sentiment. But Devrie was too quick to think it was only mockery; in that, at least, she had not changed. She clutched my arm and her fingers felt like chains, or talons.

"You found him. Seena, you found him."

"I found him."

"Tell me," she whispered.

"Sit down first, before you fall over. God, Devrie, don't you eat at all?"

*"Tell me,"* she said. So I did.

Devrie Caroline Konig had admitted herself to the Institute of the Biological Hope on the Caribbean island of Dominica eleven months ago, in late November of 2017, when her age was 23 years and 4 months. I am precise about this because it is all I can be sure of. I need the precision. The Institute of the Biological Hope is not precise; it is a mongrel, part research laboratory in brain sciences, part monastery, part school for training in the discipline of the mind. That made my baby sister guinea pig, postulant, freshman. She had always been those things, but, until now, sequentially. Apparently so had many other people, for when eccentric Nobel Prize winner James Arthur Bohentin had founded his Institute, he had been able to fund it, although precariously. But in that it did not differ from most private scientific research centers.

Or most monasteries.

I wanted Devrie out of the Institute of the Biological Hope.

"It's located on Dominica," I had said sensibly—what an ass I had been—to an unwasted Devrie a year ago, "because the research procedures there fall outside United States laws concerning the safety of research subjects. Doesn't that tell you something, Devrie? Doesn't that at least give you pause? In New York, it would be illegal to do to anyone what Bohentin does to his people."

"Do you know him?" she had asked.

"I have met him. Once."

"What is he like?"

"Like stone."

Devrie shrugged, and smiled. "All the participants in the Institute are willing. Eager."

"That doesn't make it ethical for Bohentin to destroy them. Ethical or legal."

"It's legal on Dominica. And in thinking you know better than the participants what they should risk their own lives for, aren't you playing God?"

"Better me than some untrained fanatic who offers himself up like an exalted Viking hero, expecting Valhalla."

"You're an intellectual snob, Seena."

"I never denied it."

"Are you sure you aren't really objecting not to the Institute's dangers but to its purpose? Isn't the 'Hope' part what really bothers you?"

"I don't think scientific method and pseudo-religious mush mix, no. I never did. I don't think it leads to a perception of God."

"The holotank tapes indicate it leads to a perception of *something* the brain hasn't encountered before," Devrie said, and for a moment I was silent.

I was once, almost, a biologist. I was aware of the legitimate studies that formed the basis for Bohentin's megalomania: the brain wave changes that accompany anorexia nervosa, sensory deprivation, biological feedback, and neurotransmitter stimulants. I have read the historical accounts, some merely pathetic but some disturbingly not, of the Christian mystics who achieved rapture through the mortification of the flesh and the Eastern mystics who achieved anesthesia through the control of the mind, of the faith healers who succeeded, of the carcinomas shrunk through trained will. I knew of the research of focused clairvoyance during orgasm, and of what happens when neurotransmitter number and speed are increased chemically.

And I knew all that was known about the twin trance.

Fifteen years earlier, as a doctoral student in biology, I had spent one summer replicating Sunderwirth's pioneering study of drug-enhanced telepathy in identical twins. My results were positive, except that within six months all eight of my research subjects had died. So had Sunderwirth's. Twin-trance research became the cloning controversy of the new decade, with the same panicky cycle of public outcry, legal restrictions, religious misunderstandings, fear, and demagoguery. When I received the phone call that the last of my subjects was dead—cardiac arrest, no history of heart disease, forty-three Goddamn years old—I locked myself in my apartment, with the lights off and my father's papers clutched in my hand, for three days. Then I resigned from the neurology department and became an entomologist. There is no pain in classifying dead insects.

"There is something *there*," Devrie had repeated. She was holding the letter sent to our father, whom someone at the Institute had not heard was dead. "It says the holotank tapes—"

"So there's something there," I said. "So the tanks are picking up some strange radiation. Why call it 'God'?"

"Why not call it God?"

"Why not call it Rover? Even if I grant you that the tape pattern looks like a presence—which I don't—you have no way of knowing that Bohentin's phantom isn't, say, some totally ungodlike alien being."

"But neither do I know that it *is*."

"Devrie—"

She had smiled and put her hands on my shoulders. She had—has, has always had—a very sweet smile. "Seena. *Think*. If the Institute can prove rationally that God exists—can prove it to the intellectual mind, the doubting Thomases who need something concrete to study... faith that doesn't need to be taken on faith..."

She wore her mystical face, a glowing softness that made me want to shake the silliness out of her. Instead I made some clever riposte, some sarcasm I no longer remember, and reached out to ruffle her hair. Big-sisterly, patronizing, thinking I could deflate her rapturous interest with the pin-prick of ridicule. God, I was an ass. It hurts to remember how big an ass I was.

A month and a half later Devrie committed herself and half her considerable inheritance to the Institute of the Biological Hope.

"Tell me," Devrie whispered. The Institute had no windows; outside I had seen grass, palm trees, butterflies floating in the sunshine, but inside here in the bare gray room there was nowhere to look but at her face.

"He's a student in a Master's program at a third-rate college in New Hampshire. He was adopted when he was two, nearly three, in March of 1997. Before that he was in a government-run children's home. In Boston, of course. The adopting family, as far as I can discover, never was told he was anything but one more toddler given up by somebody for adoption."

"Wait a minute," Devrie said. "I need...a minute."

She had turned paler, and her hands trembled. I had recited the information as if it were no more than an exhibit listing at my museum. Of course she was rattled. I wanted her rattled. I wanted her out.

Lowering herself to the floor, Devrie sat cross-legged and closed her eyes. Concentration spread over her face, but a concentration so serene it barely deserved that name. Her breathing slowed, her color freshened, and when she opened her eyes, they had the rested energy of a person who has just slept eight hours in mountain air. Her face even looked plumper, and an EEG, I guessed, would show damn near alpha waves. In her year at the Institute she must have mastered quite an array of biofeedback techniques to do that, so fast and with such a malnourished body.

"Very impressive," I said sourly.

"Seena—have you seen him?"

"No. All this is from sealed records."

"How did you get into the records?"

"Medical and governmental friends."

"Who?"

"What do you care, as long as I found out what you wanted to know?"

She was silent. I knew she would never ask me if I had obtained her information legally or illegally; it would not occur to her to ask. Devrie, being Devrie, would assume it had all been generously offered by my modest museum connections and our dead father's immodest research connections. She would be wrong.

"How old is he now?"

"Twenty-four years last month. They must have used your two-month tissue sample."

"Do you think Daddy knew where the…baby went?"

"Yes. Look at the timing—the child was normal and healthy, yet he wasn't adopted until he was nearly three. The researchers kept track of him, all right; they kept all six clones in a government-controlled home where they could monitor their development as long as humanly possible. The same-sex clones were released for adoption after a year, but they hung onto the cross-sex ones until they reached an age where they would become harder to adopt.

They undoubtedly wanted to study *them* as long as they could. And even after the kids were released for adoption, the researchers held off publishing until all six were placed and the records sealed. Dad's group didn't publish until April, 1998, remember. By the time the storm broke, the babies were out of its path, and anonymous."

"And the last," Devrie said.

"And the last," I agreed, although of course the researchers hadn't foreseen that. So few in the scientific community had foreseen *that*. Offense against God and man, Satan's work, natter natter. Watching my father's suddenly stooped shoulders and stricken eyes, I had thought how ugly public revulsion could be and had nobly resolved—how had I thought of it then? So long ago—resolved to snatch the banner of pure science from my fallen father's hand. Another time that I had been an ass. Five years later, when it had been my turn to feel the ugly scorching of public revulsion, I had broken, left neurological research, and fled down the road that led to the Museum of Natural History, where I was the curator of ants fossilized in amber and moths pinned securely under permaplex.

"The other four clones," Devrie said, "the ones from that university in California that published almost simultaneously with Daddy—"

"I don't know. I didn't even try to ask. It was hard enough in Cambridge."

"Me," Devrie said wonderingly. "He's *me*."

"Oh, for—Devrie, he's your twin. No more than that. No—actually less than that. He shares your genetic material exactly as an identical twin would, except for the Y chromosome, but he shares none of the congenital or environmental influences that shaped your personality. There's no mystical replication of spirit in cloning. He's merely a twin who got born eleven months late!"

She looked at me with luminous amusement. I didn't like the look. On that fleshless face, the skin stretched so taut that the delicate bones beneath were as visible as the veins of a moth wing, her amusement looked ironic. Yet Devrie was never ironic. Gentle, passionate, trusting, a little stupid, she was not capable of irony. It was beyond her, just as it was beyond her to wonder why I, who had fought her entering the Institute of the Biological Hope, had brought her this information now. Her amusement was one-lay-ered, and trusting.

God's fools, the Middle Ages had called them.

"Devrie," I said, and heard my own voice unexpectedly break, "leave here. It's physically not safe. What are you down to, ten per-cent body fat? Eight? Look at yourself, you can't hold body heat, your palms are dry, you can't move quickly without getting dizzy. Hypotension. What's your heartbeat? Do you still menstruate? It's insane."

She went on smiling at me. God's fools don't need menstrua-tion. "Come with me, Seena. I want to show you the Institute."

"I don't want to see it."

"Yes. This visit you should see it."

"Why this visit?"

"Because you *are* going to help me get my clone to come here, aren't you? Or else why did you go to all the trouble of locating him?"

I didn't answer. She still didn't see it.

Devrie said, " 'Anything for a sister.' But you were always more like a mother to me than a sister." She took my hand and pulled herself off the floor. So had I pulled her up to take her first steps, the day after our mother died in a plane crash at Orly. Now Dev-rie's hand felt cold. I imprisoned it and counted the pulse.

"Bradycardia."

But she wasn't listening.

The Institute was a shock. I had anticipated the laboratories: monotonous gray walls, dim light, heavy soundproofing, minimal fixtures in the ones used for sensory dampening; high-contrast textures and colors, strobe lights, quite good sound equipment in those for sensory arousal. There was much that Devrie, as subject rather than researcher, didn't have authority to show me, but I de-duced much from what I did see. The dormitories, divided by sex, were on the sensory-dampening side. The subjects slept in small cells, ascetic and chaste, that reminded me of an abandoned Car-melite convent I had once toured in Belgium. That was the shock: the physical plant felt scientific, but the atmosphere did not.

There hung in the gray corridors a wordless peace, a feeling so palpable I could feel it clogging my lungs. No. "Peace" was the wrong word. Say "peace" and the picture is pastoral, lazy sunshine and dreaming woods. This was not like that at all. The research subjects—students? postulants?—lounged in the corridors outside closed labs, waiting for the next step in their routine. Both men and women were anorectic, both wore gray bodysuits or caftans, both were fined down to an otherworldly ethereality when seen from a distance and a malnourished asexuality when seen up close. They talked among themselves in low voices, sitting with backs against the wall or stretched full-length on the carpeted floor, and on all their faces I saw the same luminous patience, the same certainty of being very near to something exciting that they nonetheless could wait for calmly, as long as necessary.

"They look," I said to Devrie, "as if they're waiting to take an exam they already know they'll ace."

She smiled. "Do you think so? I always think of us as travelers waiting for a plane, boarding passes stamped for Eternity."

She was actually serious. But she didn't in fact wear the same expression as the others; hers was far more intense. If they were travelers, she wanted to pilot.

The lab door opened and the students brought themselves to their feet. Despite their languid movements, they looked sharp: sharp protruding clavicles, bony chins, angular unpadded elbows that could chisel stone.

"This is my hour for biofeedback manipulation of drug effects," Devrie said. "Please come watch."

"I'd sooner watch you whip yourself in a twelfth-century monastery."

Devrie's eyes widened, then again lightened with that luminous amusement. "It's for the same end, isn't it? But they had such unsystematic means. Poor struggling God-searchers. I wonder how many of them made it."

I wanted to strike her. "*Devrie*—"

"If not biofeedback, what would you like to see?"

"You out of here."

"What else?"

There was only one thing: the holotanks. I struggled with the temptation, and lost. The two tanks stood in the middle of a roomy lab carpeted with thick gray matting and completely enclosed in a Faraday cage. That Devrie had a key to the lab was my first clue that my errand for her had been known, and discussed, by someone higher in the Institute. Research subjects do not carry keys to the most delicate brain-perception equipment in the world. For this equipment Bohentin had received his Nobel.

The two tanks, independent systems, stood as high as my shoulder. The ones I had used fifteen years ago had been smaller. Each of these was a cube, opaque on its bottom half, which held the sensing apparatus, computerized simulators, and recording equipment; clear on its top half, which was filled with the transparent fluid out of whose molecules the simulations would form. A separate sim would form for each subject, as the machine sorted and mapped all the electromagnetic radiation received and processed by each brain. *All* that each brain perceived, not only the visuals; the holograph equipment was capable of picking up all wavelengths that the brain did, and of displaying their brain-processed analogues as three-dimensional images floating in a clear womb. When all other possible sources of radiation were filtered out except for the emanations from the two subjects themselves, what the sims showed was what kinds of activity were coming from—and hence going on in—the other's brain. That was why it worked best with identical twins in twin trance: no structural brain differences to adjust for. In a rawer version of this holotank, a rawer version of myself had pioneered the recording of twin trances. The UCIC, we had called it then: What you see, I see.

What I had seen was eight autopsy reports.

"We're so *close*," Devrie said. "Mona and Marlene"—she waved a hand toward the corridor but Mona and Marlene, whichever two they had been, had gone—"had taken KX3, that's the drug that—"

"I know what it is," I said, too harshly. KX3 reacts with one of the hormones overproduced in an anorectic body. The combination is readily absorbed by body fat, but in a body without fat, much of it is absorbed by the brain.

Devrie continued, her hand tight on my arm. "Mona and Marlene were controlling the neural reactions with biofeedback, pushing the twin trance higher and higher, working it. Dr. Bohentin was monitoring the holotanks. The sims were incredibly detailed—everything each twin perceived in the perceptions of the other, in all wavelengths. Mona and Marlene forced their neurotransmission level even higher and then, in the tanks"—Devrie's face glowed, the mystic-rapture look—"a completely third sim formed. Completely separate. A third *presence*."

I stared at her.

"It was recorded in *both* tanks. It was shadowy, yes, but it was *there*. A third presence that can't be perceived except through another human's electromagnetic presence, and then only with every drug and trained reaction and arousal mode and the twin trance all pushing the brain into a supraheightened state. A third presence!"

"Isotropic radiation. Bohentin fluffed the pre-screening program and the computer hadn't cleared the background microradiation—" I said, but even as I spoke I knew how stupid that was. Bohentin didn't make mistakes like that, and isotropic radiation simulates nowhere close to the way a presence does. Devrie didn't even bother to answer me.

This, then, was what the rumors had been about, the rumors leaking for the last year out of the Institute and through the scientific community, mostly still scoffed at, not yet picked up by the popular press. This. A verifiable, replicable third presence being picked up by holography. Against all reason, a long shiver went over me from neck to that cold place at the base of the spine.

"There's more," Devrie said feverishly. "They *felt* it. Mona and Marlene. Both said afterwards that they could feel it, a huge presence filled with light, but they couldn't quite reach it. Damn—they couldn't reach it, Seena! They weren't playing off each other enough, weren't close enough. Weren't, despite the twin trance, *melded* enough."

"Sex," I said.

"They tried it. The subjects are all basically heterosexual. They inhibit."

"So go find some homosexual God-yearning anorectic incestuous twins!"

Devrie looked at me straight. "I need him. Here. He *is* me."

I exploded, right there in the holotank lab. No one came running in to find out if the shouting was dangerous to the tanks, which was my second clue that the Institute knew very well why Devrie had brought me there. "Damn it to hell, he's a human being, not some chemical you can just order up because you need it for an experiment! You don't have the right to expect him to come here, you didn't even have the right to tell anyone that he exists, but that didn't stop you, did it? There are still anti-bioengineering groups out there in the real world, religious split-brains who—how *dare* you put him in any danger? How dare you even presume he'd be interested in this insane mush?"

"He'll come," Devrie said. She had not changed expression.

"How the hell do you know?"

"He's me. And I want God. He will, too."

I scowled at her. A fragment of one of her poems, a thing she had written when she was fifteen, came to me: "Two human species/Never one—/One aching for God/One never." But she had been fifteen then. I had assumed that the sentiment, as adolescent as the poetry, would pass.

I said, "What does Bohentin think of this idea of importing your clone?"

For the first time she hesitated. Bohentin, then, was dubious. "He thinks it's rather a long shot."

"You could phrase it that way."

"But *I* know he'll want to come. Some things you just know, Seena, beyond rationality. And besides—" She hesitated again, and then went on. "I have left half my inheritance from Daddy, and the income on the trust from Mummy."

"Devrie. God, Devrie—you'd *buy* him?"

For the first time she looked angry. "The money would be just to get him here, to see what is involved. Once he sees, he'll want this as much as I do, at any price! What price can you put on God? I'm not 'buying' his life—I'm offering him the way to *find* life. What good is breathing, existing, if there's no purpose to it?

Don't you realize how many centuries, in how many ways, people have looked for that light-filled presence and never been able to be *sure*? And now we're almost there, Seena, I've seen it for myself—*almost there*. With verifiable, scientifically-controlled means. Not subjective faith this time—scientific data, the same as for any other actual phenomenon. This research stands now where research into the atom stood fifty years ago. Can you touch a quark? But it's there! And my clone can be a part of it, can *be* it, how can you talk about the money buying him under circumstances like that!"

I said slowly, "How do you know that whatever you're so close to is God?" But that was sophomoric, of course, and she was ready for it. She smiled warmly.

"What does it matter what we call it? Pick another label if it will make you more comfortable."

I took a piece of paper from my pocket. "His name is Keith Torellen. He lives in Indian Falls, New Hampshire. Address and mailnet number here. Good luck, Devrie." I turned to go.

"Seena! *I* can't go!"

She couldn't, of course. That was the point. She barely had the strength in that starved, drug-battered body to get through the day, let alone to New Hampshire. She needed the sensory-controlled environment, the artificial heat, the chemical monitoring. "Then send someone from the Institute. Perhaps Bohentin will go."

"Bo*hen*tin!" she said, and I knew that was impossible; Bohentin had to remain officially ignorant of this sort of recruiting. Too many U.S. laws were involved. In addition, Bohentin had no persuasive skills; people as persons and not neurologies did not interest him. They were too far above chemicals and too far below God.

Devrie looked at me with a kind of level fury. "This is really why you found him, isn't it? So I would have to stop the drug program long enough to leave here and go get him. You think that once I've gone back out into the world either the build-up effects in the brain will be interrupted or else the spell will be broken and I'll have doubts about coming back here!"

"Will you listen to yourself? 'Out into the world.' You sound like some archaic nun in a cloistered order!"

"You always did ridicule anything you couldn't understand," Devrie said icily, turned her back on me, and stared at the empty holotanks. She didn't turn when I left the lab, closing the door behind me. She was still facing the tanks, her spiny back rigid, the piece of paper with Keith Torellen's address clutched in fingers delicate as glass.

In New York the museum simmered with excitement. An unexpected endowment had enabled us to buy the contents of a small, very old museum located in a part of Madagascar not completely destroyed by the African Horror. Crate after crate of moths began arriving in New York, some of them collected in the days when naturalists-gentlemen shot jungle moths from the trees using dust shot. Some species had been extinct since the Horror and thus were rare; some were the brief mutations from the bad years afterward and thus were even rarer. The museum staff uncrated and exclaimed.

"Look at this one," said a young man, holding it out to me. Not on my own staff, he was one of the specialists on loan to us—De-Fabio or DeFazio, something like that. He was very handsome. I looked at the moth he showed me, all pale wings outstretched and pinned to black silk. "A perfect Thysania Africana. *Perfect*."

"Yes."

"You'll have to loan us the whole exhibit, in a few years."

"Yes," I said again. He heard the tone in my voice and glanced up quickly. But not quickly enough—my face was all professional interest when his gaze reached it. Still, the professional interest had not fooled him; he had heard the perfunctory note. Frowning, he turned back to the moths.

By day I directed the museum efficiently enough. But in the evenings, home alone in my apartment, I found myself wandering from room to room, touching objects, unable to settle to work at the oversize teak desk that had been my father's, to the reports and journals that had not. His had dealt with the living, mine with the ancient dead—but I had known that for years. The fogginess of my evenings bothered me.

"Faith should not mean fogginess."

Who had said that? Father, of course, to Devrie, when she had joined the dying Catholic Church. She had been thirteen years old. Skinny, defiant, she had stood clutching a black rosary from God knows where, daring him from scared dark eyes to forbid her. Of course he had not, thinking, I suppose, that Heaven, like any other childhood fever, was best left alone to burn out its course.

Devrie had been received into the Church in an overdecorated chapel, wearing an overdecorated dress of white lace and carrying a candle. Three years later she had left, dressed in a magenta body suit and holding the keys to Father's safe, which his executor had left unlocked after the funeral. The will had, of course, made me Devrie's guardian. In the three years Devrie had been going to Mass, I had discovered that I was sterile, divorced my second husband, finished my work in entomology, accepted my first position with a museum, and entered a drastically premature menopause.

That is not a flip nor random list.

After the funeral, I sat in the dark in my father's study, in his maroon leather chair and at his teak desk. Both felt oversize. All the lights were off. Outside it rained; I heard the steady beat of water on the window, and the wind. The dark room was cold. In my palm I held one of my father's research awards, a small abstract sculpture of a double helix, done by Harold Landau himself. It was very heavy. I couldn't think what Landau had used, to make it so heavy. I couldn't think, with all the noise from the rain. My father was dead, and I would never bear a child.

Devrie came into the room, leaving the lights off but bringing with her an incandescent rectangle from the doorway. At sixteen she was lovely, with long brown hair in the masses of curls again newly fashionable. She sat on a low stool beside me, all that hair falling around her, her face white in the gloom. She had been crying.

"He's gone. He's really gone. I don't believe it yet."

"No."

She peered at me. Something in my face, or my voice, must have alerted her; when she spoke again it was in that voice people use when they think your grief is understandably greater than theirs. A smooth dark voice, like a wave.

"You still have me, Seena. We still have each other."

I said nothing.

"I've always thought of you more as my mother than my sister, anyway. You took the place of Mother. You've been a mother to at least *me*."

She smiled and squeezed my hand. I looked at her face—so young, so pretty—and I wanted to hit her. I didn't want to be her mother; I wanted to be her. All her choices lay ahead of her, and it seemed to me that self-indulgent night as if mine were finished. I could have struck her.

"Seena—"

"Leave me alone! Can't you ever leave me alone? All my life you've been dragging behind me; why don't *you* die and finally leave me alone!"

We make ourselves pay for small sins more than large ones. The more trivial the thrust, the longer we're haunted by memory of the wound.

I believe that.


Indian Falls was out of another time: slow, quiet, safe. The Avis counter at the airport rented not personal guards but cars, and the only shiny store on Main Street sold wilderness equipment. I suspected that the small state college, like the town, traded mostly on trees and trails. That Keith Torellen was trying to take an academic degree *here* told me more about his adopting family than if I had hired a professional information service.

The house where he lived was shabby, paint peeling and steps none too sturdy. I climbed them slowly, thinking once again what I wanted to find out.

Devrie would answer none of my messages on the mailnet. Nor would she accept my phone calls. She was shutting me out, in retaliation for my refusing to fetch Torellen for her. But Devrie would discover that she could not shut me out as easily as that; we were sisters. I wanted to know if she had contacted Torellen herself, or had sent someone from the Institute to do so.

If neither, then my visit here would be brief and anonymous; I would leave Keith Torellen to his protected ignorance and shabby town. But if he *had* seen Devrie, I wanted to discover if and what he had agreed to do for her. It might even be possible that he could be of use in convincing Devrie of the stupidity of what she was doing. If he could be used for that, I would use him.

Something else: I was curious. This boy was my brother—nephew? no, brother—as well as the result of my father's rational mind. Curiosity prickled over me. I rang the bell.

It was answered by the landlady, who said that Keith was not home, would not be home until late, was "in rehearsal."

"Rehearsal?"

"Over to the college. He's a student and they're putting on a play."

I said nothing, thinking.

"I don't remember the name of the play," the landlady said. She was a large woman in a faded garment, dress or robe. "But Keith says it's going to be real good. It starts this weekend." She laughed. "But you probably already know all that! George, my husband George, he says I'm forever telling people things they already know!"

"How would I know?"

She winked at me. "Don't you think I got eyes? Sister, or cousin? No, let me guess—older sister. Too much alike for cousins."

"Thank you," I said. "You've been very helpful."

"Not sister!" She clapped her hand over her mouth, her eyes shiny with amusement. "You're checking up on him, ain't you? You're his mother! I should of seen it right off!"

I turned to negotiate the porch steps.

"They rehearse in the new building, Mrs. Torellen," she called after me. "Just ask anybody you see to point you in the right direction."

"Thank you," I said carefully.

Rehearsal was nearly over. Evidently it was a dress rehearsal; the actors were in period costume and the director did not interrupt. I did not recognize the period or the play. Devrie had been interested in theater; I was not. Quietly I took a seat in the darkened back row and waited for the pretending to end.

Despite wig and greasepaint, I had no trouble picking out Keith Torellen. He moved like Devrie: quick, light movements, slightly pigeon-toed. He had her height and, given the differences of a male body, her slenderness. Sitting a theater's length away, I might have been seeing a male Devrie.

But seen up close, his face was mine.

Despite the landlady, it was a shock. He came toward me across the theater lobby, from where I had sent for him, and I saw the moment he too struck the resemblance. He stopped dead, and we stared at each other. Take Devrie's genes, spread them over a face with the greater bone surface, larger features, and coarser skin texture of a man—and the result was my face. Keith had scrubbed off his make-up and removed his wig, exposing brown curly hair the same shade Devrie's had been. But his face was mine.

A strange emotion, unnamed and hot, seared through me.

"Who are *you*? Who the hell *are* you?"

So no one had come from the Institute after all. Not Devrie, not anyone.

"You're one of them, aren't you?" he said; it was almost a whisper. "One of my real family?"

Still gripped by the unexpected force of emotion, still dumb, I said nothing. Keith took one step toward me. Suspicion played over his face—Devrie would not have been suspicious—and vanished, replaced by a slow painful flush of color.

"You are. You *are* one. Are you...are you my mother?"

I put out a hand against a stone post. The lobby was all stone and glass. Why were all theater lobbies stone and glass? Architects had so little damn imagination, so little sense of the bizarre.

"No! I am not your mother!"

He touched my arm. "Hey, are you okay? You don't look good. Do you need to sit down?"

His concern was unexpected, and touching. I thought that he shared Devrie's genetic personality, and that Devrie had always been hypersensitive to the body. But this was not Devrie. His hand on my arm was stronger, firmer, warmer than Devrie's. I felt giddy, disoriented. This was not Devrie.

"A mistake," I said unsteadily. "This was a mistake. I should not have come. I'm sorry. My name is Dr. Seena Konig and I am a… relative of yours, but I think this now is a mistake. I have your address and I promise that I'll write you about your family, but now I think I should go." Write some benign lie, leave him in ignorance. This was a mistake.

But he looked stricken, and his hand tightened on my arm. "You can't! I've been searching for my biological family for two years! You can't just go!"

We were beginning to attract attention in the theater lobby. Hurrying students eyed us sideways. I thought irrelevantly how different they looked from the "students" at the Institute, and with that thought regained my composure. This was a student, a boy—"you can't!" a boyish protest, and boyish panic in his voice—and not the man-Devrie-me he had seemed a foolish moment ago. He was nearly twenty years my junior. I smiled at him and removed his hand from my arm.

"Is there somewhere we can have coffee?"

"Yes. Dr…"

"Seena," I said. "Call me Seena."

Over coffee, I made him talk first. He watched me anxiously over the rim of his cup, as if I might vanish, and I listened to the words behind the words. His adopting family was the kind that hoped to visit the Grand Canyon but not Europe, go to movies but not opera, aspire to college but not to graduate work, buy wilderness equipment but not wilderness. Ordinary people. Not religious, not rich, not unusual. Keith was the only child. He loved them.

"But at the same time I never really felt I belonged," he said, and looked away from me. It was the most personal thing he had knowingly revealed, and I saw that he regretted it. Devrie would not have. More private, then, and less trusting. And I sensed in him a grittiness, a tougher awareness of the world's hardness, than Devrie had ever had—or needed to have. I made my decision. Having disturbed him thus far, I owed him truth—but not the whole truth.

"Now you tell me," Keith said, pushing away his cup. "Who were my parents? Our parents? Are you my sister?"

"Yes."

"Our parents?"

"Both are dead. Our father was Dr. Richard Konig. He was a scientist. He—" But Keith had recognized the name. His readings in biology or history must have been more extensive than I would have expected. His eyes widened, and I suddenly wished I had been more oblique.

"Richard Konig. He's one of those scientists that were involved in that bioengineering scandal—"

"How did you learn about that? It's all over and done with. Years ago."

"Journalism class. We studied how the press handled it, especially the sensationalism surrounding the cloning thing twenty years—"

I saw the moment it hit him. He groped for his coffee cup, clutched the handle, didn't raise it. It was empty anyway. And then what I said next shocked me as much as anything I have ever done.

"It was Devrie," I said, and heard my own vicious pleasure, "*Devrie* was the one who wanted me to tell you!"

But of course he didn't know who Devrie was. He went on staring at me, panic in his young eyes, and I sat frozen. That tone I heard in my own voice when I said "Devrie," that vicious pleasure that it was she and not I who was hurting him...

"Cloning," Keith said. "Konig was in trouble for claiming to have done illegal cloning. Of humans." His voice had held so much dread that I fought off my own dread and tried to hold myself steady to his need.

"It's illegal now, but not then. And the public badly misunderstood. All that sensationalism—you were right to use that word, Keith—covered up the fact that there is nothing abnormal about producing a fetus from another diploid cell. In the womb, identical twins—"

"Am I a clone?"

"Keith—"

"*Am I a clone?*"

Carefully I studied him. This was not what I had intended, but although the fear was still in his eyes, the panic had gone. And curiosity—Devrie's curiosity, and her eagerness—they were there as well. This boy would not strike me, nor stalk out of the restaurant, nor go into psychic shock.

"Yes. You are."

He sat quietly, his gaze turned inward. A long moment passed in silence.

"Your cell?"

"No. My—our sister's. Our sister Devrie."

Another long silence. He did not panic. Then he said softly, "Tell me."

Devrie's phrase.

"There isn't much to tell, Keith. If you've seen the media accounts, you know the story, and also what was made of it. The issue then becomes how you feel about what you saw. Do you believe that cloning is meddling with things man should best leave alone?"

"No. I don't."

I let out my breath, although I hadn't known I'd been holding it. "It's actually no more than delayed twinning, followed by surrogate implantation. A zygote—"

"I know all that," he said with some harshness, and held up his hand to silence me. I didn't think he knew that he did it. The harshness did not sound like Devrie. To my ears, it sounded like myself. He sat thinking, remote and troubled, and I did not try to touch him.

Finally he said, "Do my parents know?"

He meant his adoptive parents. "No."

"Why are you telling me now? Why did you come?"

"Devrie asked me to."

"She needs something, right? A kidney? Something like that?"

I had not foreseen that question. He did not move in a class where spare organs were easily purchasable. "No. Not a kidney, not any kind of biological donation." A voice in my mind jeered at that, but I was not going to give him any clues that would lead to Devrie. "She just wanted me to find you."

"Why didn't she find me herself? She's my age, right?"

"Yes. She's ill just now and couldn't come."

"Is she dying?"

"No!"

Again he sat quietly, finally saying, "No one could tell me anything. For two years I've been searching for my mother, and not one of the adoptee-search agencies could find a single trace. Not one. Now I see why. Who covered the trail so well?"

"My father."

"I want to meet Devrie."

I said evenly, "That might not be possible."

"Why not?"

"She's in a foreign hospital. Out of the country. I'm sorry."

"When does she come home?"

"No one is sure."

"What disease does she have?"

*She's sick for God*, I thought, but aloud I said, not thinking it through, "A brain disease."

Instantly I saw my own cruelty. Keith paled, and I cried, "No, no, nothing you could have as well! Truly, Keith, it's not—she took a bad fall. From her hunter."

"Her hunter," he said. For the first time, his gaze flickered over my clothing and jewelry. But would he even recognize how expensive they were? I doubted it. He wore a synthetic, deep-pile jacket with a tear at one shoulder and a cheap wool hat, dark blue, shapeless with age. From long experience I recognized his gaze: uneasy, furtive, the expression of a man glimpsing the financial gulf between what he had assumed were equals. But it wouldn't matter. Adopted children have no legal claim on the estates of their biological parents. I had checked.

Keith said uneasily, "Do you have a picture of Devrie?"

"No," I lied.

"Why did she want you to find me? You still haven't said."

I shrugged. "The same reason, I suppose, that you looked for your biological family. The pull of blood."

"Then she wants me to write to her."

"Write to me instead."

He frowned. "Why? Why not to Devrie?"

What to say to that? I hadn't bargained on so much intensity from him. "Write in care of me, and I'll forward it to Devrie."

"Why not to her directly?"

"Her doctors might not think it advisable," I said coldly, and he backed off—either from the mention of doctors or from the coldness.

"Then give me your address, Seena. Please."

I did. I could see no harm in his writing me. It might even be pleasant. Coming home from the museum, another wintry day among the exhibits, to find on the mailnet a letter I could answer when and how I chose, without being taken by surprise. I liked the idea.

But no more difficult questions now. I stood. "I have to leave, Keith."

He looked alarmed. "So soon?"

"Yes."

"But why?"

"I have to return to work."

He stood, too. He was taller than Devrie. "Seena," he said, all earnestness, "just a few more questions. How did you find me?"

"Medical connections."

"Yours?"

"Our father's. I'm not a scientist." Evidently his journalism class had not studied twin-trance sensationalism.

"What do you do?"

"Museum curator. Arthropods."

"What does Devrie do?"

"She's too ill to work. I must go, Keith."

"One more. Do I look like Devrie as well as you?"

"It would be wise, Keith, if you were careful whom you spoke with about all of this. I hadn't intended to say so much."

"I'm not going to tell my parents. Not about being—not about all of it."

"I think that's best, yes."

"Do I look like Devrie as well as you?"

A little of my first, strange emotion returned with his intensity. "A little, yes. But more like me. Sex variance is a tricky thing."

Unexpectedly, he held my coat for me. As I slipped into it, he said from behind, "Thank you, Seena," and let his hands rest on my shoulders.

I did not turn around. I felt my face flame, and self-disgust flooded through me, followed by a desire to laugh. It was all so transparent. This man was an attractive stranger, was Devrie, was youth, was myself, was the work not of my father's loins but of his mind. Of course I was aroused by him. Freud outlasts cloning: a note for a research study, I told myself grimly, and inwardly I did laugh.

But that didn't help either.

In New York, winter came early. Cold winds whipped white-caps on harbor and river, and the trees in the Park stood bare even before October had ended. The crumbling outer boroughs of the shrinking city crumbled a little more and talked of the days when New York had been important. Manhattan battened down for snow, hired the seasonal increases in personal guards, and talked of Albuquerque. Each night museum security hunted up and evicted the drifters trying to sleep behind exhibits, drifters as chilled and pale as the moths under permaplex, and, it seemed to me, as detached from the blood of their own age. All of New York seemed detached to me that October, and cold. Often I stood in front of the cases of Noctuidae, staring at them for so long that my staff began to glance at each other covertly. I would catch their glances when I jerked free of my trance. No one asked me about it.

Still no message came from Devrie. When I contacted the Institute on the mailnet, she did not call back.

No letter came from Keith Torellen.

Then one night, after I had worked late and was hurrying through the chilly gloom toward my building, he was there, bulking from the shadows so quickly that the guard I had taken for the walk from the museum sprang forward in attack position.

"No! It's all right! I know him!"

The guard retreated, without expression. Keith stared after him, and then at me, his face unreadable.

"Keith, what are you doing here? Come inside!"

He followed me into the lobby without a word. Nor did he say anything during the metal scanning and ID procedure. I took him up to my apartment, studying him in the elevator.

He wore the same jacket and cheap wool hat as in Indian Falls, his hair wanted cutting, and the tip of his nose was red from waiting in the cold. How long had he waited there? He badly needed a shave.

In the apartment he scanned the rugs, the paintings, my grandmother's ridiculously ornate, ugly silver, and turned his back on them to face me.

"Seena, I want to know where Devrie is."

"Why? Keith, what has happened?"

"Nothing has happened," he said, removing his jacket but not laying it anywhere. "Only that I've left school and spent two days hitching here. It's no good, Seena. To say that cloning is just like twinning: it's no good. I want to see Devrie."

His voice was hard. Bulking in my living room, unshaven, that hat pulled down over his ears, he looked older and less malleable than the last time I had seen him. Alarm—not physical fear, I was not afraid of him, but a subtler and deeper fear—sounded through me.

"Why do you want to see Devrie?"

"Because she cheated me."

"Of what, for God's sake?"

"Can I have a drink? Or a smoke?"

I poured him a Scotch. If he drank, he might talk. I had to know what he wanted, why such a desperate air clung to him, how to keep him from Devrie. I had not seen *her* like this. She was strong-willed, but always with a blitheness, a trust that eventually her will would prevail. Desperate forcefulness of the sort in Keith's manner was not her style. But of course Devrie had always had silent money to back her will; perhaps money could buy trust as well as style.

Keith drank off his Scotch and held out his glass for another. "It was freezing out there. They wouldn't let me in the lobby to wait for you."

"Of course not."

"You didn't tell me your family was rich."

I was a little taken aback at his bluntness, but at the same time it pleased me; I don't know why.

"You didn't ask."

"That's shit, Seena."

"Keith. Why are you here?"

"I told you. I want to see Devrie."

"What is it you've decided she cheated you of? Money?"

He looked so honestly surprised that again I was startled, this time by his resemblance to Devrie. She too would not have thought of financial considerations first, if there were emotional ones possible. One moment Keith was Devrie, one moment he was not. Now he scowled with sudden anger.

"Is that what you think—that fortune hunting brought me hitching from New Hampshire? God, Seena, I didn't even know how much you had until this very—I still don't know!"

I said levelly, "Then what is it you're feeling so cheated of?"

Now he was rattled. Again that quick, half-furtive scan of my apartment, pausing a millisecond too long at the Caravaggio, subtly lit by its frame. When his gaze returned to mine it was troubled, a little defensive. Ready to justify. Of course I had put him on the defensive deliberately, but the calculation of my trick did not prepare me for the staggering naivete of his explanation. Once more it was Devrie complete, reducing the impersonal greatness of science to a personal and emotional loss.

"Ever since I knew that I was adopted, at five or six years old, I wondered about my biological family. Nothing strange in that—I think all adoptees do. I used to make up stories, kid stuff, about how they were really royalty, or lunar colonists, or survivors of the African Horror. Exotic things. I thought especially about my mother, imagining this whole scene of her holding me once before she released me for adoption, crying over me, loving me so much she could barely let me go but had to for some reason. Sentimental shit." He laughed, trying to make light of what was not, and drank off his Scotch to avoid my gaze.

"But Devrie—the fact of her—destroyed all that. I never had a mother who hated to give me up. I never had a mother at all. What

I had was a cell cut from Devrie's fingertip or someplace, something discardable, and she doesn't even know what I look like. But she's damn well going to."

"Why?" I said evenly. "What could you expect to gain from her knowing what you look like?"

But he didn't answer me directly. "That first moment I saw you, Seena, in the theater at school, I thought you were my mother."

"I know you did."

"And you hated the idea. Why?"

I thought of the child I would never bear, the marriage, like so many other things of sweet promise, gone sour. But self-pity is a fool's game. "None of your business."

"Isn't it? Didn't you hate the idea because of the way I was made? Coldly. An experiment. Weren't you a little bit insulted at being called the mother of a discardable cell from Devrie's fingertip?"

"What the hell have you been reading? An experiment—what is any child but an experiment? A random egg, a random sperm. Don't talk like one of those anti-science religious split-brains!"

He studied me levelly. Then he said, "Is Devrie religious? Is that why you're so afraid of her?"

I got to my feet, and pointed at the sideboard. "Help yourself to another drink if you wish. I want to wash my hands. I've been handling specimens all afternoon." Stupid, clumsy lie—nobody would believe such a lie.

In the bathroom I leaned against the closed door, shut my eyes, and willed myself to calm. Why should I be so disturbed by the angry lashing-out of a confused boy? I was handy to lash out against: my father, whom Keith was really angry at, was not. It was all so predictable, so earnestly adolescent, that even over the hurting in my chest I smiled. But the smile, which should have reduced Keith's ranting to the tantrum of a child—there, there, when you grow up you'll find out that no one really knows who he is—did not diminish Keith. His losses were real—mother, father, natural place in the natural sequence of life and birth. And suddenly, with a clutch at the pit of my stomach, I knew why I had told him all that I had about his origins. It was not from any ethic of fidelity to "the truth." I had told him he was a clone because I, too, had had real losses—research, marriage, motherhood—and Devrie could never have shared them with me. Luminous, mystical Devrie, too occupied with God to be much hurt by man. *Leave me alone! Can't you ever leave me alone! All my life you've been dragging behind me— why don't you die and finally leave me alone!* And Devrie had smiled tolerantly, patted my head, and left me alone, closing the door softly so as not to disturb my grief. My words had not hurt her. I could not hurt her.

But I could hurt Keith—the other Devrie—and I had. That was why he disturbed me all out of proportion. That was the bond. My face, my pain, my fault.

*Through my fault, through my fault, through my most grievous fault.* But what nonsense. I was not a believer, and the comforts of superstitious absolution could not touch me. What shit. Like all nonbelievers, I stood alone.

It came to me then that there was something absurd in thinking all this while leaning against a bathroom door. Grimly absurd, but absurd. The toilet as confessional. I ran the cold water, splashed some on my face, and left. How long had I left Keith alone in the living room?

When I returned, he was standing by the mailnet. He had punched in the command to replay my outgoing postal messages, and displayed on the monitor was Devrie's address at the Institute of the Biological Hope.

"What is it?" Keith said. "A hospital?"

I didn't answer him.

"I can find out, Seena. Knowing this much, I can find out. Tell me."

*Tell me.* "Not a hospital. It's a research laboratory. Devrie is a voluntary subject."

"Research on what? I will find out, Seena."

"Brain perception."

"Perception of what?"

"Perception of *God*," I said, torn among weariness, anger, and a sudden gritty exasperation, irritating as sand. Why not just leave him to Devrie's persuasions, and her to mystic starvation? But I knew I would not. I still, despite all of it, wanted her out of there.

Keith frowned. "What do you mean, 'perception of God'?"

I told him. I made it sound as ridiculous as possible, and as dangerous. I described the anorexia, the massive use of largely untested drugs that would have made the Institute illegal in the United States, the skepticism of most of the scientific community, the psychoses and death that had followed twin-trance research fifteen years earlier. Keith did not remember that—he had been eight years old—and I did not tell him that I had been one of the researchers. I did not tell him about the tapes of the shadowy third presence in Bohentin's holotanks. In every way I could, with every verbal subtlety at my use, I made the Institute sound crackpot, and dangerous, and ugly. As I spoke, I watched Keith's face, and sometimes it was mine, and sometimes the expression altered it into Devrie's. I saw bewilderment at her having chosen to enter the Institute, but not what I had hoped to see. Not scorn, not disgust.

When I had finished, he said, "But why did she think that *I* might want to enter such a place as a twin subject?"

I had saved this for last. "Money. She'd buy you."

His hand, his third Scotch, went rigid. "Buy me."

"It's the most accurate way to put it."

"What the hell made her think—" He mastered himself, not without effort. Not all the discussion of bodily risk had affected him as much as this mention of Devrie's money. He had a poor man's touchy pride. "She thinks of me as something to be *bought*."

I was carefully quiet.

"Damn her," he said. "*Damn* her." Then, roughly, "And I was actually considering—"

I caught my breath. "Considering the Institute? After what I've just told you? How in hell could you? And you said, I remember, that your background was not religious!"

"It's not. But I…I've wondered." And in the sudden turn of his head away from me so that I wouldn't see the sudden rapt hopelessness in his eyes, in the defiant set of his shoulders, I read more than in his banal words, and more than he could know. Devrie's look, Devrie's wishfulness, feeding on air. The weariness and anger, checked before, flooded me again and I lashed out at him.

"Then go ahead and fly to Dominica to enter the Institute yourself!"

He said nothing. But from something—his expression as he stared into his glass, the shifting of his body—I suddenly knew that he could not afford the trip.

I said, "So you fancy yourself as a believer?"

"No. A believer manqué." From the way he said it, I knew that he had said it before, perhaps often, and that the phrase stirred some hidden place in his imagination.

"What is wrong with you," I said, "with people like you, that the human world is not enough?"

"What is wrong with people like you, that it is?" he said, and this time he laughed and raised his eyebrows in a little mockery that shut me out from this place beyond reason, this glittering escape. I knew then that somehow or other, sometime or other, despite all I had said, Keith would go to Dominica.

I poured him another Scotch. As deftly as I could, I led the conversation into other, lighter directions. I asked about his childhood. At first stiffly, then more easily as time and Scotch loosened him, he talked about growing up in the Berkshire Hills. He became more light-hearted, and under my interest turned both shrewd and funny, with a keen sense of humor. His thick brown hair fell over his forehead. I laughed with him, and broke out a bottle of good port. He talked about amateur plays he had acted in; his enthusiasm increased as his coherence decreased. Enthusiasm, humor, thick brown hair. I smoothed the hair back from his forehead. Far into the night I pulled the drapes back from the window and we stood together and looked at the lights of the dying city ten stories below. Fog rolled in from the sea. Keith insisted we open the doors and stand on the balcony; he had never smelled fog tinged with the ocean. We smelled the night, and drank some more, and talked, and laughed.

And then I led him again to the sofa.

"Seena?" Keith said. He covered my hand, laid upon his thigh, with his own, and turned his head to look at me questioningly. I leaned forward and touched my lips to his, barely in contact, for a long moment. He drew back, and his hand tried to lift mine. I tightened my fingers.

"Seena, no…"

"Why not?" I put my mouth back on his, very lightly. He had to draw back to answer, and I could feel that he did not want to draw back. Under my lips he frowned slightly; still, despite his drunkenness—so much more than mine—he groped for the word.

"Incest…"

"No. We two have never shared a womb."

He frowned again, under my mouth. I drew back to smile at him, and shifted my hand. "It doesn't matter anymore, Keith. Not in New York. But even if it did—I am not your sister, not really. You said so yourself—remember? Not family. Just…here."

"Not family," he repeated, and I saw in his eyes the second before he closed them the flash of pain, the greed of a young man's desire, and even the crafty evasions of the good port. Then his arms closed around me.

He was very strong, and more than a little violent. I guessed from what confusions the violence flowed but still I enjoyed it, that overwhelming rush from that beautiful male-Devrie body. I wanted him to be violent with me, as long as I knew there was no real danger. No real danger, no real brother, no real child. Keith was not my child but Devrie was my child-sister, and I had to stop her from destroying herself, no matter how… didn't I? "The pull of blood." But this was necessary, was justified…was a necessary gamble. For Devrie.

So I told myself. Then I stopped telling myself anything at all, and surrendered to the warm tides of pleasure.

But at dawn I woke and thought—with Keith sleeping heavily across me and the sky cold at the window—*what the hell am I doing?*

When I came out of the shower, Keith was sitting rigidly against the pillows. Sitting next to him on the very edge of the bed, I pulled a sheet around my nakedness and reached for his hand. He snatched it away.

"Keith. It's all right. Truly it is."

"You're my sister."

"But nothing will come of it. No child, no repetitions. It's not all that uncommon, dear heart."

"It is where I come from."

"Yes. I know. But not here."

He didn't answer, his face troubled.

"Do you want breakfast?"

"No. No thank you."

I could feel his need to get away from me; it was almost palpable. Snatching my bodysuit off the floor, I went into the kitchen, which was chilly. The servant would not arrive for another hour. I turned up the heat, pulled on my bodysuit—standing on the cold floor first on one foot and then on the other, like some extinct species of water fowl—and made coffee. Through the handle of one cup I stuck two folded large bills. He came into the kitchen, dressed even to the torn jacket.

"Coffee."

"Thanks."

His fingers closed on the handle of the cup, and his eyes widened. Pure, naked shock, uncushioned by any defenses whatsoever: the whole soul, betrayed, pinned in the eyes.

"Oh God, no, Keith—how can you even think so? It's for the trip back to Indian Falls! A gift!"

An endless pause, while we stared at each other. Then he said, very low, "I'm sorry. I should have...seen what it's for." But his cup trembled in his hand, and a few drops sloshed onto the floor. It was those few drops that undid me, flooding me with shame. Keith had a right to his shock, and to the anguish in his/my/Devrie's face. She wanted him for her mystic purposes, I for their prevention. Fanatic and saboteur, we were both better defended against each other than Keith, without money nor religion nor years, was against either of us. If I could have seen any other way than the gamble I had taken...but I could not. Nonetheless, I was ashamed.

"Keith. I'm sorry."

"Why did we? Why did *we*?"

I could have said: *we* didn't; I did. But that might have made it worse for him. He was male, and so young.

Impulsively I blurted, "Don't go to Dominica!" But of course he was beyond listening to me now. His face closed. He set down the coffee cup and looked at me from eyes much harder than they had been a minute ago. Was he thinking that because of our night together I expected to influence him directly? *I* was not that young. He could not foresee that I was trying to guess much farther ahead than that, for which I could not blame him. I could not blame him for anything. But I did regret how clumsily I had handled the money. That had been stupid.

Nonetheless, when he left a few moments later, the handle of the coffee cup was bare. He had taken the money.

The Madagascar exhibits were complete. They opened to much press interest, and there were both favorable reviews and celebrations. I could not bring myself to feel that it mattered. Ten times a day I went through the deadening exercise of willing an interest that had deserted me, and when I looked at the moths, ashy white wings outstretched forever, I could feel my body recoil in a way I could not name.

The image of the moths went home with me. One night in November I actually thought I heard wings beating against the window where I had stood with Keith. I yanked open the drapes and then the doors, but of course there was nothing there. For a long time I stared at the nothingness, smelling the fog, before typing yet another message, urgent-priority personal, to Devrie. The mailnet did not bring any answer.

I contacted the mailnet computer at the college at Indian Falls. My fingers trembled as they typed a request to leave an urgent-priority personal message for a student, Keith Torellen. The mailnet typed back:

> TORELLEN, KEITH ROBERT. 64830016. ON MEDICAL LEAVE
> OF ABSENCE. TIME OF LEAVE: INDEFINITE. NO FORWARD-
> ING MAILNET NUMBER. END.

The sound came again at the window. Whirling, I scanned the dark glass, but there was nothing there, no moths, no wings, just the lights of the decaying city flung randomly across the blackness and the sound, faint and very far away, of a siren wailing out somebody else's disaster.

I shivered. Putting on a sweater and turning up the heat made me no warmer. Then the mail slot chimed softly and I turned in time to see the letter fall from the pneumatic tube from the lobby, the apartment house sticker clearly visible, assuring me that it had been processed and found free of both poison and explosives. Also visible was the envelope's logo: INSTITUTE OF THE BIOLOGICAL HOPE, all the O's radiant golden suns. But Devrie never wrote paper mail. She preferred the mailnet.

The note was from Keith, not Devrie. A short note, scrawled on a torn scrap of paper in nearly indecipherable handwriting. I had seen Keith's handwriting in Indian Falls, across his student notebooks; this was a wildly out-of-control version of it, almost psychotic in the variations of spacing and letter formation that signal identity. I guessed that he had written the note under the influence of a drug, or several drugs, his mind racing much faster than he could write. There was neither punctuation nor paragraphing.

> Dear Seena Im going to do it I have to know my parents are angry but I have to know I have to all the confusion is gone
> Seena    Keith

There was a word crossed out between "gone" and "Seena," scratched out with erratic lines of ink. I held the paper up to the light, tilting it this way and that. The crossed-out word was "mother."

*all the confusion is gone mother*
Mother.

Slowly I let out the breath I had not known I was holding. The first emotion was pity, for Keith, even though I had intended this. We had done a job on him, Devrie and I. Mother, sister, self. And when he and Devrie artificially drove upward the number and speed of the neurotransmitters in the brain, generated the twin trance, and then Keith's pre-cloning Freudian-still mind reached for Devrie to add sexual energy to all the other brain energies fueling Bohentin's holotanks—

Mother. Sister. Self.

All was fair in love and war. A voice inside my head jeered: And which is this? But I was ready for the voice. This was both. I didn't think it would be long before Devrie left the Institute to storm to New York.

It was nearly another month, in which the snow began to fall and the city to deck itself in the tired gilt fallacies of Christmas. I felt fine. Humming, I catalogued the Madagascar moths, remounting the best specimens in exhibit cases and sealing them under permaplex, where their fragile wings and delicate antennae could lie safe. The mutant strains had the thinnest wings, unnaturally tenuous and up to twenty-five centimeters each, all of pale ivory, as if a ghostly delicacy were the natural evolutionary response to the glowing landscape of nuclear genocide. I catalogued each carefully.

"Why?" Devrie said. "*Why?*"

"You look like hell."

"Why?"

"I think you already know," I said. She sagged on my white velvet sofa, alone, the PGs that I suspected acted as much as nurses as guards, dismissed from the apartment. Tears of anger and exhaustion collected in her sunken eye sockets but did not fall. Only with effort was she keeping herself in a sitting position, and the effort was costing her energy she did not have. Her skin, except for two red spots of fury high on each cheekbone, was the color of old eggs. Looking at her, I had to keep my hands twisted in my lap to keep myself from weeping.

"Are you telling me you *planned* it, Seena? Are you telling me you located Keith and slept with him because you knew that would make him impotent with me?"

"Of course not. I know sexuality isn't that simple. So do you."

"But you gambled on it. You gambled that it would be one way to ruin the experiment."

"I gambled that it would…complicate Keith's responses."

"Complicate them past the point where he knew who the hell he was with!"

"He'd be able to know if you weren't making him glow out of his mind with neurotransmitter kickers! He's not stupid. But he's not ready for whatever mystic hoops you've tried to make him jump through—if anybody ever *can* be said to be ready for that!—and no, I'm not surprised that he can't handle libidinal energies on top of all the other artificial energies you're racing through his brain. Something was bound to snap."

"You caused it, Seena. As cold-bloodedly as that."

A sudden shiver of memory brought the feel of Keith's hands on my breasts. No, not as cold-bloodedly as that. No. But I could not say so to Devrie.

"I trusted you," she said. " 'Anything for a sister'—God!"

"You were right to trust me. To trust me to get you out of that place before you're dead."

"Listen to yourself! Smug, all-knowing, self-righteous…do you know how *close* we were at the Institute? Do you have any idea what you've destroyed?"

I laughed coldly. I couldn't help it. "If contact with God can be destroyed because one confused kid can't get it up, what does that say about God?"

Devrie stared at me. A long moment passed, and in the moment the two red spots on her cheeks faded and her eyes narrowed. "Why, Seena?"

"I told you. I wanted you safe, out of there. And you are."

"No. No. There's something else, something more going on here. Going on with you."

"Don't make it more complicated than it is, Devrie. You're my sister, and my only family. Is it so odd that I would try to protect you?"

"Keith is your brother."

"Well, then, protect both of you. Whatever derails that experiment protects Keith, too."

She said softly, "Did you want him so much?"

We stared at each other across the living room, sisters, I standing by the mailnet and she supported by the sofa, needing its support, weak and implacable as any legendary martyr to the faith. Her weakness hurt me in some nameless place; as a child Devrie's body had been so strong. The hurt twisted in me, so that I answered her with truth. "Not so much. Not at first, not until we...no, that's not true. I wanted him. But that was not the reason, Devrie—it was not a rationalization for lust, nor any lapse in self-control."

She went on staring at me, until I turned to the sideboard and poured myself a Scotch. My hand trembled.

Behind me Devrie said, "Not lust. And not protection either. Something else, Seena. You're afraid."

I turned, smiling tightly. "Of you?"

"No. No, I don't think so."

"What then?"

"I don't know. Do you?"

"This is your theory, not mine."

She closed her eyes. The tears, shining all this time over her anger, finally fell. Head flung back against the pale sofa, arms limp at her side, she looked the picture of desolation, and so weak that I was frightened. I brought her a glass of milk from the kitchen and held it to her mouth, and I was a little surprised when she drank it off without protest.

"Devrie. You can't go on like this. In this physical state."

"No," she agreed, in a voice so firm and prompt that I was startled further. It was the voice of decision, not surrender. She straightened herself on the sofa. "Even Bohentin says I can't go on like this. I weigh less than he wants, and I'm right at the edge of not having the physical resources to control the twin trance. I'm having racking withdrawal symptoms even being on this trip, and at this very minute there is a doctor sitting at Father's desk in your study, in case I need him. Also, I've had my lawyers make over most of my remaining inheritance to Keith. I don't think you knew that. What's left has all been transferred to a bank on Dominica, and if I die it goes to the Institute. You won't be able to touch it, nor touch Keith's portion either, not even if I die. And I will die, Seena, soon, if I don't start eating and stop taking the program's drugs. I'll just burn out body and brain both. You've guessed that I'm close to that, but you haven't guessed how close. Now I'm telling you. I can't handle the stresses of the twin trance much longer."

I just went on holding her glass, arm extended, unable to move.

"You gambled that you could destroy one component in the chain of my experiment at the Institute by confusing my twin sexually. Well, you won. Now *I'm* making a gamble. I'm gambling my life that you can undo what you did with Keith, and without his knowing that I made you. You said he's not stupid and his impotency comes from being unable to handle the drug program; perhaps you're partly right. But he is me—*me*, Seena—and I know you've thought I was stupid all my life, because I wanted things you don't understand. Now Keith wants them, too—it was inevitable that he would—and you're going to undo whatever is standing in his way. I had to fight myself free all my life of your bullying, but Keith doesn't have that kind of time. Because if you don't undo what you caused, I'm going to go ahead with the twin trance anyway—the *twin trance*, Seena—without the sexual component and without letting Bohentin know just how much greater the strain is in trance than he thinks it is. He doesn't know, he doesn't have a twin, and neither do the doctors. But I know, and if I push it much farther I'm going to eventually die at it. *Soon* eventually. When I do, all your scheming to get me out of there really will have failed and you'll be alone with whatever it is you're so afraid of. But I don't think you'll let that happen.

"I think that instead you'll undo what you did to Keith, so that the experiment can have one last real chance. And in return, after that one chance, I'll agree to come home, to Boston or here to New York, for one year.

"That's my gamble."

She was looking at me from eyes empty of all tears, a Devrie I had not ever seen before. She meant it, every demented word, and she would do it. I wanted to scream at her, to scream a jumble of suicide and moral blackmail and warped perceptions and outrage, but the words that came out of my mouth came out in a whisper.

"What in God's name is worth *that*?"

Shockingly, she laughed, a laugh of more power than her wasted frame could have contained. Her face glowed, and the glow looked both exalted and insane. "You said it, Seena—in God's name. To finally know. To *know*, beyond the fogginess of faith, that we're not alone in the universe…Faith should not mean fogginess."

She laughed again, this time defensively, as if she knew how she sounded to me. "You'll do it, Seena." It was not a question. She took my hand.

"You would *kill* yourself?"

"No. I would die trying to reach God. It's not the same thing."

"I never bullied you, Devrie."

She dropped my hand. "All my life, Seena. And on into now. But all of your bullying and your scorn would look rather stupid, wouldn't it, if there really can be proved to exist a rational basis for what you laughed at all those years!"

We looked at each other, sisters, across the abyss of the pale sofa, and then suddenly away. Neither of us dared speak.

My plane landed on Dominica by night. Devrie had gone two days before me, returning with her doctor and guards on the same day she had left, as I had on my previous visit. I had never seen the island at night. The tropical greenery, lush with that faintly menacing suggestion of plant life gone wild, seemed to close in on me. The velvety darkness seemed to smell of ginger, and flowers, and the sea—all too strong, too blandly sensual, like an overdone perfume ad. At the hotel it was better; my room was on the second floor, above the dark foliage, and did not face the sea. Nonetheless, I stayed inside all that evening, all that darkness, until I could go the next day to the Institute of the Biological Hope.

"Hello, Seena."

"Keith. You look—"

"Rotten," he finished, and waited. He did not smile. Although he had lost some weight, he was nowhere near as skeletal as Devrie, and it gave me a pang I did not analyze to see his still-healthy body in the small gray room where last I had seen hers. His head was shaved, and without the curling brown hair he looked sterner, prematurely middle-aged. That, too, gave me a strange emotion, although it was not why he looked rotten. The worst was his eyes. Red-veined, watery, the sockets already a little sunken, they held the sheen of a man who was not forgiving somebody for something. Me? Himself? Devrie? I had lain awake all night, schooling myself for this insane interview, and still I did not know what to say. What does one say to persuade a man to sexual potency with one's sister so that her life might be saved? I felt ridiculous, and frightened, and—I suddenly realized the name of my strange emotion—humiliated. How could I even start to slog toward what I was supposed to reach?

"How goes the Great Experiment?"

"Not as you described it," he said, and we were there already. I looked at him evenly.

"You can't understand why I presented the Institute in the worst possible light."

"I can understand that."

"Then you can't understand why I bedded you, knowing about Bohentin's experiment."

"I can also understand that."

Something was wrong. Keith answered me easily, without restraint, but with conflict gritty beneath his voice, like sand beneath blowing grass. I stepped closer, and he flinched. But his expression did not change.

"Keith. What is this about? What am I doing here? Devrie said you couldn't...that you were impotent with her, confused enough about who and what..." I trailed off. He still had not changed expression.

I said quietly, "It was a simplistic idea in the first place. Only someone as simplistic as Devrie..." Only someone as simplistic as Devrie would think you could straighten out impotency by talking about it for a few hours. I turned to go, and I had gotten as far as laying my hand on the doorknob before Keith grasped my arm. Back to him, I squeezed my eyes shut. What in God would I have *done* if he had not stopped me?

"It's not what Devrie thinks!" With my back to him, not able to see his middle-aged baldness but only to hear the anguish in his voice, he again seemed young, uncertain, the boy I had bought coffee for in Indian Falls. I kept my back to him, and my voice carefully toneless.

"What is it, then, Keith? If not what Devrie thinks?"

"I don't know!"

"But you do know what it's not? It's not being confused about who is your sister and who your mother and who you're willing to have sex with in front of a room full of researchers?"

"No." His voice had gone hard again, but his hand stayed on my arm. "At first, yes. The first time. But, Seena—I *felt* it. *Almost.* I almost felt the presence, and then all the rest of the confusion—it didn't seem as important anymore. Not the confusion between you and Devrie."

I whirled to face him. "You mean God doesn't care whom you fuck if it gets you closer to fucking with Him."

He looked at me hard then—at me, not at his own self-absorption. His reddened eyes widened a little. "Why, Seena—*you* care. You told me the brother-sister thing didn't matter anymore—but *you* care."

Did I? I didn't even know anymore. I said, "But, then, I'm not deluding myself that it's all for the old Kingdom and the Glory."

"Glory," he repeated musingly, and finally let go of my arm. I couldn't tell what he was thinking.

"Keith. This isn't getting us anywhere."

"Where do you want to get?" he said in the same musing tone. "Where did any of you, starting with your father, want to get with me? Glory...glory."

Standing this close to him, seeing close up the pupils of his eyes and smelling close up the odor of his sweat, I finally realized what I should have seen all along: he was glowing. He was of course constantly on Bohentin's program of neuro-transmitter manipulation, but the same chemicals that made the experiments possible also raised the threshold of both frankness and suggestibility. I guessed it must be a little like the looseness of being drunk, and I wondered if perhaps Bohentin might have deliberately raised the dosage before letting this interview take place. But no, Bohentin wouldn't be aware of the bargain Devrie and I had struck; she would not have told him. The whole bizarre situation was hers alone, and Keith's drugged musings a fortunate side-effect I would have to capitalize on.

"Where do you think my father wanted to get with you?" I asked him gently.

"Immortality. Godhead. The man who created Adam without Eve."

He was becoming maudlin. "Hardly 'the man,' " I pointed out. "My father was only one of a team of researchers. And the same results were being obtained independently in California."

"Results. I am a 'result.' What do *you* think he wanted, Seena?"

"Scientific knowledge of cell development. An objective truth."

"That's all Devrie wants."

"To compare bioengineering to some mystic quest—"

"Ah, but if the mystic quest is given a laboratory answer? Then it, too, becomes a scientific truth. You really hate that idea, don't you, Seena? You hate science validating anything you define as non-science."

I said stiffly, "That's rather an oversimplification."

"Then what do you hate?"

"I hate the risk to human bodies and human minds. To Devrie. To you."

"How nice of you to include me," he said, smiling. "And what do you think Devrie wants?"

"Sensation. Romantic religious emotion. To be all roiled up inside with delicious esoterica."

He considered this. "Maybe."

"And is that what you want as well, Keith? You've asked what everyone else wants. What do you want?"

"I want to feel at home in the universe. As if I belonged in it. And I never have."

He said this simply, without self-consciousness, and the words themselves were predictable enough for his age—even banal. There was nothing in the words that could account for my eyes suddenly filling with tears. "And 'scientifically' reaching God would do that for you?"

"How do I know until I try it? Don't cry, Seena."

"I'm not!"

"All right," he agreed softly. "You're not crying." Then he added, without changing tone, "I am more like you than like Devrie."

"How so?"

"I think that Devrie has always felt that she belongs in the universe. She only wants to find the...the coziest corner of it to curl up in. Like a cat. The coziest corner to curl up in is God's lap. Aren't you surprised that I should be more like you than like the person I was cloned from?"

"No," I said. "Harder upbringing than Devrie's. I told you that first day: cloning is only delayed twinning."

He threw back his head and laughed, a sound that chilled my spine. Whatever his conflict was, we were moving closer.

"Oh no, Seena. You're so wrong. It's more than delayed twinning, all right. You can't buy a real twin. You either have one or you don't. But you can buy yourself a clone. Bought, paid for, kept on the books along with all the rest of the glassware and holotanks and electron microscopes. You said so yourself, in your apartment, when you first told me about Devrie and the Institute. 'Money. She'd buy you.' And you were right, of course. Your father bought me, and she did, and you did. But of course you two women couldn't have bought if I hadn't been selling."

He was smiling still. Stupid—we had both been stupid, Devrie and I, we had both been looking in the wrong place, misled by our separate blinders-on training in the laboratory brain. My training had been scientific, hers humanistic, and so I looked at Freud and she looked at Oedipus, and we were equally stupid. How did the world look to a man who did not deal in laboratory brains, a man raised in a grittier world in which limits were not what the mind was capable of but what the bank book would stand? "Your genes are too expensive for you to claim except as a beggar; your sisters are too expensive for you to claim except as a beggar; God is too expensive for you to claim except as a beggar." To a less romantic man it would not have mattered, but a less romantic man would not have come to the Institute. What dark humiliations and resentments did Keith feel when he looked at Devrie, the self who was buyer and not bought?

Change the light you shine onto a mind, and you see different neural patterns, different corridors, different forests of trees grown in soil you could not have imagined. Run that soil through your fingers and you discover different pebbles, different sand, different leaf mold from the decay of old growths. Devrie and I had been hacking through the wrong forest.

Not Oedipus, but Marx.

Quick lines of attack came to me. Say: Keith it's a job like any other with high-hazard pay why can't you look at it like that a very dangerous and well-paid job for which you've been hired by just one more eccentric member of the monied class. Say: You're entitled to the wealth you're our biological brother damn it consider it rationally as a kinship entitlement. Say: Don't be so nicey-nice it's a tough world out there and if Devrie's giving it away take it don't be an impractical chump.

I said none of that. Instead I heard myself saying, coolly and with a calm cruelty, "You're quite right. You were bought by Devrie, and she is now using her own purchase for her own ends. You're a piece of equipment bought and paid for. Unfortunately, there's no money in the account. It has all been a grand sham."

Keith jerked me to face him with such violence that my neck cracked. "What are you saying?"

The words came as smoothly, as plausibly, as if I had rehearsed them. I didn't even consciously plan them: how can you plan a lie you do not know you will need? I slashed through this forest blind, but the ground held under my feet.

"Devrie told me that she has signed over most of her inheritance to you. What she didn't know, because I haven't yet told her, is that she doesn't have control of her inheritance any longer. It's not hers. I control it. I had her declared mentally incompetent on the grounds of violent suicidal tendencies and had myself made her legal guardian. She no longer has the legal right to control her fortune. A doctor observed her when she came to visit me in New York. So the transfer of her fortune to you is invalid."

"The lawyers who gave me the papers to sign—"

"Will learn about the New York action this week," I said smoothly. How much inheritance law did Keith know? Probably very little. Neither did I, and I invented furiously; it only needed to *sound* plausible. "The New York courts only handed down their decision recently, and Dominican judicial machinery, like everything else in the tropics, moves slowly. But the ruling will hold, Keith. Devrie does not control her own money, and you're a pauper again. But *I* have something for you. Here. An airline ticket back to Indian Falls. You're a free man. Poor, but free. The ticket is in your name, and there's a check inside it—that's from me. You've earned it, for at least trying to aid poor Devrie. But now you're going to have to leave her to me. I'm now her legal guardian."

I held the ticket out to him. It was wrapped in its airline folder; my own name as passenger was hidden. Keith stared at it, and then at me.

I said softly, "I'm sorry you were cheated. Devrie didn't mean to. But she has no money, now, to offer you. You can go. Devrie's my burden now."

His voice sounded strangled. "To remove from the Institute?"

"I never made any secret of wanting her out. Although the legal papers for that will take a little time to filter through the Dominican courts. She wouldn't go except by force, so force is what I'll get. Here."

I thrust the ticket folder at him. He made no move to take it, and I saw from the hardening of his face—my face, Devrie's face—the moment when Devrie shifted forests in his mind. Now she was without money, without legal control of her life, about to be torn from the passion she loved most. The helpless underdog. The orphaned woman, poor and cast out, in need of protection from the powerful who had seized her fortune.

Not Marx, but Cervantes.

"You would do that? To your own sister?"

Anything for a sister. I said bitterly, "Of course I would."

"She's not mentally incompetent!"

"Isn't she?"

"No!"

I shrugged. "The courts say she is."

Keith studied me, resolve hardening around him. I thought of certain shining crystals, that will harden around any stray piece of grit. Now that I was succeeding in convincing him, my lies hurt—or perhaps what hurt was how easily he believed them.

"Are you sure, Seena," he said, "that *you* aren't just trying a grab for Devrie's fortune?"

I shrugged again, and tried to make my voice toneless. "I want her out of here. I don't want her to die."

"Die? What makes you think she would die?"

"She looks—"

"She's nowhere near dying," Keith said angrily—his anger a release, so much that it hardly mattered at what. "Don't you think I can tell in twin trance what her exact physical state is? And don't you know how much control the trance gives each twin over the bodily processes of the other? Don't you even know that? Devrie isn't anywhere near dying. And I'd pull her out of trance if she were." He paused, looking hard at me. "Keep your ticket, Seena."

I repeated mechanically, "You can leave now. There's no money." *Devrie had lied to me.*

"That wouldn't leave her with any protection at all, would it?" he said levelly. When he grasped the doorknob to leave, the tendons in his wrist stood out clearly, strong and taut. I did not try to stop his going.

Devrie had lied to me. With her lie, she had blackmailed me into yet another lie to Keith. The twin trance granted control, in some unspecified way, to each twin's body; the trance I had pioneered might have resulted in eight deaths unknowingly inflicted on each other out of who knows what dark forests in eight fumbling minds. Lies, blackmail, death, more lies.

Out of these lies they were going to make scientific truth. Through these forests they were going to search for God.

"Final clearance check of holotanks," an assistant said formally. "Faraday cage?"

"Optimum."

"External radiation?"

"Cleared," said the man seated at the console of the first tank.

"Cleared," said the woman seated at the console of the second.

"Microradiation?"

"Cleared."

"Cleared."

"Personnel radiation, Class A?"

"Cleared."

"Cleared."

On it went, the whole tedious and crucial procedure, until both tanks had been cleared and focused, the fluid adjusted, tested, adjusted again, tested again. Bohentin listened patiently, without expression, but I, standing to the side of him and behind the tanks, saw the nerve at the base of his neck and just below the hairline pulse in some irregular rhythm of its own. Each time the nerve pulsed, the skin rose slightly from under his collar. I kept my eyes on that syncopated crawling of flesh, and felt tension prickle over my own skin like heat.

Three-quarters of the lab, the portion where the holotanks and other machinery stood, was softly dark, lit mostly from the glow of console dials and the indirect track lighting focused on the tanks. Standing in the gloom were Bohentin, five other scientists, two medical doctors—and me. Bohentin had fought my being allowed there, but in the end he had had to give in. I had known too many threatening words not in generalities but in specifics: reporters' names, drug names, cloning details, twin trance tragedy, anorexia symptoms, bio-engineering amendment. He was not a man who much noticed either public opinion or relatives' threats, but no one else outside his Institute knew so many specific words—some people knew some of the words, but only I had them all. In the end he had focused on me his cold, brilliant eyes, and given permission for me to witness the experiment that involved my sister.

I was going to hold Devrie to her bargain. I was not going to believe anything she told me without witnessing it for myself.

Half the morning passed in technical preparation. Somewhere Devrie and Keith, the human components of this costly detection circuit, were separately being brought to the apex of brain activity. Drugs, biofeedback, tactile and auditory and kinaesthetic stimulation—all carefully calculated for the maximum increase of both the number of neurotransmitters firing signals through the synapses of the brain and of the speed at which the signals raced. The more rapid the transmission through certain pathways, the more intense both perception and feeling. Some neurotransmitters, under this pressure, would alter molecular structure into natural hallucinogens; that reaction had to be controlled. Meanwhile other drugs, other biofeedback techniques, would depress the body's natural enzymes designed to either reabsorb excess transmitters or to reduce the rate at which they fired. The number and speed of neurotransmitters in Keith's and Devrie's brains would mount, and mount, and mount, all natural chemical barriers removed. The two of them would enter the lab with their whole brains—rational cortex, emotional limbic, right and left brain functions—simultaneously aroused to an unimaginable degree. *Simultaneously.* They would be feeling as great a "rush" as a falling skydiver, as great a glow as a cocaine user, as great a mental clarity and receptivity as a da Vinci whose brush is guided by all the integrated visions of his unconscious mind. They would be white-hot.

Then they would hit each other with the twin trance.

The quarter of the lab which Keith and Devrie would use was softly and indirectly lit, though brighter than the rest. It consisted of a raised, luxuriantly padded platform, walls and textured pillows in a pink whose component wavelengths had been carefully calculated, temperature in a complex gradient producing precise convection flows over the skin. The man and woman in that womb-colored, flesh-stimulating environment would be able to see us observers standing in the gloom behind the holotanks only as vague shapes. When the two doors opened and Devrie and Keith moved onto the platform, I knew that they would not even try to distinguish who stood in the lab. Looking at their faces, that looked only at each other, I felt my heart clutch.

They were naked except for the soft helmets that both attached hundreds of needles to nerve clumps just below the skin and also held the earphones through which Bohentin controlled the music that swelled the cathedrals of their skulls. "Cathedrals"—from their faces, transfigured to the ravished ecstasy found in paintings of medieval saints, that was the right word. But here the ecstasy was controlled, understood, and I saw with a sudden rush of pain at old memories that I could recognize the exact moment when Keith and Devrie locked onto each other with the twin trance. I recognized it, with my own more bitter hyperclarity, in their eyes, as I recognized the cast of concentration that came over their features, and the intensity of their absorption. The twin trance. They clutched each other's hands, faces inches apart, and suddenly I had to look away.

Each holotank held two whorls of shifting colors, the outlines clearer and the textures more sharply delineated than any previous holographs in the history of science. Keith's and Devrie's perceptions of each other's presence. The whorls went on clarifying themselves, separating into distinct and mappable layers, as on the platform Keith and Devrie remained frozen, all their energies focused on the telepathic trance. Seconds passed, and then minutes. And still, despite the clarity of the holographs in the tank, a clarity that fifteen years earlier I would have given my right hand for, I sensed that Keith and Devrie were holding back, were deliberately confining their unimaginable perceptiveness to each other's radiant energy, in the same way that water is confined behind a dam to build power.

But how could *I* be sensing that? From a subliminal "reading" of the mapped perceptions in the holotanks? Or from something else?

More minutes passed. Keith and Devrie stayed frozen, facing each other, and over her skeletal body and his stronger one a flush began to spread, rosy and slow, like heat tide rising.

"Jesus H. Christ," said one of the medical doctors, so low that only I, standing directly behind her, could have heard. It was not a curse, nor a prayer, but some third possibility, unnameable.

Keith put one hand on Devrie's thigh. She shuddered. He drew her down to the cushions on the platform and they began to caress each other, not frenzied, not in the exploring way of lovers but with a deliberation I have never experienced outside a research lab, a slow care that implied that worlds of interpretation hung on each movement. Yet the effect was not of coldness nor detachment but of intense involvement, of tremendous energy joyously used, of creating each other's bodies right then, there under each other's hands. They were *working*, and oblivious to all but their work. But if it was a kind of creative work, it was also a kind of primal innocent eroticism, and, watching, I felt my own heat begin to rise. "Innocent"—but if innocence is unknowingness, there was nothing innocent about it at all. Keith and Devrie knew and controlled each heartbeat, and I felt the exact moment when they let their sexual energies, added to all the other neural energies, burst the dam and flood outward in wave after wave, expanding the scope of each brain's perceptions, inundating the artificially-walled world.

A third whorl formed in each holotank.

It formed suddenly: one second nothing, the next brightness. But then it wavered, faded a bit. After a few moments it brightened slightly, a diffused golden haze, before again fading. On the platform Keith gasped, and I guessed he was having to shift his attention between perceiving the third source of radiation and keeping up the erotic version of the twin trance. His biofeedback techniques were less experienced than Devrie's, and the male erection more fragile. But then he caught the rhythm, and the holograph brightened.

It seemed to me that the room brightened as well, although no additional lights came on and the consoles glowed no brighter. Sweat poured off the researchers. Bohentin leaned forward, his neck muscle tautening toward the platform as if it were his will and not Keith/Devrie's that strained to perceive that third presence recorded in the tank. I thought, stupidly, of mythical intermediaries: Merlyn never made king, Moses never reaching the Promised Land. Intermediaries—and then it became impossible to think of anything at all.

Devrie shuddered and cried out. Keith's orgasm came a moment later, and with it a final roil of neural activity so strong the two primary whorls in each holotank swelled to fill the tank and inundate the third. At the moment of break-through Keith screamed, and in memory it seems as if the scream was what tore through the last curtain—that is nonsense. How loud would microbes have to scream to attract the attention of giants? How loud does a knock on the door have to be to pull a sleeper from the alien world of dreams?

The doctor beside me fell to her knees. The third presence— or some part of it—swirled all around us, racing along our own unprepared synapses and neurons, and what swirled and raced was astonishment. A golden, majestic astonishment. We had finally attracted Its attention, finally knocked with enough neural

145

force to be just barely heard—and It was astonished that we could, or did, exist. The slow rise of that powerful astonishment within the shielded lab was like the slow swinging around of the head of a great beast to regard some butterfly it has barely glimpsed from the corner of one eye. But this was no beast. As Its attention swung toward us, pain exploded in my skull—the pain of sound too loud, lights too bright, charge too high. My brain was burning on overload. There came one more flash of insight—wordless, pattern without end—and the sound of screaming. Then, abruptly, the energy vanished.

Bohentin, on all fours, crawled toward the holotanks. The doctor lay slumped on the floor; the other doctor had already reached the platform and its two crumpled figures. Someone was crying, someone else shouting. I rose, fell, dragged myself to the side of the platform and then could not climb it. I could not climb the platform. Hanging with two hands on the edge, hearing the voice crying as my own, I watched the doctor bend shakily to Keith, roll him off Devrie to bend over her, turn back to Keith.

Bohentin cried, "The tapes are intact!"

"Oh God oh God oh God oh God oh God," someone moaned, until abruptly she stopped. I grasped the flesh-colored padding on top of the platform and pulled myself up onto it.

Devrie lay unconscious, pulse erratic, face cast in perfect bliss. The doctor breathed into Keith's mouth—what strength could the doctor himself have left?—and pushed on the naked chest. Breathe, push, breathe, push. The whole length of Keith's body shuddered; the doctor rocked back on his heels; Keith breathed.

"It's all on tape!" Bohentin cried. "It's all *on tape!*"

"God damn you to hell," I whispered to Devrie's blissful face. "It didn't even know we were there!"

Her eyes opened. I had to lean close to hear her answer.

"But now…we know He…is there."

She was too weak to smile. I looked away from her, away from that face, out into the tumultuous emptiness of the lab, anywhere.

They will try again.

Devrie has been asleep, fed by glucose solution through an IV, for fourteen hours. I sit near her bed, frowned at by the nurse, who can see my expression as I stare at my sister. Somewhere in another bed Keith is sleeping yet again. His rest is more fitful than Devrie's; she sinks into sleep as into warm water, but he cannot. Like me, he is afraid of drowning.

An hour ago he came into Devrie's room and grasped my hand. "How could It—He—It not have been aware that we existed? Not even have *known*?"

I didn't answer him.

"You felt it too, Seena, didn't you? The others say they could, so you must have too. It…created us in some way. No, that's wrong. How could It create us and not *know*?"

I said wearily, "Do *we* always know what we've created?" and Keith glanced at me sharply. But I had not been referring to my father's work in cloning.

"Keith. What's a Thysania Africana?"

"A what?"

"Think of us," I said, "as just one more biological side-effect. One type of being acts, and another type of being comes into existence. Man stages something like the African Horror, and in doing so he creates whole new species of moths and doesn't even discover they exist until long afterward. If man can do it, why not God? And why should He be any more aware of it than we are?"

Keith didn't like that. He scowled at me, and then looked at Devrie's sleeping face: Devrie's sleeping bliss.

"Because she is a fool," I said savagely, "and so are you. You won't leave it alone, will you? Having been noticed by It once, you'll try to be noticed by It again. Even though she promised me otherwise, and even if it kills you both."

Keith looked at me a long time, seeing clearly—finally—the nature of the abyss between us, and its dimensions. But I already knew neither of us could cross. When at last he spoke, his voice held so much compassion that I hated him. "Seena. Seena, love. There's no more doubt now, don't you see? Now rational belief is no harder than rational doubt. Why are you so afraid to even believe?"

I left the room. In the corridor I leaned against the wall, palms spread flat against the tile, and closed my eyes. It seemed to me that I could hear wings, pale and fragile, beating against glass.

They will try again. For the sake of sure knowledge that the universe is not empty, Keith and Devrie and all the others like their type of being will go on pushing their human brains beyond what the human brain has evolved to do, go on fluttering their wings against that biological window. For the sake of sure knowledge: belief founded on experiment and not on faith. And the Other: being/alien/God? It, too, may choose to initiate contact, if It can and now that It knows we are here. Perhaps It will seek to know us, and even beyond the laboratory Devrie and Keith may find any moment of heightened arousal subtly invaded by a shadowy Third. Will they sense It, hovering just beyond consciousness, if they argue fiercely or race a sailboat in rough water or make love? How much arousal will it take, now, for them to sense those huge wings beating on the other side of the window?

And windows can be broken.

Tomorrow I will fly back to New York. To my museum, to my exhibits, to my moths under permaplex, to my empty apartment, where I will keep the heavy drapes drawn tightly across the glass.

For—*oh God*—all the rest of my life.

# MARGIN OF ERROR

PAULA CAME BACK in a blaze of glory, her Institute uniform with its pseudo-military medals crisp and bright, her spine straight as an engineered diamond-fiber rod. I heard her heels clicking on the sidewalk and I looked up from the bottom porch step, a child on my lap. Paula's face was genemod now, the blemishes gone, the skin fine-pored, the cheekbones chiseled under green eyes. But I would have known that face anywhere. No matter what she did to it.

"Karen?" Her voice held disbelief.

"Paula," I said.

"*Karen*?" This time I didn't answer. The child, my oldest, twisted in my arms to eye the visitor. The slight movement made the porch step creak.

It was the kind of neighborhood where women sat all morning on porches or stoops, watching children play on the sidewalk. Steps sagged; paint peeled; small front lawns were scraped bare by feet and tricycles and plastic wading pools. Women lived a few doors down from their mothers, both of them growing heavier every year. There were few men. The ones there were, didn't seem to stay long.

I said, "How did you find me?"

"It wasn't hard," Paula said, and I knew she didn't understand my smile. Of course it wasn't hard. I had never intended it should be. This was undoubtedly the first time in nearly five years that Paula had looked.

She lowered her perfect body gingerly onto the porch steps. My little girl, Lollie, gazed at her from my lap. Then Lollie opened her cupped hands and smiled. "See my frog, lady?"

"Very nice," Paula said. She was trying hard to hide her contempt, but I could see it. For the sad imprisoned frog, for Lollie's dirty face, for the worn yard, for the way I looked.

"Karen," Paula said, "I'm here because there's a problem. With the project. More specifically, with the initial formulas, we think. With a portion of the nanoassembler code from five years ago, when you were...still with us."

"A problem," I repeated. Inside the house, a baby wailed. "Just a minute."

I set Lollie down and went inside. Lori cried in her crib. Her diaper reeked. I put a pacifier in her mouth and cradled her in my left arm. With the right arm I scooped Timmy from his crib. When he didn't wake, I jostled him a little. I carried both babies back to the porch, deposited Timmy in the portacrib, and sat down next to Paula.

"Lollie, go get me a diaper, honey. And wipes. You can carry your frog inside to get them."

Lollie went; she's a sweet-natured kid. Paula stared incredulously at the twins. I unwrapped Lori's diaper and Paula grimaced and slid farther away.

"Karen—are you listening to me? This is important!"

"I'm listening."

"The nanocomputer instructions are off, somehow. The major results check out, obviously—" *Obviously.* The media had spent five years exclaiming over the major results.

"—but there are some odd foldings in the proteins of the twelfth-generation nanoassemblers."

Twelfth generation. The nanocomputer attached to each assembler replicates itself every six months. That was one of the project's checks and balances on the margin of error. It had been five and a half years. Twelfth generation was about right.

"Also," Paula continued, and I heard the strain in her voice, "there are some unforeseen macro-level developments. We're not sure yet that they're tied to the nanocomputer protein folds. There might not be any connection. What we're trying to do now is cover all the variables."

"You must be working on fairly remote variables if you're reduced to asking me."

"Well, yes, we are. Karen, do you have to do that *now*?"

"Yes." I scraped the shit off Lori with one edge of the soiled diaper. Lollie danced out of the house with a clean one. She sat beside me, whispering to her frog.

Paula said, "What I need…what the project needs—"

I said, "Do you remember the summer we collected frogs? We were maybe eight and ten. You'd become fascinated reading about that experiment where they threw a frog in boiling water but it jumped out, and then they put a frog in cool water and gradually increased the temperature to boiling until the stupid frog just sat there and died. Remember?"

"Karen—"

"I collected sixteen frogs for you, and when I found out what you were going to do with them, I cried and tried to let them go. But you boiled eight of them anyway. The other eight were controls. I'll give you that—proper scientific method. To reduce the margin of error, you said."

"Karen—we were just kids…"

I put the clean diaper on Lori. "Not all kids behave like that. Lollie doesn't. But you wouldn't know that, would you? Nobody in your set has children. You should have had a baby, Paula."

She barely hid her shudder. But, then, most of the people we knew felt the same way.

She said, "What the project needs is for you to come back and work on the same small area you did originally. Looking for something—anything—you might have missed in the protein-coded instructions to successive generations of nanoassemblers."

"No," I said.

"It's not really a matter of choice. The macrolevel problems—I'll be frank, Karen. It looks like a new form of cancer, one nobody's ever seen. Unregulated replication of some very weird cells."

"So take the cellular nanomachinery out." I crumpled the stinking diaper and set it out of the baby's reach. Closer to Paula.

"You know we can't do that! The project's irreversible!"

"Many things are irreversible," I said. Lori started to fuss. I picked her up, opened my blouse, and gave her the breast. She sucked greedily. Paula glanced away. She has had nanomachinery in her perfect body, making it perfect, for five years now. Her breasts will never look swollen, blue-veined, sagging.

"Karen, listen—"

"No—you listen," I said quietly. "Eight years ago you convinced Zweigler I was only a minor member of the research team, included only because I was your sister. I've always wondered, by the way, how you did that—were you sleeping with him, too? Seven years ago you got me shunted off into the minor area of the project's effect on female gametes—which nobody cared about because it was already clear there was no way around sterility as a side effect. Nobody thought it was too high a price for a perfect, self-repairing body, did they? Except me."

Paula didn't answer. Lollie carried her frog to the wading pool and set it carefully in the water.

I said, "I didn't mind working on female gametes, even if it was a backwater, even if you got star billing. I was used to it, after all. As kids, you were always the cowboy; I got to be the horse. You were the astronaut, I was the alien you conquered. Remember? One Christmas you used up all the chemicals in your first chemistry set and then stole mine."

"I don't think trivial childhood incidents matter in—"

"Of course you don't. And I never minded. But I did mind when five years ago you made copies of all my notes and presented them as yours, while I was so sick during my pregnancy with Lollie. You claimed my work. Stole it. Just like the chemistry set. And then you eased me off the project."

"What you did was so minor—"

"If it was so minor, why are you here asking for my help now? And why would you imagine for half a second I'd give it to you?"

She stared at me, calculating. I stared back coolly. Paula wasn't used to me cool, I could see that. I'd always been the excitable one. Excitable, flighty, unstable—that's what she'd told Zweigler. A security risk.

Timmy fussed in his portacrib. I stood up, still nursing Lori, and scooped him up with my free arm. Back on the steps, I juggled Timmy to lie across Lori on my lap, pulled back my blouse, and gave him the other breast. This time Paula didn't permit herself a grimace.

She said, "Karen, what I did was wrong. I know that now. But for the sake of the project, not for me, you have to—"

"You *are* the project. You have been from the first moment you grabbed the headlines away from Zweigler and the others who gave their life to that work. 'Lovely Young Scientist Injects Self With Perfect-Cell Drug!' 'No Sacrifice Too Great To Circumvent FDA Shortsightedness, Heroic Researcher Declares.' "

Paula said flatly, "You're jealous. You're obscure and I'm famous. You're a mess and I'm beautiful. You're—"

"A milch cow? While you're a brilliant researcher? Then solve your own research problems."

"This was your area—"

"Oh, Paula, they were *all* my areas. I did more of the basic research than you did, and you know it. But you knew how to position yourself with Zweigler, to present key findings at key moments, to cultivate the right connections…all that stuff you do so well. And, of course, I was still under the delusion we were partners. I just didn't realize it was a barracuda partnering a goldfish."

From the wading pool Lollie watched us with big eyes. "Mommy…"

"It's okay, honey. Mommy's not mad at you. Look, better catch your frog—he's hopping away."

She shrieked happily and dove for the frog. Paula said softly, "I had no idea you were so angry after all this time. You've changed, Karen."

"But I'm not angry. Not anymore. And you never knew what I was like before. You never bothered to know."

"I knew you never wanted a scientific life. Not the way I did. You always wanted kids. Wanted…*this*." She waved her arm around the shabby yard. David left eighteen months ago. He sends money. It's never enough.

"I wanted a scientific establishment that would let me have both. And I wanted credit for my work. I wanted what was mine. How did you do it, Paula—end up with what was yours and what was mine, too?"

"Because you were distracted by babyshit and frogs!" Paula yelled, and for the first time I saw how scared she really was. Paula didn't make admissions like that. A tactical error. I watched her stab desperately for a way to regain the advantage. A way to seize the offensive.

I seized it first. "You should have left David alone. You already had Zweigler; you should have left me David. Our marriage was never the same after that."

She said, "I'm dying, Karen."

I turned my head from the nursing babies to look at her.

"It's true. My cellular machinery is running wild. Just in the last few months. The nanoassemblers are creating weird structures, destructive enzymes. For five years they replicated perfectly and now…For five years it all performed *exactly* as it was programmed to—"

I said, "It still is."

Paula sat very still. Lori had fallen asleep. I juggled her into the portacrib and nestled Timmy more comfortably on my lap. Lollie chased her frog around the wading pool. I squinted to see if Lollie's lips were blue; the weather was really too cool for her to be in the water very long.

Paula choked out, "You programmed the assembler machinery in the ovaries to—"

"Nobody much cares about women's ovaries. Only fourteen percent of college-educated women want to muck up their lives with kids. Recent survey result. Less than one percent margin of error."

"—you actually sabotaged…hundreds of women have been injected by now, maybe *thousands*—"

"Oh, there's a reverser enzyme," I said. "Completely effective if you take it before the twelfth-generation replication. You're the only person that's been injected that long. I just discovered the reverser a few months ago, tinkering with my old notes for something to do in what your friends probably call my idle domestic prison. That's provable, incidentally. All my notes are computer-dated."

Paula whispered, "Scientists don't *do* this—"

"Too bad you wouldn't let me be one."

"Karen—"

"Don't you want to know what the reverser is, Paula? It's engineered from human chorionic gonadotropin. The pregnancy hormone. Too bad you never wanted a baby."

She went on staring at me. Lollie shrieked and splashed with her frog. Her lips *were* turning blue. I stood up, laid Timmy next to Lori in the portacrib, and buttoned my blouse.

"You made an experimental error twenty-five years ago," I said to Paula. "Too small a sample population. Sometimes a frog jumps out."

I went to lift my daughter from the wading pool.

# DANCING ON AIR

*"When a man has been guilty of a mistake, either in ordering his own affairs, or in directing those of the State, or in commanding an army, do we not always say, So-and-so has made a false step in this affair? And can making a false step derive from anything but lack of skill in dancing?"*

—Moliere

## 1.

SOMETIMES I UNDERSTAND THE WORDS. Sometimes I do not understand the words.

Eric brings me to the exercise yard. A man and a woman stand there. The man is tall. The woman is short. She has long black fur on her head. She smells angry.

Eric says, "This is Angel. Angel, this is John Cole and Caroline Olson."

"Hello," I say.

"I'm supposed to understand that growl?" the woman says. "Might as well be Russian!"

"Caroline," the man says, "you promised…"

"I know what I promised." She walks away. She smells very angry. I don't understand. My word was *hello. Hello* is one of the easy words.

The man says, "Hello, Angel." He smiles. I sniff his shoes and bark. He smells friendly. I smell two cats and a hot dog and street tar and a car. I feel happy. I like cars.

The woman comes back. "If we have to do this, then let's just do it, for Chrissake. Let's sign the papers and get out of this hole."

John Cole says, "The lawyers are all waiting in Eric's office."

Eric's office smells of many people. I go to my place beside the door. I lie down. Maybe later somebody takes me in the car.

A woman looks at many papers and talks. "A contract between Biomod Canine Protection Agency, herein referred to as the party of the first part, and the New York City Ballet, herein referred to as the party of the second part, in fulfillment of the requirements of Columbia Insurance Company, herein referred to as the party of the third part, as those requirements are set forth in Policy 438-69, Section 17, respecting prima ballerina Caroline Olson. The party of the first part shall furnish genetically-modified canine protection to Caroline Olson under, and not limited to, the following conditions…"

The words are hard.

I think words I can understand.

My name is Angel. I am a dog. I protect. Eric tells me to protect. No people can touch the one I protect except safe people. I love people I protect. I sleep now.

"Angel," Eric says from his chair, "Wake up now. You must protect."

I wake up. Eric walks to me. He sits next to me. He puts his voice in my ear.

"This is Caroline. You must protect Caroline. No one must hurt Caroline. No one must touch Caroline except safe people. Angel— *protect Caroline.*"

I smell Caroline. I am very happy. I protect Caroline.

"Jesus H. Christ," Caroline says. She walks away.

I love Caroline.

We go in the car. We go very far. Many people. Many smells. John drives the car. John is safe. He may touch Caroline. John stops the car. We get out. There are many tall buildings and many cars.

"You sure you're going to be okay?" John Cole says.

"You've protected your investment, haven't you?" Caroline snarls. John drives away.

A man stands by the door. The man says, "Evening, Miss Olson."

"Evening, Sam. This is my new guard dog. The company insists I have one, after…what's been happening. They say the insurance company is paranoid. Yeah, sure. I need a dog like I need a knee injury."

"Yes, ma'am. Doberman, isn't he? He looks like a goooood ol' dog. Hey, big fella, what's your name?"

"Angel," I say.

The man jumps and makes a noise. Caroline laughs.

"Bioenhanced. Great for my privacy, right? Rover, Sam is safe. Do you hear me? Sam is *safe*."

I say, "My name is Angel."

Caroline says, "Sam, you can relax. Really. He only attacks on command, or if I scream, or if he hasn't been told a person is safe and that person touches me."

"Yes, Ma'am." Sam smells afraid. He looks at me hard. I bark and my tail moves.

Caroline says, "Come on, Fido. Your spy career is about to begin."

I say, "My name is Angel."

"Right," Caroline says.

We go in the building. We go in the elevator. I say, "Sam has a cat. I smell Sam's cat."

"Who the fuck cares," Caroline says.

I am a dog.

I must love Caroline.


# 2.

TWO DAYS AFTER THE SECOND ballerina was murdered, Michael Chow, senior editor of *New York Now* and my boss, called me into his office. I already knew what he wanted, and I already knew I didn't want to do it. He knew that, too. We both knew it wouldn't make any difference.

"You're the logical reporter, Susan," Michael said. He sat behind his desk, always a bad sign. When he thought I'd want an assignment, he leaned casually against the front of the desk. Its top was cluttered with print-outs; with disposable research cartridges, some with their screens alight; with pictures of Michael's six children. *Six.* They all looked like Michael: straight black hair and a smooth face like a peeled egg. At the apex of the mess sat a hardcopy of the *Times* 3:00 p.m. on-line lead: AUTOPSY DISCOVERS BIOENHANCERS IN CITY BALLET DANCER. "You have an in. Even Anton Privitera will talk to you."

"Not about this. He already gave his press conference. Such as it was."

"So? You can get to him as a parent and leverage from there."

My daughter Deborah was a student in the School of American Ballet, the juvenile province of Anton Privitera's kingdom. For thirty years he had ruled the New York City Ballet like an anointed tyrant. Sometimes it seemed he could even levy taxes and raise armies, so exalted was his reputation in the dance world, and so good was his business manager John Cole at raising funds and enlisting corporate patrons. Dancers had flocked to the City Ballet from Europe, from Asia, from South America, from the serious ballet schools in the patrolled zones of America's dying cities. Until bioenhancers, the New York City Ballet had been the undisputed grail of the international dance world.

Now, of course, that was changing.

Privitera was dynamic with the press as long as we were content with what he wished us to know. He wasn't going to want to discuss the murder of two dancers, one of them his own.

A month ago Nicole Heyer, a principal dancer with the American Ballet Theater, had been found strangled in Central Park. Three days ago the body of Jennifer Lang had been found in her modest apartment. Heyer had been a bioenhanced dancer who had come to the ABT from the Stuttgart Ballet. Lang, a minor soloist with the City Ballet, had of course been natural. Or so everybody thought until the autopsy. The entire company had been bioscanned only three weeks ago, Artistic Director Privitera had told the press, but apparently these particular viro-enhancers were so new and so different that they hadn't even shown up on the scan.

I wondered how to make Michael understand the depth of my dislike for all this.

"Don't cover the usual police stuff," Michael said, "nor the scientific stuff on bioenhancement. Concentrate on the human angle you do so well. What's the effect of these murders on the other dancers? Has it affected their dancing? Does Privitera seem more confirmed in his company policy now, or has this shaken him enough to consider a change? What's he doing to protect his dancers? How do the parents feel about the youngsters in the ballet school? Are they withdrawing them until the killer is caught?"

I said, "You don't have any sensitivity at all, do you, Michael?"

He said quietly, "Your girl's seventeen, Susan. If you couldn't get her to leave dancing before, you're not going to get her to leave now. Will you do the story?"

I looked again at the scattered pictures of Michael's children. His oldest was at Harvard Law. His second son was a happily married househusband, raising three kids. His third child, a daughter, was doing six-to-ten in Rock Mountain Maximum Security State Prison for armed robbery. There was no figuring it out. I said, "I'll do the story."

"Good," he said, not looking at me. "Just hold down the metaphors, Susan. You're still too given to metaphors."

"*New York Now* could use a few metaphors. A feature magazine isn't supposed to be a TV holo bite."

"A feature magazine isn't art, either," Michael retorted. "Let's all keep that in mind."

"You're in luck," I said. "As it happens, I'm not a great lover of art."

I couldn't decide whether to tell Deborah I had agreed to write about ballet. She would hate my writing about her world under threat.

Which was a reason both for and against.

* * *

September heat and long, cool shadows fought it out over the wide plaza of Lincoln Center. The fountain splashed, surrounded by tourists and students and strollers and derelicts. I thought Lincoln Center was ugly, shoe-box architecture stuck around a charmless expanse of stone unredeemed by a little splashing water. Michael said I only felt that way because I hated New York. If Lincoln Center had been built in Kentucky, he said, I would have admired it.

I had remembered to get the electronic password from Deborah. Since the first murder, the New York State Theater changed it weekly. Late afternoon was heavy rehearsal time; the company was using the stage as well as the studios. I heard the Spanish bolero from the second act of *Coppelia*. Deborah had been trying to learn it for weeks. The role of Swanilda, the girl who pretends to be a doll, had first made the brilliant Caroline Olson a superstar.

Privitera's office was a jumble of dance programs, costume swatches, and computers. He made me wait for him twenty minutes. I sat and thought about what I knew about bioenhanced dancers, besides the fact that there weren't supposed to have been any at City Ballet.

There were several kinds of bioenhancement. All of them were experimental, all of them were illegal in The United States, all of them were constantly in flux as new discoveries were made and rushed onto the European, South American, and Japanese markets. It was a new science, chaotic and contradictory, like physics at the start of the last century, or cancer cures at the start of this one. No bioenhancements had been developed specifically for ballet dancers, who were an insignificant portion of the population. But European dancers submitted to experimental versions, as did American dancers who could travel to Berlin or Copenhagen or Rio for the very expensive privilege of injecting their bodies with tiny, unproven biological "machines."

Some nanomachines carried programming that searched out deviations in the body and repaired them to match surrounding tissue. This speeded the healing of some injuries some of the time, or only erratically, or not at all, depending on whom you believed. Jennifer Lang had been receiving these treatments, trying desperately to lessen the injury rate that went hand-in-hand with ballet. The nanomachines were highly experimental, and nobody was sure what long-term effect they might have, reproducing themselves in the human body, interacting with human DNA.

Bone builders were both simpler and more dangerous. They were altered viruses, reprogrammed to change the shape or density of bones. Most of the experimental work had been done on old women with advanced osteoporosis. Some grew denser bones after treatment. The rest didn't. In ballet, the legs are required to rotate 180 degrees in the hip sockets—the famous "turn out" that had destroyed so many dancers' hips and knees. If bones could be altered to swivel 180 degrees *naturally* in their sockets, turn out would cause far less strain and disintegration. Extension could also be higher, making easier the spectacular *arabesques* and *grand battement* kicks.

If the bones of the foot were reshaped, foot injuries could be lessened in the unnatural act of dancing on toe.

Bioenhanced leg muscles could be stronger, for higher jumps, greater speed, more stamina.

Anything that helped metabolic efficiency or lung capacity could help a dancer sustain movements. They could also help her keep down her weight without anorexia, the secret vice of the ballet world.

Dancers in Europe began to experiment with bioenhancement. First cautiously, clandestinely. Then scandalously. Now openly, as a mark of pride. A dancer with the Royal Ballet or the Bolshoi or the Nederlands Dans Theater who didn't have his or her body enhanced was considered undevoted to movement. A dancer at the New York City Ballet who did have his or her body enhanced was considered undevoted to art.

Privitera swept into his office without apology for being late. "Ah, there you are. What can I do for you?" His accent was very light, but still the musical tones of his native Tuscany were there. It gave his words a deceptive intimacy.

"I've come about my daughter, Deborah Anders. She's in the D level at SAB. She's the one who—"

"Yes, yes, yes, I know who she is. I know all my dancers, even the very young ones. Of course. But shouldn't you be talking with Madame Alois? She is the director of our School."

"But you make all the important decisions," I say, trying to smile winningly.

Privitera sat on a wing chair. He must have been in his seventies, yet he moved like a young man: straight strong back, light movements. The famous bright blue eyes met mine shrewdly. His vitality and physical presence on stage had made him a legendary dancer; now he was simply a legend. Whatever he decided the New York City Ballet should be, it became. I didn't like him. That absolute power bothered me—even though it was merely power over an art form seen by only a fraction of the people who watched soccer or football.

"I have three questions about Deborah, Mr. Privitera. First—and I'm sure you hear this all the time—can you give me some idea of her chances as a professional dancer? She'll have to apply to college this fall, if she's going to go, and although what she really wants is to dance professionally, if that's not going to happen then we need to think about other—"

"Yes, yes," Privitera said, swatting away this question like the irrelevancy he considered it to be. "But dance is never a second choice, Ms. Anders."

"Matthews," I said. "Susan Matthews. Anders is Deborah's name."

"If Deborah has it in her to be a dancer, that's what she will be. If not—" He shrugged. People who were not dancers ceased to exist for Anton Privitera.

"That's what I want to know. Does she have it in her to be a professional dancer? Her teachers say she has good musicality and rhythm, but..."

My hands gripped together so tightly the skin was gray.

"Perhaps. Perhaps. You must leave it to me to judge when the time comes."

"But that's what I'm saying," I said, as agreeably as I could. "The time *has* come. College—"

"You cannot hurry art. If Deborah is meant to be a dancer, she will become one. Leave it to me, dear."

*Dear.* It was what he called all his dancers. I saw that it had just slipped out. *Leave it to me, dear. I know best.* How often did he say that in class, in rehearsal, during a choreography session, before a performance?

The muted strains of *Coppelia* drifted through the walls. I said, "Then let me ask my second question. As a parent, I'm naturally concerned about Deborah's safety since these awful murders. What steps has City Ballet taken to ensure the safety of the students and dancers?"

The intense eyes contracted to blue shards. But I could see the moment he decided the question was within a parent's right to ask. "The police do not think there is danger to the students. This… madman, this *bestia*, apparently attacks only full-fledged dancers, soloists and principals who have tried to reach art through medicine and not through dancing. No dancer in my company or my school is bioenhanced. My dancers believe as I do: You can achieve art only through talent and work, through opening yourself to the dance, not through mechanical aids. What they do at the ABT— that is *not art!* Besides," he added, with an abrupt descent to the practical, "students cannot afford bioenhancing operations."

Idealism enforced by realism—I saw the combination that kept the City Ballet a success, despite the technically superior performances of bioenhanced dancers. I could almost hear dancers and patrons alike: *"The only real ballet." "Dance that preserves the necessary illusion that the performers' bodies and the audience's are fundamentally the same." "My dear, he's simply the most wonderful man, saving the precious traditions that made dance great in the first place. We've pledged $20,000—"*

I decided to push. "But Jennifer Lang apparently found a way to afford illegal bioenhancements that—"

"That has nothing to do with your Deborah," Privitera said, standing in one fluid movement. His blue eyes were arctic. "Now if you will excuse me, many things call me."

"But you haven't said what you *are* doing for the students' safety," I said, not rising from my chair, trying to sound as if my only interest were parental. "Please, I need to know. Deborah..."

He barely repressed a sigh. "We have increased security, Ms. Anders. Electronic surveillance both at SAB and Lincoln Center has been added to, with specifics that I cannot discuss. We have hired additional escorts for those students performing small professional roles who must leave Lincoln Center after ten at night. We have created new emphasis on teaching our young dancers the importance, the complete *necessity*, of training their bodies for dance, not relying on drugs and operations that can only offer tawdry imitations of the genuine experience of art."

I doubted City Ballet had actually done all that: it had only been three days since Jennifer Lang's murder. But Privitera's rhetoric helped me ask my last questions.

"Have any other parents withdrawn their sons and daughters from SAB? For that matter, have any of your dancers altered their performance schedules? How has the company as a whole been affected?"

Privitera looked at me with utter scorn. "If a dancer—even a student dancer—leaves me because some *bestia* is killing performers who do what I have insisted my dancers *not* do—such a so-called dancer should leave. There is no place for such a dancer in my school or my company. Don't you understand, Ms. Anders—this is the *New York City Ballet*."

He left. Through the open door the music was clear: still the Spanish dance from *Coppelia*. The girl who turned herself into a beautiful doll.

Michael was right. I was definitely too given to metaphors.

As I walked down the hall, it occurred to me that Privitera hadn't mentioned increased bioscanning. Surely that would make the most sense—discover which dancers were attaining their high jumps and strong *developpés* through bioenhancement, and then eliminate those dancers from the purity of the company? Before some *bestia* did it first.

Deborah, I knew, was taking an extra class in Studio 3. I shouldn't go. If I went, we would only fight again. I pushed open the door to Studio 3.

I sat on a hard small chair with the ballet mothers waiting for the class to end. I knew better than to talk to any of them. They all wanted their daughters to succeed in ballet.

Barre warm-ups were over. The warm air smelled of rosin on wood. Dancers worked in the center of the floor, sweat dripping off their twirling and leaping bodies. *Bourées, pirouettes, entrechats.* "*Non, non!*" the teacher called, a retired French dancer whom I had never seen smile. "When you jump, your arms must help. They must pull you through from left to right. Like this."

Deborah did the step wrong. "*Non, non!*" the teacher called. "Like this!"

Deborah still did it wrong. She grimaced. I felt my stomach tighten.

Deborah tried again. It was still wrong. The teacher gestured toward the back of the room. Deborah walked to the barre and practiced the step alone while the rest of the class went on leaping. *Plié, relevé,* then...I didn't know the names of the rest of these steps. Whatever they were, she was still doing them wrong. Deborah tried over and over again, her face clenched. I couldn't watch.

When Deborah was fourteen, she ran away from home in St. Louis to her father's hovel in New York, the same father she had not seen since she was three. She wanted to dance for Anton Privitera, she said. I demanded that Pers, whom I had divorced for desertion, send her back. He refused. Deborah moved into his rat-trap on West 110th, way outside Manhattan's patrolled zone. The lack of police protection didn't deter her, the filthy toilet down the hall didn't deter her, the nine-year-old who was shot dealing sunshine on the stoop next door didn't deter her. When I flew to New York, she cried but refused to go home. She wanted to dance for Anton Privitera.

You can't physically wrestle a fourteen-year-old onto a plane. You can argue, and scream, and threaten, and plead, and cry, but you cannot physically move her. Not without a court order. I filed for breach of custody.

Pers did the most effective thing you can do in the New York judicial system: nothing. Since Pers was an indigent periodically on public assistance, the court appointed a public defender for him. The public defender had 154 cases. He asked for three continuances in a row. The judge had a docket full six months ahead. In less than a year and a half Deborah would be sixteen, legally entitled to leave home. She auditioned for Privitera, and the School of American Ballet accepted her.

Another kid was shot, this one on the subway just before Pers's stop. She was twelve. A boy was knifed, a young mother was raped, houses were torched. Pers's lawyer resigned. Another was appointed, who immediately filed for a continuance.

I quit my job with *St. Louis On-Line* and moved to New York. I left behind a new promotion, a house I loved, and a man I had just started to care about. I found work on Michael's magazine, for half the prestige and two-thirds the salary, in a city twice as expensive and three times as dangerous. I took a two-room apartment on West Seventy-fifth, shabby but decent, just inside the patrolled zone. From my living room window I could see the shimmer of the electronic fence marking the zone. The shimmer bent to exclude all of Central Park south of Seventieth. I bought a gun.

After a few tense weeks, Deborah moved in with me. We lived with piles of toe shoes and surgical tape, with leotards and tights drying on a line strung across the living room, with *Dance* magazine in tattered third-hand copies that would go on to be somebody else's fourth-hand copies, with bunions and inflamed tendons and pulled ligaments. We lived with Deborah's guilt and my anger. At night I lay awake on the pull-out sofa, staring at the ceiling, remembering the day Deborah had started kindergarten and I had opened a college fund for her. She refused now to consider college. She wanted to dance for Anton Privitera.

Privitera had not yet invited her to join the company. She had just turned seventeen. This was her last year with the School. If she weren't invited into the corps de ballet this year, she could forget about dancing for the New York City Ballet.

I sat with the ballet mothers and watched. Deborah's extension was not as high as some of the other girls', her strength not always enough to sustain a slow, difficult move.

So glamorous! the ballet mothers screeched. So beautiful! So wonderful for a girl to know so young what she wants to do with her life! The ballet mothers apparently never saw the constant injuries, the fatigue, the competition that made every friend a deadly rival, the narrowing down of a young world until there is only one definition of success: Do I get to dance for Privitera? Everything else is failure. Life and death, determined at seventeen. "I don't know what I'll do if Jeannie isn't asked to join the company," Jeannie's mother told me. "It would be like we both died. Maybe we would."

"You're so unfair, Mom!" Deborah shouted at me periodically in the tiny, jammed apartment. "You never see the good side of dancing! You're so against me!"

Is it so unfair to hope that your child will be forced out of a life that can only break her body and her heart? A life whose future will belong only to those willing to become human test tubes for inhuman biological experiments?

Nicole Heyer, the dead ABT dancer, had apparently come to the United States from Germany because she could not compete with the dazzlingly bioenhanced dancers in her own country. Jennifer Lang, an ordinary girl from an ordinary Houston family, had lacked the money for major experimentation. To finance her bioenhancements in European labs, she had rented herself out as a glamorous and expensive call girl. Fuck a ballerina! That was how her killer had gotten into her apartment.

In her corner of Studio 3, Deborah finally got the sequence of steps straight, although I could see she was wobbly. She rejoined the class. The room had become as steamy as a Turkish bath. Students ran and leapt the whole length of the hall, corner to corner, in groups of six. "*Grand jeté* in third *arabesque*," Madame called. "*Non, non*, more extension, Lisa. Victoria, more quick—*vite! vite!* One, two…next group."

Deborah ran, jumped, and crashed to the ground.

I stood. Jeannie's mother put a hand on my arm. "You can't go to her," she said matter-of-factly. "You'll interfere with her discipline."

Madame ran gnarled hands over Deborah's ankle. "Lisa, help her to the side. Ninette, go tell the office to send the doctor. *Alors*, next group, *grand jeté* in third *arabesque...*"

I shook off Jeannie's mother's hand and walked slowly to where Deborah sat, her face twisted in pain.

"It's nothing, Mom."

"Don't move it until the doctor gets here."

"I said it's nothing!"

It was a sprain. The doctor taped it and said Deborah shouldn't dance for a week.

At home she limped to her room. An hour later I found her at the barre.

"Deborah! You heard what the doctor said!"

Her eyes were luminous with tears: Odette as the dying swan, Giselle in the mad scene. "I have to, Mom! You don't understand! They're casting *Nutcracker* in two weeks! I have to be there, dancing!"

"Deborah—"

"I can dance through the injury! Leave me alone!"

Deborah had never yet been cast in Privitera's *Nutcracker*. I watched her transfer her weight gingerly to the injured ankle, wince, and *plié*. She wouldn't meet my eyes in the mirror.

Slowly I closed the door.

That night we had tickets to see *Coppelia*. Caroline Olson skimmed across the stage, barely seeming to touch ground. Her *grand jetés* brought gasps from the sophisticated New York ballet audience. In the final act, when Swanilda danced a tender *pas de deux* with her lover Franz, I could see heads motionless all over the theater, lips slightly parted, barely breathing. Franz turned her slowly in a liquid *arabesque*, her leg impossibly high, followed by *pirouettes*. Swanilda melted from one pose to another, her long silken legs forming a perfect line with her body, flesh made light and strong and elegant as the music itself.

Beside me, I felt Deborah's despair.

## 3.

CAROLINE JUMPS. SHE JUMPS with her hind legs out straight, one in front and one in back. She runs in circles and jumps again. Dmitri catches her.

"No, no," Mr. Privitera says. "Not like that. *Promenade en couronne, attitude, arabesque effacé.* Now the lift. Dmitri, you are handling her like a sack of grain. Like this."

Mr. Privitera picks up Caroline. My ears raise. But Mr. Privitera is safe. Mr. Privitera can touch Caroline. Dmitri can touch Caroline. Carlos can touch Caroline.

Dmitri says, "It's the damn *dog.* How am I supposed to learn the part with him staring at me, ready to tear me from limb to limb? How the hell am I supposed to concentrate?"

John Cole sits next to me. John says, "Dmitri, there's no chance Angel will attack you. His biochip is state-of-the-art programming. I told you. If you're in his 'safe' directory, you'd have to actually attack Caroline yourself before Angel would act, unless Caroline told you otherwise. There's no real danger to break your concentration."

Dmitri says, "And what if I drop her accidentally? How do I know that won't look like an attack to that dog?"

Caroline sits down. She looks at John. She looks at Dmitri. She does not look at me. She smiles.

John says, "A drop is not an attack. Unless Caroline screams—and we all know she never does, no matter what the injury—there's no danger. Believe me."

"I don't," Dmitri says.

Everybody stands quiet.

Mr. Privitera says, "Caroline, dear, let me drop you. Stand up. Ready—lift."

Caroline smells surprised. She stands. Mr. Privitera picks up Caroline. She jumps a little. He picks her up over his head. She falls down hard. My ears raise. Caroline does not scream. She is not hurt. Mr. Privitera is safe. Caroline said Mr. Privitera is safe.

"See?" Mr. Privitera says. He breathes hard. "No danger. Positions, please. *Promenade en couronne, attitude, arabesque effacé,* lift."

Dmitri picks up Caroline. The music gets loud. John says in my ear, "Angel—did Caroline go away from her house last night?"

"Yes," I say.

"Where did Caroline go?"

"Left four blocks, right one block. Caroline gave money."

"The bakery," John says. "Did she go away to any more places, or did she go home?"

"Caroline goes home last night."

"Did anyone come to Caroline's house last night?"

"No people come to Caroline's house last night."

"Thank you," John says. He pats me. I feel happy.

Caroline looks at us. A woman ties a long cloth on Caroline's waist. The woman gives Caroline a piece of wood. Yesterday I ask John what the wood is. Yesterday John says it is a fan. The music starts, faster. Caroline does not jump. Yesterday Caroline jumps with the fan.

"Caroline?" Mr. Privitera says. "Start here, dear."

Caroline jumps. She still looks at John. He looks at me.

Some woman here smells of yogurt and a bitch collie in heat.

Caroline opens the bedroom door. She comes out. She wears jeans on her hind legs. She wears a hat on her head. It covers all her fur. She walks to the door. She says to me, "Stay, you old fleabag. You hear me? Stay!"

I walk to the door.

"Christ." Caroline opens the door a little way. She pushes her body through the door. She closes the door. I push through the door hard with her.

"I said stay!" Caroline opens the door again. She pushes me. I do not go inside. Caroline goes inside. I follow Caroline.

"Take two," Caroline says. She opens the door. She walks away. She goes back. She closes the door. She opens the door. She closes the door. She turns around. She goes through the door and closes it hard. She is very fast. I am inside alone.

"Gotcha, Fido!" Caroline says through the door.

I howl. I throw me against the door. I bark and howl. The light goes on in my head. I howl and howl.

Soon Caroline comes through the door. A man holds her arm. He smells of iron. He talks to a box.

"Subject elected to return to her apartment, sir, rather than have me accompany her to her destination. We're in here now."

Caroline grabs the box. "John, you shit, how *dare* you! You had the dog bio-wired! That's an invasion of privacy, I'll sue your ass off, I'll quit the company, I'll—"

"Caroline," John's voice said. I look. There is no John smell. John is not here. Only John's voice is here. "You have no legal grounds. This man is allowed to accompany you, according to the protection contract you signed. *You* signed it, my dear. As for quitting the City Ballet...That's up to you. But while you dance for us, Angel goes where you do. If he gets too excited over not seeing you, the biosignal triggers. Just where were you going that you didn't want Angel with you?"

"To turn tricks on street corners!" Caroline yells. "And I bet he has a homing device embedded in him, too, doesn't he?"

She smells very angry. She is angry at me. I lie on the floor. I put my paws on my head. It is not happy here.

The man says, "Departing the apartment now, sir." He leaves. He takes the small box.

Caroline sits on the floor. Her back is against the door. She looks at me. My paws are on my head. Caroline smells angry.

Nothing happens.

A little later Caroline says, "I guess it's you and me, then. They set it up that way. I'm stuck with you."

I do not move my paws. She still smells angry.

"All right, let's try another approach. Disarm the enemy from within. Psychological sabotage. You don't have any idea what I'm talking about, do you? What did they give you, a five-year-old's IQ? Angel..."

I look at Caroline. She says my right name.

"...tell me about Sam's cat."

"What?"

"Sam's cat. You said that first day you came home with me that you smelled a cat on Sam, the day doorman. Do you still smell it? Can you tell what kind of cat it is?"

I am confused. Caroline says nice words. Caroline smells angry. Her back is too straight. Her fur is wrong.

"Is it a male cat or a female cat? Can you tell that?"

"A female cat," I say. I remember the cat smell. My muscles itch.

"Did you want to chase it?"

"I must never chase cats. I must protect Caroline."

Caroline's smell changes. She leans close to my ear.

"But did you *want* to chase it, Angel? Did you want to get to behave like a dog?"

"I want to protect Caroline."

"Hoo boy. They did a job on you, didn't they, boy?"

The words are too hard. Caroline still smells a little angry. I do not understand.

"It's nothing compared to what they're doing in South America and Europe," she says. Her body shakes.

"Are you hurt?" I say.

Caroline puts a hand on my back. The hand is very soft. She says no words.

I am happy. Caroline talks to me. She tells me about dancing. Caroline is a dancer. She jumps and runs in circles. She stands high on her hind legs. People come in cars to watch her. The people are happy when Caroline dances.

We walk outside. I protect Caroline. We go many places. Caroline gives me cake and hot dogs. There are many smells. Sometimes Caroline and I follow the smells. We see many dogs and many cats. The man with the small box comes with us sometimes. John says the man is safe.

"What if I tell Angel you're not 'safe'?" Caroline says to the man. He follows us on a long walk. "What if I order him to tear you limb to limb?" She smells angry again.

"You don't have programming override capacity. The biochip augmenting his bioenhancement is very specific, Ms. Olson. I'm hardwired in."

"I'll bet," Caroline says. "Did anybody ask Angel if he wants this life?"

The man smiles.

We go to Lincoln Center every day. Caroline dances there. She dances in the day. She dances at night. More people watch at night.

John asks me where Caroline and I go. Every day I tell him.

Nobody tries to touch Caroline. I protect her.

"I can't do it," Caroline tells a man on the street corner. The man stands very close to Caroline. I growl soft. "For God's sake, Stan, don't touch me. The dog. And I'm probably being watched."

"Do they care *that* much?"

"I could blow the whistle on the whole unofficial charade," Caroline says. She smells tired. "No matter what Privitera's delusions are. But then we'd lose our chance, wouldn't we?"

"Thanks for the time," the man says, loud. He smiles. He walks away.

Later John says, "Who did Caroline talk to?"

"A man," I say. "He wants the time."

Later Caroline says, "Angel, we're going tonight to see my mother."

# 4.

DEMONSTRATORS DYED THE FOUNTAIN at Lincoln Center blood red.

They marched around the gruesome jets of water, shouting and resisting arrest. I sprinted across the plaza, trying to get there to see which side they were on before the police carted all of them away. Even from this distance I could tell they weren't dancers, not with those thick bodies. The electronic placards dissolved from HOW MANY MUST DIE FROM DENYING EVOLUTION! to FREE MEDICAL RESEARCH FROM GOVERNMENT STRAIGHTJACKETS! to MY BODY BELONGS TO ME! Pro-human bioenhancement, then. A holograph projector, which a cop was shutting down, spewed out a ten-foot high holo of Jane and June Welsh, Siamese twins who had been successfully separated only after German scientists had bioenhanced their bodies to force alterations in major organs. The holo loop showed the attached twins dragging each other around, followed by the successfully separated twins waving gaily. The cop did something and Jane and June disappeared.

"They died," I said to a demonstrator, a slim boy wearing a FREE MY BODY! button. "Ultimately, neither of their hearts could stand the stress of bioenhancement."

He glared at me. "That was their risk to take, wasn't it?"

"Their combined IQ didn't equal your weight. How could they evaluate risk?"

"This is a *revolution*, lady. In any revolution you have casualties that—" A cop grabbed his arm. The boy took a wild swing at him and the cop pressed his nerve gun to the boy's neck. He dropped peacefully, smiling.

Abruptly more people gathered, some of them wilier than the boy. Demonstrators stood with their hands on their heads, singing slogans. Media robocams zoomed in from the sky; the live crews would be here in minutes. A group of counter-demonstrators formed across the plaza, in front of the Met. I backed away slowly, hands on my head, not singing—and stopped abruptly halfway across the chaotic plaza.

An old woman in a powerchair was watching the demonstration with the most intense expression I had ever seen. It was as if she were watching a horrifying execution, judging it judiciously as art. Bodyguards flanked the chair. She wore an expensive, pale blue suit and large, perfectly-matched pearls. Her wrinkled, cold face was completely familiar. This was how Caroline Olson would look in forty years, if she refused all cosmetic treatment.

She caught me watching her. Her expression didn't change. It passed over me as if I didn't exist.

I took the chance. "Ms. Olson?"

She didn't deny the name. "Yes?"

"I'm a reporter with *New York Now*, doing an article on the New York City Ballet. I'd like to ask you a few questions about your daughter Caroline, if that's all right."

"I never give interviews."

"Yes, ma'am. Just a few informal questions—you must be so proud of Caroline. But are you worried about her safety in light of the recent so-called ballerina murders?"

She shocked me. She smiled. "No, not at all."

"You're *not?*"

She gazed at the break-up of the demonstration. "Do you know the work on dancers' bodies they're doing in Berlin?"

"No, I—"

"Then you have no business interviewing anyone on the subject." She watched the last of the demonstrators being dragged away by the cops. "The New York City ballet is finished. The future of the art lies with bioenhancement."

I must have looked like a fish, staring at her with my mouth working. "But Caroline is the prima ballerina, she's only twenty-six—"

"Caroline had a good run. For a dancer." She made a signal, an imperious movement of her hand, and one of the bodyguards turned her chair and wheeled it away.

I trotted after it. "But, Ms. Olson, are you saying you think your daughter and her whole company *should* be replaced by bio-enhanced dancers because they can achieve higher lifts, fewer injuries, more spectacular turn out—"

"I never give interviews," she said, and the other bodyguard moved between us.

I gazed after her. She had spoken about Caroline as if her daughter were an obsolete Buick. It took me a moment to remember to pull out a notebook and tell it what she had said.

Someone dumped something into the fountain. Immediately the red disappeared and the water spouted clear once more. A bio-enhanced dog trotted over and lapped at the water, the dog's owner patiently holding the leash while his pink-furred, huge-eyed poodle drank its fill.

After an hour at a library terminal at *New York Now*, I knew that Anna Olson was a major contributor to the American Ballet Theater but not to the New York City Ballet, where her daughter had chosen to dance. Caroline's father was dead. He had left his widow an East Side mansion, three Renoirs, and a fortune invested in Peruvian sugar, Japanese weather-control equipment, and German pharmaceuticals. According to *Ballet News*, mother and daughter were estranged. To find out more than that, I'd need professional help.

Michael didn't want to do it. "There's no money for that kind of research, Susan. Not to even mention the ethics involved."

"Oh, come on, Michael. It's no worse than using criminal informers for any other story."

"This isn't your old newspaper job, Susie. We're a feature magazine, remember? We don't use informants, and we don't do investigative reporting." He leaned against his desk, his peeled-egg face troubled.

"The magazine doesn't have to do any investigating at all. Just give me the number. I know you know it. If I'd been doing the job I should have for the last two years instead of sulking because I hate New York, I'd know it, too. Just the number, Michael. That's all. Neither you nor the magazine will even be mentioned."

He ran his hand through his hair. For the first time, I noticed that it was thinning. "All right. But Susan—don't get obsessed. For your own sake." He looked at the picture of his daughter doing time in Rock Mountain.

I called the Robin Hood and arranged to see him. He was young—they all are—maybe as young as twenty, operating out of a dingy apartment in Tribeca. I couldn't judge his equipment: beyond basic literacy, computers are as alien to me as dancers. Like dancers, they concentrate on one aspect of the world, dismissing the rest.

The Robin Hood furnished the usual proofs that he could tap into private databanks, that he could access government records, and that his translation programs could handle international airline d-bases. He promised a two-day turnaround. The price was astronomical by my standards, although probably negligible by his. I transferred the credits from my savings account, emptying it.

I said, "You do know that the original Robin Hood transferred goods for free?"

He said, not missing a beat, "The original Robin Hood didn't have to pay for a Seidman-Nuwer encrypter."

I really hadn't expected him to know who the original Robin Hood was.

When I got home, Deborah had fallen asleep across her bed, still dressed in practice clothes. The toes of her tights were bloody. A new pair of toe shoes were shoved between the bedroom door and the door jamb; she softened the stiff boxes by slamming the door on them. There were three email messages for her from SAB, but I erased them all. I covered her, closed her door, and let her sleep.

I met with the Robin Hood two days later. He handed me a sheaf of hardcopy. "The City Ballet injury records show two injuries for Caroline Olson in the last four years, which is as far back as the files are kept. One shin splint, one pulled ligament. Of course, if she had other injuries and saw a private doctor, that wouldn't show up on their records, but if she did see one it wasn't anybody on the City Ballet Recommended Physician List. I checked that."

"Two injuries? In four *years?*"

"That's what the record shows. These here are four-year records of City Ballet bioscans. All negative. Nobody shows any bioenhancement, not even Jennifer Lang. These are the City Ballet attendance figures over ten years, broken down by subscription and single-event tickets."

I was startled; the drop in attendance over the last two years was more dramatic than the press had ever indicated.

"This one is Mrs. Anna Olson's tax return for last year. All that income—all of it—is from investments and interests, and none of it is tied up in trusts or entails. She controls it all, and she can waste the whole thing if she wants to. You asked about unusual liquidation of stock in the last ten years: There wasn't any. There's no trust fund for Caroline Olson. This is Caroline's tax return—only her salary with City Ballet, plus guest appearance fees. Hefty, but nothing like what the old lady controls.

"This last is the air flight stuff you wanted: No flights on major commercial airlines out of the country for Caroline in the last six years, except when the City Ballet did its three international tours, and then Caroline flew pretty much with everybody else in the group. Of course if she did go to Rio or Copenhagen or Berlin, she could have gone by chartered plane or private jet. My guess is private jet. Those aren't required to file passenger lists."

It wasn't what I'd hoped to find. Or rather, it was half of what I'd hoped. No dancer is injured that seldom. It just doesn't happen. I pictured Caroline Olson's amazing extension, her breathtaking leaps; she reached almost the height expected of male superstars. And her crippled horror of a mother had huge amounts of money. *"Caroline had a good run."*

I would bet my few remaining dollars that Caroline Olson was bioenhanced, no matter what her bioscans said. Jennifer Lang's had been negative, too. Apparently the DNA hackers were staying one step ahead of the DNA security checkers. Although it was odd that the records didn't show a single dancer trying to get away with bioenhancement, not even once, even in the face of Privitera's fervency. There are always some people who value their own career advancement over the received faith.

But I had assumed that Caroline would have needed to leave the country. Bioenhancement labs are large, full of sensitive and costly and nonportable equipment, and dozens of technicians. Not easy to hide. Police investigators had traced both Jennifer Lang and Nicole Heyer to Danish labs. I didn't think one could exist illegally in New York.

Maybe I was wrong.

The Robin Hood watched me keenly. In the morning light from the window he looked no older than Deborah. He had thick brown hair, nice shoulders. I wondered if he had a life outside his lab. So many of them didn't.

"Thanks," I said.

"Susan—"

"What?"

He hesitated. "I don't know what you're after with this data. But I've worked with friends of Michael's before. If you're thinking about trying to leverage anything to do with human bioenhancement..."

"Yeah?"

"Don't." He looked intently at his console. "That's out of both our leagues. Magazine reporters are very small against the kind of high-stakes shit those guys are into."

"Thanks for the advice," I said. And then, on impulse, "Would you by any chance like a home-cooked meal? I have a daughter about your age, seventeen, she's a dancer…"

He stared at me in disbelief. He shook his head. "You're a *client*, Susan. And anyway, I'm twenty-six. And I'm married." He shook his head again. "And if you don't know enough not to ask a Robin Hood to dinner, you really don't know enough to mess around with bioenhancement. That stuff's life or death."

Life or death. Enough for a bioenhancement corporation to murder two dancers?

But I rejected that idea. It was always too easy to label the corporations the automatic bad guys. That was the stuff of cheap holovids. Most corporate types I knew just tried to keep ahead of the IRS.

I said, "Most life-and-death stuff originates at home."

I could feel him shaking his head as I left, but I didn't turn around.

## 5.

CAROLINE AND I RIDE in a taxi. It is late at night. We ride across the park. Then we ride more. Caroline says words to a gate. A man opens the door to a very big house. He smells surprised. He wears pajamas. "Miss Caroline!"

"Hello, Seacomb. Is my mother in?"

"She's asleep, of course. If there's an emergency—"

"No emergency. But my apartment pipes sprung a leak and I'll be spending the night here. This is my dog, Angel. Angel, Seacomb is safe."

"Of course, Miss," Seacomb says. He smells very unhappy. "It's just—"

"Just that you have orders not to let me use this house?"

"No, Miss," the man says. "My orders are to let you use the house as you choose. Only—"

"Of course they are," Caroline says. "My mother wants me to grovel back here. She's been panting for that. Well, here I am. Only she's taken a sleeping pill and is out cold until morning, right?"

"Yes, Miss," the man says. He smells very unhappy. There are no cats or dogs in this place, but there are mice. The mice droppings smell interesting.

"I'll sleep in the downstairs study. And, oh, Seacomb, I'm expecting guests. Please disable the electric gate. They'll use the back entrance, and I'll let them in myself. You needn't take any trouble about it."

"It's no trouble to—"

"I said I'll let them in myself."

"Yes, Miss," Seacomb says. He smells very very unhappy.

He leaves. Caroline and I go down stairs. Caroline drinks. She gives me water. I smell a mouse in a cupboard. My ears raise. There are interesting things here.

"Well, Angel, here we are at my mother's house. Do you remember your mother, boy?"

"No," I say. I am confused. The words are a little hard.

"There are some people coming for a party. Some dancers. Kristine Meyers is coming. You remember Kristine Meyers?"

"Yes," I say. Kristine Meyers dances with Caroline. They run in circles and jump high. Caroline jumps higher.

"We're going to talk about dancing, Angel. This is a prettier house than mine to talk about dancing. This is a good house for a party, which is what we're going to have. My mother lets me use her house for parties. Remember that, boy."

Later Caroline opens the door. Some people stand there. We go into the basement. Kristine Meyers is there. She smells frightened. Some men are with her. They carry papers. They talk a long time.

"Here, Angel, have a pretzel," a man says. "It's a party."

Some people dance to a radio. Kristine smells angry and confused. Her fur stands up. Caroline says words to her. The words are hard. The words are long. I have a pretzel. Nobody touches Caroline.

We are there all night. Kristine cries.

"Her boyfriend is gone," Caroline says to me.

In early morning we go home. We go in a taxi. Somebody is sick in the taxi yesterday. It smells bad. Caroline sleeps. I sleep. Caroline does not go to class.

In the afternoon we go to Lincoln Center. Kristine is there. She sleeps on a couch in the lounge. Caroline dances with Dmitri.

John Cole bends close to my ear. "You went out with Caroline all last night."

"Yes," I say.

"Where did you go?"

"We go to Caroline's mother's house. We go to a party. Caroline's mother lets Caroline use her house for parties."

"Who was at this party?"

"Dancers. Kristine is at the party. Kristine is safe."

John looks at Kristine. She still sleeps on the couch.

"Who else was at the party? What did they do?"

I remember hard. "Dancers are at the party. We eat pretzels. We talk about dancing. People dance to the radio. Nobody touches Caroline. There is music."

John's body relaxes. "Good," he says. "Okay."

"I like pretzels," I say. But John does not give me a pretzel today.

Caroline and I walk in the park. There are many good smells. Caroline sits under a tree. The long fur on her head falls down. She pats my head. She gives me a cookie.

"It's easy for you, isn't it, Angel?" Caroline says.

I say, "The words are hard."

"You like being a dog? A bioenhanced servant dog?"

"The words are hard."

"Are you happy, Angel?"

"I am happy. I love Caroline."

She pats my head again. The sun is warm. The smells are good. I close my eyes.

"I love to dance," Caroline says. "And I hate that I love it."

I open my eyes. Caroline smells unhappy.

"Goddamn it, I love it anyway. I do. Even though it wasn't my choice. You didn't choose what you are, either, did you, Angel?

They goddamn made you what they needed you to be. Yet you love it. And for you there's no account due."

The words are too hard. I put my nose into Caroline's front legs. She puts her front legs around me. She holds me tight.

"It's not *fair*," Caroline whispers into my fur.

Caroline does not hold me yesterday. She holds me today. I am happy. But Caroline smells unhappy.

Where is my happy if Caroline smells unhappy?

I do not understand.

## 6.

DEBORAH DIDN'T GET CAST in *Nutcracker*. An SAB teacher told her she might want to consider auditioning for one of the regional companies rather than City Ballet—a death sentence, from her point of view. She told me this quietly, without histrionics, sitting cross-legged on the floor sewing ribbons onto a pair of toe shoes. Not wanting to say the wrong thing, I said nothing, contenting myself with touching her hair, coiled at the nape of her neck into the ballerina bun. Two days later she told me she was dropping out of high school.

"I need the time to dance," she said. "You just don't understand, Mom."

The worst thing I could do was let her make me into the enemy. "I do understand, honey. But there will be lots of time to dance after you finish school. And if you don't—"

"Finishing is a year away! I can't afford the time. I have to take more classes, work harder, get asked into the company. *This year*. I'm sorry, Mom, but I just can't waste my time on all that useless junk in school."

I locked my hands firmly on my lap. "Well, let's look at this reasonably. Suppose after all you do get asked to join the company—"

"I *will* be asked! I'll work so hard they'll have to ask me!"

"All right. Then you dance with them until, say, you're thirty-five. At thirty-five you have over half your life left. You saw what happened to Carla Cameri and Maura Jones." Carla's hip had disintegrated; Maura's Achilles tendon had forced her into retirement at thirty-two. Both of them worked in a clothing store, for pitifully small salaries. Dancers didn't get pensions unless they'd been with the same company for ten years, a rarity in the volatile world of artistic directors with absolute power, who often fired dancers because they were remaking a company into a different "look."

I pressed my point. "What will you do at thirty or thirty-five with your body debilitated and without even a high school education?"

"I'll teach. I'll coach. I'll go back to school. Oh, Mom, how do I know? That's decades away! I have to think about what I need to do for my career now!"

No mother love is luminous enough to make a sixteen-year-old see herself at thirty-five.

I said, "No, Deborah. You can't quit school. I'd have to sign for you, and I won't."

"Daddy already did."

We looked at each other. It was too late; she'd already made me into the enemy. Because she needed one.

She said, in a sudden burst of passion, "You don't understand! You never felt about your job the way I feel about ballet! You never loved anything enough to give up everything else for it!" She rushed to her room and slammed the door. I put my head in my hands.

After a while, I started to laugh. I couldn't help it. *Never loved anything enough to give up everything else for it.*

Right.


Pers wasn't available to yell at. I phoned six times. I left messages on email, even though I had no idea whether he had a terminal. I made the trip out of the protected zone to his apartment. The area was worse than I remembered: glass, broken machinery, shit, drug paraphernalia. The cab driver was clearly eager to leave, but I made him wait while I questioned a kid who came out of Pers's building. The boy, about eight, had a long pus-encrusted cut down one cheek.

"Do you know when Pers Anders usually comes home? He lives in 2C."

The kid stared at me, expressionless. The cab driver leaned out and said, "One more minute and I'm leaving, lady."

I pulled out a twenty-dollar bill and held it close to me. "When does Pers Anders usually come home?"

"He moved."

"Moved?"

"Left his stuff. He say he go someplace better than this shithole. I hear him say it. Don't you try to prong me, lady. You give me that money."

"Do you know the address?"

He greeted this with the scorn it deserved. I gave him the money.

Deborah left school and started spending all day and much of the night at Lincoln Center. Finally I walked over to SAB and caught her just before a partnering class. She had twisted a bright scarf around her waist, over her leotard, and her sweaty hair curled in tendrils where it had escaped her bun.

"Deborah, why didn't you tell me your father had moved?"

She looked wary, wiping her face with a towel to gain time. "I didn't think you'd care. You hate him."

"As long as you still visit him, I need to know where he is."

She considered this. Finally she gave me the address. It was a good one, in the new luxury condos where the old main library had been.

"How can Pers afford *that*?"

"He didn't say. Maybe he's got a job. Mom, I have class."

"Pers is allergic to jobs."

"Mom, Mr. Privitera is teaching this class *himself*!"

I didn't stay to watch class. On the way out, I passed Privitera, humming to himself on his way to elate or cast down his temple virgins.

The police had released no new information on the ballerina murders.

I turned in the article on the New York City Ballet. It seemed to me neither good nor bad; everything important about the subject didn't fit the magazine's focus. There weren't too many metaphors. Michael read it without comment. I worked on an article about computerized gambling, and another about holographic TV. I voted in the Presidential election. I bought Christmas presents.

But every free minute, all autumn and early winter, I spent at the magazine library terminals, reading about human bioenhancement, trying to guess what Caroline Olson was having done to herself. What might someday lie in Deborah's future, if she were as big a fool then as she was being now.

"Don't get obsessed," Michael had said.

The literature was hard to interpret. I wasn't trained in biology, and as far as I could see, the cutting-edge research was chaotic, with various discoveries being reported one month, contradicted the next. All the experiments were carried out in other countries, which meant they were reported in other languages, and I didn't know how far to trust the biases of the translators. Most of them seemed to be other scientists in the same field. This whole field seemed to me like a canoe rushing toward the falls: nobody in charge, both oars gone, control impossible.

I read about splendid, "revolutionary" advances in biological nanotechnology that always seemed under development, or not quite practical yet, or hotly disputed by people practicing other kinds of revolutionary advances. I read about genesplicing retroviruses and setting them loose in human organs to accomplish potentially wonderful things. Elimination of disease. Perfect metabolic functioning. Immortality. The studies were always concerned with one small, esoteric facet of scientific work, but the "Conclusions" sections were often grandiose, speculating wildly.

I even picked up hints of experimental work on altering genetic makeup *in vitro*, instead of trying to reshape adult bodies. Some scientists seemed to think this might actually be easier to accomplish. But nowhere in the world was it legal to experiment on an embryo not destined for abortion, an embryo that would go on to become a human being stuck with the results of arbitrary and untested messing around with his basic cellular blueprints. Babies were not tinker toys—or dogs. The Copenhagen Accord, signed twenty-seven years by most technologically civilized countries, had seen to that. The articles on genetic modification *in vitro* were carefully speculative.

But then so was nearly everything else I read. The proof was walking around in inaccessible foreign hospitals, or living anonymously in inaccessible foreign cities—the anonymity of the experimental subjects seemed to be a given, which also made me wonder how many of them were experimental casualties. And if so, of what kind.

Michael wasn't going to want any article built on this tentative speculation. Lawsuits would loom. But I was beyond caring what Michael wanted.

I learned that the Fifth International Conference on Human Bioenhancement was going to be held in Paris in late April. After paying the Robin Hood, I had no money left for a trip to Paris. Michael would have to pay for it. I would have to give him a reason.

One night in January I did a stupid thing. I went alone to Lincoln Center and waited by the stage door of the New York State Theater. Caroline Olson came out at 11:30, dressed in jeans and parka, accompanied only by a huge black Doberman on the most nominal of leashes. They walked south on Broadway, to an all-night restaurant. I sat myself at the next table.

For the last few months, her reviews had not been good. "A puzzling and disappointing degeneration," said *The New Yorker*. "Technical sloppiness not associated with either Olson or Privitera," said *Dance Magazine*. "This girl is in trouble, and Anton Privitera had better find out what kind of trouble and move to correct it," said the *Times On-Line*.

Caroline ate abstractedly, feeding bits to the dog, oblivious to the frowns of a fastidious waiter who was undoubtedly an out-of-work actor. Up close, the illusion of power and beauty I remembered from *Coppelia* evaporated. She looked like just another mildly pretty, self-absorbed, overly thin young woman. Except for the dog, the waiter/actor didn't give her a second glance.

"We go now?" the dog said.

I choked on my sandwich. Caroline glanced at me absently. "Soon, Angel."

She went on eating. I left, waited for her, and followed her home. She and the dog lived on Central Park South, a luxury building where the late-night electronic surveillance system greeted them both by name.

I took a cab home. Deborah had never mentioned that the City Ballet prima ballerina was protected by a bioenhanced Doberman. She knew I'd written the story about the ballerina murders. Anton Privitera hadn't mentioned it, either, in his press conference about dancer safety. I wondered why not. While I was parceling out wonder, I devoted some to the question of City Ballet's infrequent, superficial, and always-positive bioscans. Shouldn't a company devoted to the religion of "natural art" be more zealous about ferreting out heretics?

Unless, of course, somebody didn't really want to know.

Privitera? But that was hard to reconcile with his blazing, intolerant sincerity.

It occurred to me that I had never seen an admittedly bioenhanced dancer perform. Until tonight, I'd gone to finished performances rarely and only with Deborah, who of course scorned such perverts and believed that they had nothing to teach her.

She was out when I got back to our apartment. Each week, it seemed, she was gone more. I fell asleep, waiting for her to come home.

# 7.

SNOW FALLS. IT IS COLD. Caroline and I walk to Lincoln Center. A man takes Caroline's purse. He runs. Caroline says "Shit!" Then she says, "Angel? Go stop him!" She drops my leash.

I run and jump on the man. He screams. I do not hurt him. Caroline says *stop him*. She does not say *attack him*. So I stand on the man's chest and growl and nip at his foreleg. He brings out a knife. Then I bite him. He drops the knife and screams again. The police come.

"Holy shit," Caroline says to me. "You really do that. You really do."

"I protect Caroline," I say.

Caroline talks to police. Caroline talks to reporters. I get a steak to eat.

I am happy.

The snow goes away. The snow is there many many days, but it goes away. We visit Caroline's mother's house for two more parties in the basement. It gets warm in the park. Ducks live in the water again. Flowers grow. Caroline says not to dig up flowers.

I lie backstage. Caroline dances on stage. John and Mr. Privitera stand beside me. They smell unhappy. John's shoes smell of tar and food and leaves and cats and other good things. I sniff John's shoes.

"She looks exhausted," John says. "She's giving it everything she's got, but it's just not there, Anton."

Mr. Privitera says no words. He watches Caroline dance.

"William Scholes attacked again in the *Times*. He said that watching her had become painful—'like watching a reed grown stiff and brittle.'"

"I will talk to her again," Mr. Privitera says.

"Scholes called the performance 'a travesty,'" John says.

Caroline comes backstage. She limps. She wipes her face with a towel. She smells afraid.

"Dear, I'd like to see you," Mr. Privitera says.

We go to Caroline's dressing room. Caroline sits down. She trembles. Her body smells sick. I growl. Caroline puts a hand on my head.

Mr. Privitera says, "First of all, dear, I have good news for all of us. The police have caught that unspeakable murderer who killed Jennifer Lang and the ABT dancer."

Caroline sits up a little straighter. Her smell changes. "They did! How?"

"They caught him breaking into the Plaza Hotel room where Marie D'Arbois is staying while she guests with ABT."

"Is Marie—"

"She's fine. She wasn't alone, she had a lover or something with her. The madman just got careless. The police are holding back the details. Marie, of course, is another of those bioenhanced dancers. I don't know if you ever saw her dance."

"I did," Caroline says. "I thought she was wonderful."

Caroline and Mr. Privitera look hard at each other. They smell ready to attack. But they do not attack. I am confused. Mr. Privitera is safe. He may touch Caroline.

Mr. Privitera says, "We must all be grateful to the police. Now there's something else I need to discuss with you, dear."

Caroline closes her hand on my fur. She says, "Yes?"

"I want you to take a good long rest, dear. You know your dancing has deteriorated. You tell me you're not doing drugs or working sketchily, and I believe you. Sometimes it helps a dancer to take a rest from performing. Take class, eat right, get strong. In the fall we'll see."

"You're telling me you're cutting me from the summer season at Saratoga."

"Yes, dear."

Caroline is quiet. Then she says, "There's nothing wrong with me. My timing has just been a little off, that's all."

"Then take the summer to work on your timing. And everything else."

Mr. Privitera and Caroline look hard at each other again. Caroline's hand still pulls my fur. It hurts a little. I do not move.

Mr. Privitera leans close to Caroline. "Listen, dear. *Jewels* was one of your best roles. But tonight...And not just *Jewels*. You wobbled and wavered through *Starscape*. Your Nikiya in the 'Shades' section of *La Bayadère* was...embarrassing. There is no other word. You danced as if you had never learned the steps. And you couldn't even complete the *Don Quixote pas de deux* at the gala."

"I fell! Dancers get injured all the time! My injury rate compared to—"

"You've missed rehearsals and even performances," Mr. Privitera said. He stands up. "I'm sorry, dear. Take the summer. Rest. Work. In the fall, we'll see."

Caroline says, "What about the last two weeks of the season?"

Mr. Privitera says, "I'm sorry, dear."

He walks to the door. He puts his hand on the door. He says, "Oh, at least you won't have to be burdened with that dog anymore. Now that the madman's been caught, I'll have John notify the protection agency to come pick it up."

Caroline raises her head. Her fur all stands up. She smells angry. Soon she runs out the door. Mr. Privitera is gone. She runs to the offices. "John! John, you bastard!"

The office hall is dark. The doors do not open. John is not here.

Caroline runs up steps to the offices. She falls. She falls down some of the steps and hits the wall. She lies on the floor. She holds her hind foot and smells hurt.

"Angel," she says. "Go get somebody to help me."

I go to the lounge. One dancer is there. She says, "Oh! I'm sorry, I didn't know that anybody—Angel?"

"Caroline is hurt," I say. "Come. Come fast."

She comes. Caroline says, "Who are you? No, wait—Deborah, right? From the corps?"

"No, I'm not...I haven't been invited to join the corps yet. I'm a student at SAB. I'm just here a lot...Are you hurt? Can you stand?"

"Help me up," Caroline says. "Angel, Deborah is safe."

Deborah tries to pick up Caroline. Caroline makes a little noise. She cannot stand. Deborah gets John. He picks up Caroline.

"It's nothing," she says. "No doctor. Just get me a cab...dammit, John, don't fuss, it's nothing!" She looks at John hard. "You want to take Angel away from me."

John smells surprised. He says, "Who told you that?"

"His Majesty himself. But now you've decided whatever you thought I was doing so privately doesn't matter anymore, is that right?"

"It's a mistake. Of course you can keep the dog. Anton doesn't understand," John says. He smells angry.

"No, I'll just bet he doesn't," Caroline says. "You might have picked a kinder way to tell me I'm through at City Ballet."

"You're not through, Caroline," John says. Now he smells bad. His words are not right. He smells like the man who takes Caroline's purse.

"Right," Caroline says. She sits in the cab.

Deborah steps back. She smells surprised.

"I'm keeping the dog," Caroline says. "So we're in agreement, aren't we, John? Come on, Angel. Let's go home."

\* \* \*

We go to class. Caroline cannot dance. She tries and then stops. She sits in a corner. Mr. Privitera sits in another corner. Caroline watches Deborah. The dancers raise one hind leg. They spin and jump.

Madame holds up her hand. The music stops. "Deborah, let us see that again, *s'il vous plaît*. Alone."

The other dancers move away. They look at each other. They smell surprised. The music starts again and Deborah raises one hind leg very high. She spins and jumps.

Mr. Privitera says, "Let me see the bolero from *Coppelia*. Madame says you know it."

"Y-yes," Deborah says. She dances alone.

"Very nice, dear," Mr. Privitera says. "You are much improved."

The other dancers look at each other again.

Everybody dances.

Caroline watches Deborah hard.

## 8.

DEBORAH'S FACE LOOKED LIKE every Christmas morning in the entire world. She grabbed both my hands. "They invited me to join the company!"

My suitcase lay open on the bed, surrounded by discarded clothes I wasn't taking to the bioenhancement conference in Paris. My daughter picked up a pile of spidersilk blouses and hurled them into the air. In the soft April air from the open window the filmy, artificial material drifted and danced. "I can't believe it! They asked me to join the company! I'm in!"

She whirled around the tiny room, rising on toe in her street shoes, laughing and exclaiming. My silence went unnoticed. Deborah did an *arabesque* to the bedpost, then plopped herself down on my best dress. "Don't you want to know what happened, Mom?"

"What happened, Deborah?"

"Well, Mr. Privitera came to watch class, and Madame asked me to repeat the variation alone. God, I thought I'd die. Then *Mr. Privitera*—not Madame—asked me to do the bolero from *Cop-*

*pelia*. For an awful minute I couldn't remember a single step. Then I did, and he said it was very nice! He said I was much improved!"

Accolades from the king. But even in my numbness I could see there was something she wasn't telling me.

"I thought you told me the company doesn't choose any new dancers this close to the end of the season?"

She sobered immediately. "Not usually. But Caroline Olson was fired. She missed rehearsals and performances, and she wasn't even taking the trouble to prepare her roles. Her reviews have been awful."

"I saw them," I said.

Deborah looked at me sharply. "Ego, I guess. Caroline's always been sort of a bitch. So apparently they're not letting her go to Saratoga, because Tina Patrochov and a guest artist are dividing her roles, and Mr. Privitera told Jill Kerrigan to learn Tina's solo from *Sleeping Beauty*. So that left a place in the corps de ballet, and they chose me!"

I had had enough time to bring myself to say it.

"Congratulations, sweetheart."

"When does your plane for Paris leave?"

This non sequitur—if it was that—turned me back to my packing. "Seven tonight."

"And you'll be gone ten days. You'll have a great time in Paris. Maybe the next time the company goes on tour, I'll go with them!"

She whirled out of the room.

I sat at the end of the bed, holding onto the bedpost. When Deborah was three, she'd wanted a ride on a camel. Somehow it had become an obsession. She talked about camels in daycare, at dinnertime, at bedtime. She drew pictures of camels, misshapen things with one huge hump. Camels were in short supply in St. Louis. Ignore it, everyone said, kids forget these things, she'll get over it. Deborah never forgot. She didn't get over it. Pers had just left us, and I was consumed with the anxiety of a single parent. Finally I paid a friend to tie a large wad of hay under a blanket on his very old, very swaybacked horse. A Peruvian camel, I told my three-year-old. A very special kind. You can have a ride.

"That's not a camel," Deborah had said, with nostril-lifted disdain. "That's a heffalunt!"

I read last week in *World* that the animal-biotech scientists have built a camel with the flexible trunk of an elephant. The trunk can lift up to forty-five pounds. It was expected to be a useful beast of burden in the Sahara.

I finished packing for Paris.

Paris in April was an unending gray drizzle. The book and software stalls along the Seine kept up their electronic weather shields, giving them the hazy, streaming-gutter look of abandoned outhouses. The gargoyles on Notre Dame looked insubstantial in the rain, irrelevant in the face of camels with trunks. The French, as usual, conspired to make Americans—especially Americans who speak only rudimentary French—feel crass and barbaric. My clothes were wrong. My desire for a large breakfast was wrong. The Fifth International Conference on Human Bioenhancement had lost my press credentials.

The conference was held in one of the huge new hotels in Neuilly, near the Eurodisney Gene Zoo. I couldn't decide if this was an attempt to provide entertainment or irony. Three hundred scientists and doctors, a hundred press, and at least that many industrial representatives, plus groupies, thronged the hotel. The scientists presented papers; the industrial reps, mostly from biotech or pharmaceutical firms, presented "infoforums." The moment I walked in, carrying provisional credentials, I felt the tension, a peculiar kind of tension instantly recognizable to reporters. Something big was going on. Big and unpleasant.

From the press talk in the bar I learned that the presentation to not miss was Thursday night by Dr. Gerard Taillebois of the Pasteur Research Institute, in conjunction with Dr. Greta Erbland of Steckel und Osterhoff. This pairing of a major research facility with a commercial biotech firm was common in Europe. Sometimes the addition of a hospital made it a triumvirate. A handwritten addendum on the program showed that the presentation had been moved from the Napoleon Room to the Grand Ballroom.

I checked out the room; it was approximately the size of an airplane hangar. Hotel employees were setting up acres of chairs.

I asked a *garçon* to point out Dr. Taillebois to me. He was a tall, bald man in his sixties or seventies who looked like he hadn't slept or eaten in days.

Wednesday night I went to the Paris Opera Ballet. The wet pavement in front of the Opera House gleamed like black patent leather. Patrons dripped jewels and fur. This gala was why Michael had funded my trip; my first ballet article for *New York Now* had proved popular, despite its vapidity. Or maybe because of it. Tonight the famous French company was dancing an eclectic program, with guest artists from the Royal Ballet and the Kirov. Michael wanted 5,000 words on the oldest ballet company in the world.

I watched bioenhanced British dancers perform the wedding *pas de deux* from *Sleeping Beauty*, with its famous fishdives; Danish soloists in twentieth-century dances by Georges Balanchine; French ballerinas in contemporary works by their brilliant choreographer Louis Dufort. All of them were breathtaking. In the new ballets, especially choreographed for these bioenhanced bodies, the dancers executed sustained movements no natural body would have been capable of making at all, at a speed that never looked machine-like. Instead the dancers were flashes of light: lasers, optic signals, nerve impulses surging and across the stage and triggering pleasure centers in the brains of the delighted audience.

I gaped at one *pas de trois* in which the male dancer lifted two women at once, holding them aloft in swallow lifts over his head, one on each palm, then turning them slowly for a full ninety seconds. It wasn't a bench-pressing stunt. It was the culmination of a yearning, lyrical dance, as tender as any in the great nineteenth-century ballets. The female dancers were lowered slowly to the floor, and they both flowed through a *fouette of adage* as if they hadn't any bones.

Not one dancer had been replaced in the evening's program due to injury. I tried to remember the last time I'd seen a performance of the New York City Ballet without a last-minute substitution.

During intermission, profoundly depressed, I bought a glass of wine in the lobby. The eddying crowd receded for a moment, and I was face to face with Anna Olson, seated regally in her powerchair and flanked by her bodyguards. Holding tight to her hand was a little girl of five or six, dressed in a pink party dress and pink tights, with wide blue eyes, black hair, and a long slim neck. She might have been Caroline Olson fifteen years ago.

"Ms. Olson," I said.

She looked at me coldly, without recognition.

"I'm Susan Matthews. We met at the private reception for Anton Privitera at Georgette Allen's," I lied.

"Yes?" she said, but her eyes raked me. My dress wasn't the sort that turned up at the private fundraisers of New York billionaires. I didn't give her a chance to cut me.

"This must be your—" granddaughter? Caroline, an only child, had never interrupted her dancing career for pregnancy. niece? grandniece? "—your ward."

"*Je m'appelle Marguerite*," the child said eagerly. "*Nous regardons le ballet.*"

"Do you study ballet, Marguerite?"

"*Mais oui!*" she said scornfully, but Anna Olson made a sign and the bodyguards deftly cut me off from both of them. By maneuvering around the edge of the hall, I caught a last, distant glimpse of Marguerite. She waited patiently in line to go back to her seat. Her small feet in pink ballet slippers turned out in a perfect fifth position.

Thursday afternoon I drove into Paris to rent an electronic translator for the presentation by Taillebois and Erbland. The translators furnished by the conference were long since claimed. People who had rented them for the opening talks simply hung onto them, afraid to miss anything. The Taillebois/Erbland presentation would include written handouts in French, English, German, Spanish, Russian, and Japanese, but not until the session was over. I was afraid to miss anything, either.

I couldn't find an electronic translator with a brand name I trusted. I settled for a human named Jean-Paul, from a highly recommended commercial agency. He was about four feet ten, with sad brown eyes and a face wrinkled into fantastic crevasses. He told me he had translated for Charles de Gaulle during the crisis in Algeria. I believed him. He looked older than God.

We drove back to Neuilly in the rain. I said, "Jean-Paul, do you like ballet?"

"*Non*," he said immediately. "It is too slippery an art for me."

"Slippery?"

"Nothing is real. Girls are spirits of the dead, or joyous peasants, or other silly things. Have you ever seen any real peasants, Mademoiselle? They are not joyous. And girls lighter than air land on stage with a thump!" He illustrated by smacking the dashboard with his palm. "Men die of love for those women. Nobody dies for love. They die for money, or hate, but not love. *Non*."

"But isn't all art no more than illusion?"

He shrugged. "Not all illusion is worth creating. Not silly illusions. Dancers wobbling on tippy toes...*non, non*."

I said carefully, "French dancers can be openly bioenhanced. Not like in the United States. To some of us, that gives the art a whole new excitement. Technical, if not artistic."

Jean-Paul shrugged again. "Anybody can be bioenhanced, if they have the money. Bioenhancement, by itself it does not impress me. My grandson is bioenhanced."

"What does he do?"

Jean-Paul twisted his body toward me in the seat of the car. "He is a soccer player! One of the best in the world! If you followed the sport, you would know his name. Claude Despreaux. Soccer—now *there* is illusion worth creating!"

His tone was exactly Anton Privitera's, talking about ballet.

Thursday evening, just before the presentation, I finally caught Deborah at home. Her face on the phonevid was drawn and strained. "What's wrong?"

"Nothing, Mom. How's Paris?"

"Wet. Deborah, you're not telling me the truth."

"Everything's fine! I just...just had a complicated rehearsal today."

The corps de ballet does not usually demand complicated rehearsals. The function of the corps is to move gracefully behind the soloists and principal dancers; it's seldom allowed to do anything that will distract from their virtuosity. I said carefully, "Are you injured?"

"No, of course not. Look, I have to go."

"Deborah..."

"They're waiting for me!" The screen went blank.

Who was waiting for her? It was 1:00 a.m. in New York.

When I called back, there was no answer.

I went to the Grand Ballroom. Jean-Paul had been holding both our seats, lousy ones, since noon. An hour later, the presentation still had not started.

The audience fidgeted, tense and muttering. Finally a woman dressed in a severe suit entered. She spoke German. Jean-Paul translated into my ear.

"Good evening. I am Katya Waggenschauser. I have an announcement before we begin. I regret to inform you that Dr. Taillebois will not appear. Dr. Taillebois...He..." Abruptly she ran off the stage.

The muttering rose to an astonished roar.

A man walked on stage. The crowd quieted immediately. Jean-Paul translated from the French, "I am Dr. Valois of the Pasteur Institute. Shortly Dr. Erbland will begin the presentation. But I regret to inform you that Dr. Taillebois will not appear. There has been an unfortunate accident. Dr. Taillebois is dead."

The murmuring rose, fell again. I heard reporters whispering into camphones in six languages.

"In a few moments Dr. Erbland will make her and Dr. Taillebois's presentation. Please be patient just a few moments longer."

Eventually someone introduced Dr. Erbland, a long and fulsome introduction, and she walked onto the stage. A thin, tall woman in her sixties, she looked shaken and pale. She opened by speaking about how various kinds of bioenhancement differed from each other in intent, procedure, and biological mechanism. Most bioenhancements were introduced into an adult body that had already finished growing. A few, usually aimed at correcting hereditary problems, were carried out on infants. Those procedures were somewhat closer to the kinds of genetic re-engineering—it was not referred to merely as "bioenhancement"—that produced new strains of animals. And as with animals, science had long known that it was possible to manipulate pre-embryonic human genes in the same way, *in vitro*.

The audience grew completely quiet.

*In vitro* work, Dr. Erbland said, offered by its nature fewer guides and guarantees. There were much coded redundancies in genetic information, and that made it difficult to determine long-term happenings. The human genome map, the basis of all embryonic re-engineering, had been complete for forty years, but "complete" was not the same as "understood." The body had many genetic behaviors that researchers were only just beginning to understand. No one could have expected that when embryonic re-engineering first began, as a highly experimental undertaking, that genetic identity would be so stubborn.

Stubborn? I didn't know what she meant. Apparently, neither did anybody else in the audience. People scarcely breathed.

This experimental nature of embryonic manipulation in humans did not, of course, stop experimentation, Dr. Erbland continued. Before such experimentation was declared illegal by the Copenhagen Accord, many laboratories around the world had advanced science with the cooperation of voluntary subjects. Completely voluntary, she said. She said it three times.

I wondered how an embryo volunteered.

These voluntary subjects had been re-engineered using variants of the same techniques that produced *in vitro* bioenhancements in other mammals. Her company, in conjunction with the Pasteur Research Institute, had been pioneers in the new techniques. For over thirty years.

Thirty years. My search of the literature had found nothing going back that far. At least not those available on the standard scientific nets. If such "re-engineered" embryos had been allowed to fully gestate, and had survived, they were just barely within the cut-off date for legal existence. Were we talking about embryos or people here?

Dr. Erbland made a curious gesture: raising both arms from the elbow, then letting them fall. It looked almost like a plea. Was she making a public confession of breaking international law? Why would she do that?

Over such a long time, Dr. Erbland continued, the human genetic identity, encoded in "jumping genes" in many unsuspected redundant ways, reasserted itself. This was the subject of her and Dr. Taillebois's work. Unfortunately, the effect on the organism—completely unanticipated by anyone—could be biologically devastating. This first graphic showed basal DNA changes in a re-engineered embryo created twenty-five years ago. The subject, a male, was—

A holograph projected a complicated, three-dimensional genemap. The scientists in the audience leaned forward intently. The non-scientists looked at each other.

As the presentation progressed, anchored in graphs and formulas and genemap holos, it became clear even to me what Dr. Erbland was actually saying.

European geneticists had been experimenting on embryos as long as thirty years ago, and never stopped. They had allowed some of those embryos to become people. Against international law, and without knowing the long-term effects. And now the long-term effects, like old bills, were coming due, and those people's bodies were destroying themselves at the genetic level.

We had engineered a bioenhanced cancer to replace the natural one we had conquered.

It was a few moments before I noticed that Jean-Paul had stopped translating. He sat like stone, his wrinkled face lengthened in sorrow.

The audience forgot this was a scientific conference. "How many people have been re-engineered at an embryonic level?" someone shouted in English. "Total number worldwide!"

Someone else shouted, "*Y todos van a morir?*"

"*Les lois internationales—*"

"*Der sagt—*"

Dr. Erbland broke into a long, passionate speech, clearly not part of the prepared presentation. I caught the word "sagt" several times: *law*. I remembered that Dr. Erbland worked for a commercial biotech firm wholly owned by a pharmaceutical company.

The same company in which Anna Olson owned a fortune in stock.

Jean-Paul said quietly, "My grandson. Claude. He was one of those embryos. They told us it was safe…"

I looked at the old man, slumped forward, and I couldn't find any sympathy for him. That appalled me. A cherished grandson… But they had agreed, Claude's parents, to roulette with a child's life. In order to produce a superior soccer player. *"Soccer—now there is an illusion worth creating."*

I remembered Anna Olson at the demonstration by the Lincoln Center fountain: *"Caroline had a good run. For a dancer."* Caroline Olson, Deborah said, had been fired because she missed rehearsals and performances. The *Times* had called her last performance "a travesty." Because her body was eating itself at a genetic level, undetectable by the City Ballet bioscans that assumed you could compare new DNA patterns to the body's original, which no procedure completely erased. But for Caroline, the original itself had carried the hidden blueprint for destruction. For twenty-six years.

The ultimate ballet mother had made Caroline into what Anna Olson needed her to be. For as long as Caroline might last.

And then I remembered little Marguerite, standing with her perfect turn out in fifth position.

I stood and pushed my way to the exit. I had to get out of that room. Nobody else left. Dr. Erbland, rattled and afraid, tried to answer questions shouted in six languages. I shoved past a woman who was punching her neighbor. Gendarmes appeared as if conjured from the floorboards. Maybe that would be next.

The hardcopies of Dr. Taillebois's original presentation were stacked neatly on tables in the lobby. I took one in English. As I went out the door, I heard a gendarme say clearly to somebody, *"Oui, il s'a suicide, Dr. Taillebois."*

I didn't want to stay an hour longer in Paris. I packed at the hotel and changed my ticket at Orly. On the plane home I made myself read the Taillebois/Erbland paper. Most of it was incomprehensible to me; what I understood was obscene. I kept seeing Marguerite in her pink ballet slippers, Caroline staggering on stage. If my lack of sympathy for Taillebois and Erbland was a lack in me, then so be it.

For the first time since Deborah had entered the School of American Ballet, and despite the dazzling performances at the Paris Opera, I found myself respecting Anton Privitera.

When I landed at Kennedy, at almost midnight, there was a message from the electronic gate keeper, "Call this number immediately. Urgent and crucial." I didn't recognize the number.

Deborah. An accident. I raced to the nearest public phone. But it wasn't a hospital; it was an attorney's office.

"Ms. Susan Matthews? Hold, please."

A man's face came on the screen. "This is James Beecher, Ms. Matthews. I'm attorney for Pers Anders. He's being held without bail, pending trial. He left a message for you, most urgent. The message is—"

"Trial? On what charges?" But I think I already knew. The well-cut suit on the lawyer. The move to an expensive neighborhood. Pers was working for somebody, and there weren't very many things he knew how to do.

"The charges are dealing in narcotics. First-degree felony. The message is—"

"Sunshine, right? No, that wouldn't have been expensive enough for Pers," I said bitterly. "Designer viruses? Pleasure center beanos?"

"The message is, 'Don't look in the caverns of the moon.' That's all." The screen went blank.

I stared at it anyway. When Deborah was tiny, in the brief period a million years ago when Pers and I were still together and raising her, she had a game she loved. She'd hide a favorite toy somewhere and call out, "Don't look in the closet! Don't look under the bed! Don't look in the sock drawer!" The toy was always wherever she said not to look. The caverns of the moon was what she called her bedroom, but that was much later, long after Pers had deserted us both but before she tracked him down in New York. I didn't know that he even knew about it.

*Don't look in the caverns of the moon.*

I took a helo right to the Central Park landing stage, charging it to the magazine. The last five blocks I ran, past the automated stores that never sleep and the night people who had just gotten up. Deborah wasn't home; she didn't expect me back from Paris until tomorrow. I tore apart her bedroom, and in an old dance bag I found it, flattened between the mattress and box spring. No practiced criminal, my Deborah.

The powder was pinkish, with no particular odor. There was a lot of it. I had no idea what it was; probably it had a unique name to go with a unique formula matched to some brain function. What kind of father would use his own daughter as a courier for this designer-gene abyss? Would the cops have already been here if I'd come home a day later? An hour later?

I flushed it all down the toilet, including the dance bag, which I first cut into tiny pieces. Then I searched the rest of the apartment, and then I searched it again. There were no more drugs. There was no money.

She wasn't running stuff for Pers for free. Not Deborah. She had spent the money somewhere.

*"They asked me to join the company! He said it was very nice! He said I was much improved!"*

I made myself sit and think. It was one o'clock in the morning. Lincoln Center would be locked and dark. She might be at a restaurant with other dancers; she might be staying the night with a friend. I called other SAB students. Each answered sleepily. Deborah wasn't there. Ninette told me that after the evening performance Deborah had said she was going home.

"Well, yes, Ms. Matthews, she did seem a little tense," Ninette said, stifling a yawn, her long hair tousled on the shoulders of her nightgown. "But it was only her second night in actual performance, so I thought..." The young voice trailed off. I wasn't going to be told whatever this girl thought. Clearly I was an interfering mother.

You bet I was.

I waited another hour. Deborah didn't come home. I called a cab and went to Caroline Olson's apartment on Central Park South.

It had to be Caroline. She must have known she herself was bioenhanced, and I had seen her dance before her downfall: the complete abandon to ballet, the joy. Maybe she thought that helping other dancers to illegal bioenhancement was a favor to them, a benefit. She might be making a distinction—the same one Dr. Erbland had made—between the ultimately destructive re-engineering done to her *in vitro* and the bioenhancements done to European dancers. Or maybe she didn't connect her own sudden deterioration with how her mother had genetically consecrated her to ballet.

Or maybe she did. Maybe she knew that her meteoric success was what was now killing her. Maybe she was so sick and so enraged that she *wanted* to destroy other dancers along with her. If she couldn't dance out her full career, then neither would they.

Or maybe she thought it was worth it. A short life but a brilliant one. Anything for art. Most dancers ended up crippling their bodies anyway, although more slowly. The great Suzanne Farrell had ended up with a plastic hip, her pelvis destroyed by constant turnout. Mikhail Baryshnikov ruined his knees. Miranda Mains was unable to walk by the time she was twenty-eight. Maybe Caroline Olson thought no sacrifice was too great for ballet, even a life.

But not my Deborah's.

I buzzed the security system of Caroline's apartment for five solid minutes. There was no answer. Finally the system said politely, "Your party does not answer. Further buzzing may constitute legal harassment. You should leave now."

I got back in the cab, chewing on my thumb. I felt that kind of desperation you think you can't live through; it consumes your belly, chokes your breath. The driver waited indifferently. *Where?* God, in New York they could be anywhere.

Anywhere nobody would think to look for illegal medical operations. Anywhere safe, and protected, and easily accessible by dancers, without suspicion.

I gave the driver Anna Olson's address, remembered from the tax return pirated by the Robin Hood. Then I transferred the gun from my purse to my pocket.

I think I wasn't quite sane.

# 9.

CAROLINE AND I RIDE in a taxi. I like taxis. I put my head out the window. The taxi has many smells. We stop at Deborah's house. Caroline and I go get Deborah.

"I've changed my mind," Deborah says. Her door is open only a little. She stands behind her door. "I'm not going."

"Yes, you are," Caroline says.

Deborah says, "You're not my mother!"

Caroline changes her smell. She has a cane to walk. She leans on her cane. Her voice gets soft. "No, I'm not your mother. And I'm not going to push you like a mother. Believe me, Deborah, I know what that's like. But as a senior dancer, I'm going to ask you to come with me. I'm willing to beg you to come. It's that important. Not just to you, but to me."

Deborah looks at the floor.

"Don't be embarrassed. Just understand that I mean it. I'll beg, I'll grovel. But first I'm asking, as a senior member of the company."

Deborah looks up. She smells angry. "Why do you care? It's my life!"

"Yes. Yours and Privitera's." Caroline closes her eyes. "You owe him something, too. No, don't consider that. Just come because I'm asking you."

Deborah still smells angry. But she comes.

We ride in the taxi to Caroline's mother's house. I say, "Is there a party tonight?"

Deborah laughs. It sounds funny. Caroline says, "Yes, Angel. Another party. With music and dancers and talking. And you can have some pretzels."

"I like pretzels," I say. "Does Deborah like pretzels?"

"No," Deborah says, and now she smells scared.

We go in the back way. Caroline has a key. People come to the basement. Someone starts music. "Not so loud!" a man says.

"No, it's all right," Caroline says. "My mother's still in Europe and the staff is on vacation while she's gone. We have the place to ourselves."

A woman brings me a pretzel. People talk. Caroline and Deborah and two men talk in the corner. I don't hear the words. The words at parties are very hard. I watch Caroline, and eat pretzels, and watch two people dance to the radio.

"Christ," the man dancer says, "is this fake revelry really necessary?"

"Yes," the woman says. She looks at me. "Caroline says yes."

In the corner, two men show Deborah some papers. Caroline sits with them. Deborah starts to cry.

I watch Caroline. Deborah may touch Caroline. The two men may touch Caroline. But Caroline says parties are happy. No people smell happy. I do not understand.

The buzzer rings.

Nobody moves. People look at each other. Caroline says, "Is the gate still open? Let it go. It's probably kids. There's nobody home but us."

The buzzer rings and rings. Then it stops. Caroline talks to Deborah. The door opens at the top of the stairs.

A man with Caroline takes a bottle from his pocket very fast. He puts the papers on the floor and pours the bottle on it. The papers disappear. "All right, everybody, this is a party," he says.

Steps run down the stairs. A voice calls, "Wait! You can't go down there! Young woman! You can't go down there!" The voice is angry. It is Caroline's mother.

I walk to Caroline. She smells surprised.

A woman comes into the basement. She holds a gun. My ears raise. I stand next to Caroline.

"Nobody move," the woman says. Deborah says, "Mom!"

Caroline looks at the woman, then at Deborah, then at the woman. She walks with her cane to the woman.

"Stay right there," the woman says. She smells angry and scared. I move with Caroline.

"Christ, you sound like a bad holovid," Caroline says. "You're Deborah's mother? What the hell do you think you're doing here?"

From the top of the stairs Caroline's mother calls, "Caroline! What is the meaning of this?"

The woman says very fast, "Deborah, you're making a terrible mistake. Bioenhancement may help your dancing for a while, but it could also kill you. The conference on genetics in Paris—they presented scientific proof that one kind of bioenhancement kills, and if they're just finding that out now about enhancements done twenty-five years ago—then who knows what kind of insane risk you're running with these other kinds? Don't take my word for it, it's on-line this morning. Pers was arrested, damn him, and I found your drug stash just before the police did. That's how you're paying for this, isn't it? Debbie—how could you be such a damn *fool*?"

"Wait a minute," Caroline says. She leans on her cane. "You thought we brought Deborah here *to bioenhance her*?" Caroline starts to laugh. She puts her hand on her face. "Oh my God!"

Caroline's mother calls from the top of the stairs, "I'm phoning the police."

Caroline says, very fast, "Go bring her down here, James. You'll have to lift her out of her chair and carry her. Keith, get her chair." The two men run up the stairs.

Caroline is shaking. I stand beside her. I growl. The woman still has the gun. She points the gun at Caroline. I wait for Caroline to tell me *Attack*.

The woman says, "Don't try to deny it. You'd do anything for ballet, wouldn't you? All of you. You're sick—but you're not murdering my daughter!"

Caroline's face changes. Her smell changes. I feel her hand on my head. Her hand shakes. Her body shakes. I smell anger bigger than other angers. I wait for *Attack*.

Deborah says, "You're all wrong, Mom! Just like you always are! Does this look like a bioenhancement lab? *Does it*? These people aren't enhancing me—they're trying to talk me out of it! These two guys are doctors and they're trying to 'deprogram' me—just like you tried to program me all my life! You never wanted me to dance, you always tried to make me into this cute little college-bound student that *you* needed me to be. Never what *I* needed!"

The men carry Caroline's mother and Caroline's mother's chair down the steps. They put Caroline's mother in the chair. Caroline's mother also smells angry. But Caroline smells more angry than everybody.

Caroline says, "Sound familiar, Mother dear? What Deborah's saying? What did *you* learn at the genetic conference? What I've been telling you for months, right? Your gift to dance is dying. Because you wanted a prima ballerina at any price. Even if I'm the one to pay it."

Caroline's mother says, "You love dance. You wanted it as much as I did. You were a star."

"I never got to find out if I would have been one anyway! That isn't so inconceivable, is it? And then I might have still been dancing! But instead I was…*made*. Molded, sewed, carpentered. Into what you needed me to be."

Deborah's mother lowers her gun. Her eyes are big. Caroline's mother says, "You were a star. You had a good run. Without me, you might have been nothing. Worthless."

A man says, very soft, "Jesus H. Christ."

Caroline is shaking hard. I am afraid she will fall again. Her hand is on her cane. The cane shakes. Her other hand is on me.

Caroline says, "You cold, self-centered bitch—"

A little girl runs down the stairs.

The little girl says, "*Tante Anna! Tante Anna! Ou êtes-vous?*" She stops at the bottom of the steps. She smells afraid. "*Qui sont tout ces gens?*"

Caroline looks at the little girl. The little girl has no shoes. She has long black fur on her head. Her hind feet go out like Caroline's feet when Caroline dances. The toes look strange. I don't understand the little girl's feet.

Caroline says again, "You cold, self-centered bitch." Her voice is soft now. She stops shaking. "When did you have her made? Five years ago? Six? A new model with improved features? Who will decay all the sooner?"

Caroline's mother says, "You are a hysterical fool."

Caroline says, "Angel—attack. Now."

I attack Caroline's mother. I knock over the chair. I bite her foreleg. Someone screams, "Caroline! For God's sake! Caroline!" I bite Caroline's mother's head. I must protect Caroline. This person hurts Caroline. I must protect Caroline.

A gun fires and I hurt and hurt and hurt—

I love Caroline.

# 10.

THE TOWN OF SARATOGA, where the American Ballet Theater is dancing its summer season, is itself a brightly-colored stage. Visitors throng the racetrack, the brand-new Electronics Museum, the historical battle sites. In 1777, right here, Benedict Arnold and his half-trained revolutionaries stopped British forces under General John Burgoyne. It was the first great victory of freedom over the old order.

Until this year, the New York City Ballet danced here every summer. But the Performing Arts Center chose not to renew the City Ballet contract. In New York, too, City Ballet attendance is half of what it was only a few years ago.

The Saratoga pavilion is open to the countryside. Ballet lovers fill the seats, spread blankets up the sloping lawn, watch dancers accompanied not only by Tchaikovsky or Chopin but also by crickets and robins. In Saratoga, the ballet smells of freshly mown grass. The classic "white ballets"—*Swan Lake, Les Sylphides*—are remembered green. Small girls whose first taste of dance is at Saratoga will dream, for the rest of their lives, of toe shoes skimming over wildflowers.

I take my seat, in the back of the regular seating, as the small orchestra finishes tuning up. The conductor enters to the usual thunderous applause, even though nobody here knows his name and very few care. They have come to see the dancers.

Debussy floats out over the countryside. *Afternoon of a Faun*: slow, melting. On the nearly bare stage, furnished only with barre and mirrors, a male dancer in practice clothes wakes up, stretches, warms up his muscles in a series of low, languorous moves.

A girl appears in the mirror, which isn't really a mirror but an empty place in the backdrop. A void. She, too, stretches, poses, *pliés*.

Both dancers watch the mirrors. They are so absorbed in their own reflections that they only gradually become aware of each other's presence. Even then, they exist for each other only as foils, presences to dance to. In the end the girl will step back through the mirror. There is the feeling that for the boy, she may not really have existed at all, except as a dream.

It is Deborah's first lead in a one-act ballet. Her extension is high, her turnout perfect, her movements sure and strong and sustained, filled with the joy of dancing. I can barely stand to look at her. This is her reward, her grail, for continuing her bioenhancement. She isn't dancing for Anton Privitera, but she is dancing. A year and a half of bioenhancement, bought legally now in Copenhagen and paid for by selling her story to an eager press, has given her the physical possibilities to match her musicality, and her rhythm, and her drive.

The faun finally touches the girl, turning her slowly *en attitude*. Deborah smiles. This is her afternoon. She's willing to pay whatever price the night demands, even though science has no idea yet what, for her kind of treatments, it might be.

Privitera must have known that some of his dancers were bioenhanced. The completely inadequate bioscans at City Ballet, the phenomenally low injury rate of his prima ballerina—Privitera must have known. Or maybe his staff let him remain in official ignorance, keeping from him any knowledge of heresy in the ranks. There was a rumor that Privitera's business manager John Coles even tried to keep Caroline from "deprogramming" dancers who wanted bioenhancement. The rumor about Coles was never substantiated. But in the last year, City Ballet has been struggling to survive. Too many patrons have withdrawn their favor. The mystique of natural art, like other mystiques, didn't last forever. It had a good run.

"If you could have chosen, and that was the *only* way you could have had the career, would you have chosen the embryonic engineering anyway?" was the sole thing Deborah asked Caroline in jail, through bullet-proof plastic glass and electronic speaking systems, under the hard eyes of matrons. Caroline, awaiting trial for second-degree murder, didn't seem to mind Deborah's brusqueness, her self-absorption. Caroline was silent a long time, her gaunt face lengthened from the girlish roundness I remembered. Then she said to Deborah, "No."

"I would," Deborah said.

Caroline only looked at her.

They're here, Caroline and her dog. Somewhere up on the grass, Caroline in a powerchair, Angel hobbling on the three legs my bullet left him. Caroline was acquitted by reason of temporary insanity. They didn't let Angel stay with her during the trial. Nor did they let him testify, which would have been abnormal but not impossible. Five-year-olds can testify under some circumstances, and Angel has the biochip-and-reengineered intelligence of a five-year-old. Maybe it wouldn't have been so abnormal. Or maybe all of us, not just Anton Privitera, will have to change our definition of abnormal.

Five-year-olds know a lot. It was Marguerite who cried out, "*Vous avez assassiné ma tante Anna!*" She knew whom I was aiming at, even if the police did not. But Marguerite couldn't know how much I loathed the old woman who had made her daughter into what the mother needed her to be—just as I, out of love, had tried to do to mine.

On stage Deborah *pirouettes*. Maybe her types of bioenhancement will be all right, despite the growing body of doubts collected by Caroline's doctor allies. When the first cures for cancer were developed from reengineered retroviruses, dying and desperate patients demanded they be administered without long, drawn-out FDA testing. Some of the patients died even sooner, possibly from the cures. Some lived until 90. The edge of anything is a lottery, and protection doesn't help—not against change, or madmen, or errors of judgement. *I protect Caroline*, Angel kept saying after I shot him, yelping in pain between sentences. *I protect Caroline.*

Deborah flows into a *retiré*, one leg bent at the knee, and rises on toe. Her face glows. Her partner lifts her above his head and turns her slowly, her feet perfectly arched in their toe shoes, dancing on air.

# AND NO SUCH THINGS GROW HERE

*Here life has death for neighbor,*
*And far from eye or ear*
*Wan waves and wet winds labor,*
*Weak ships and spirits steer;*
*They drive adrift, and wither*
*They wot not who make thither;*
*But no such winds blow hither*
*And no such things grow here.*
  —Algernon Charles Swinburne,
    "The Garden of Proserpine"

"DEE, I HAVE A PROBLEM," Perri said.

Dee Stavros held the phone away from her ear and yawned hugely.

What the hell time was it, anyway? The clock had stopped in the night: another power outage. Her one window was still dark. The air was thick and hot.

"Dee, are you there?"

"I'm here," Dee said to her sister. "So you've got a problem. What else is new?"

"This is different."

"They're all different." Only they weren't, really. Deadbeat boy-friends, a violent ex-husband, cars "stolen," a last-minute abortion, bad checks for overdue rent…Perri's messy life changed only in the details. Dee yawned again.

Perri said, "I've been arrested for GMFA," and Dee woke fully and sat up on the edge of the bed.

GMFA. Genetic Modification Felony Actions. The newest crime-fighting tool, newest draconian set of laws, newest felonies to catch the attention of a blood-crazy public who needed a scapegoat for…everything. But Perri? Feckless, bumbling, *dumb* Perri? Not possible.

Professional training took over. Dee said levelly, "Where are you now?"

"Rikers Island," Perri said, and at the relief in her voice—*It'll be all right, Dee will clean up after me again*—Dee had to struggle to hold her anger in check.

"Do you have a lawyer?"

"No. I thought you'd take care of that."

Of course. And now that she was listening, Dee heard behind Perri all the muted miserable cacophony of Rikers Island, that chaotic hellhole where alleged perps for the larger hellhole of Manhattan were all taken, processed and mishandled. But Perri didn't live in Manhattan. Nobody who could avoid it lived in Manhattan. The last time Dee had heard from her sister, Perri had been heading for the beaches of North Carolina.

For once, Perri anticipated her. "I think they took me to Rikers because it was an offshore offense. On a boat. A ship, really….Get away! I'm not done, you bitch!"

Dee said rapidly, "Relinquish the phone, Perri, before you get hurt. You had your two minutes. I'll be there as soon as I can."

"Oh, Dee, I'm—" The phone went dead.

Dee stood holding it uselessly. Perri was what? Sorry? Scared? Innocent? But Perri was always those things in her own mind. Maybe Dee should just leave her there. Get out of Perri's life once and for all. Teach Perri a lesson. Just leave her there to fend for herself for once….

But Dee was all too familiar with Rikers. She'd retired from the force less than a year ago. She started to dress.

"Why me?" Eliot Kramer said when he appeared at her fourth-floor, one-room apartment door just after dawn. Grimy sunshine glared through Dee's big south window, the only nice thing about her room, other than its being on the far edge of Queens rather than the near edge. Many people were afraid of sunshine indoors. Ultraviolet, skin cancers—even though they'd been told that glass filtered out the danger. Most people never listened to what they were told.

"Why you? Because you're the only decent lawyer I know."

"Twenty years with NYPD and you know *one* decent lawyer? Come on, Dee."

"Decent in both senses, Eliot. Usually the moral ones are incompetent and the competent ones have been bought."

He shook his head. "Boy, I'm glad I don't have your outlook on life."

"You will. You're just not old enough yet."

"And how is old is this sister of yours?" Eliot asked as they hurried down the stairs. "What's her name again?"

"Perri Stavros. She's twenty-seven. My kid sister—I raised her after our parents died in a train wreck."

"And what exactly happened?"

"Haven't any idea," Dee said. "And after she tells us, we still might not know."

"Wonderful," Eliot said unhappily.

They emerged into the street, into the pale green light under the thick trees. Young trees, saplings, twigs…this section of Queens had only been planting for six years, since the Crisis, and there were none of the large trees that richer neighborhoods had immediately imported from God-knew-where. Trees grew up through holes jackhammered into the aging sidewalk, up beside crumbling stoops, up from buckets until they were big enough to transplant. A whole row struggled to thrive in the street itself, which had been narrowed to one lane now that cars were so unaffordable. Fast-growing trees, poplars and aspens and cottonwoods, although all trees (and everything else green) grew rapidly now. Whenever possible, trees with broad leaves for the maximum amount of photosynthesis, maximum amount of carbon dioxide scrubbed from the thick and overheated air.

"Not too bad this morning," Eliot said. "Pretty breathable."

"Not if we don't get rain," Dee said. Enough water, always, was the concern. Will it rain today? Don't you think it's clouding up? Might it rain tomorrow? Water meant biomass growth, giving mankind a chance of getting back into control the atmospheric $O_2/CO_2$ loop so dangerously rising toward 1 percent of $CO_2$, the upper limit of breathability.

"It'll rain," Eliot said. "Put on your mask, we're almost at the subway. One more question—do you at least know what class of contraband your sister was caught with?"

"No," Dee said. "It's all felony, isn't it?"

"There's felonies and there's felonies," Eliot said, and put on his mask.

Perri had been caught with class-two contraband, which meant five to ten.

"But there are extenuating circumstances," Perri said, looking pleadingly at Eliot, who merely nodded, dazed.

Dee was used to Perri's effect on men. Even in the smelly, hot (God, it was hot, and only early June), windowless interrogation room, and even dirty and smelly herself, Perri's beauty blazed. The perfect body, the long long legs, the thick honey-colored hair and full lips. But it was the eyes that always did it. Blue-green, larger than any other human eyes Dee had ever seen, fringed with long dark lashes. Perri's eyes sparkled, never the same two seconds in a row, unless you counted their unchanging sweetness of expression. How did Perri keep that sweet expression, with the life she'd led? Dee didn't know, hadn't ever known.

Eliot said, his tone not quite professional, "Why don't you just tell me the entire story from the beginning, Miss Stavros."

"Perri, please." She put her hand on his arm. "You will help me, won't you, Eliot?" The gesture was unstudied, genuine. It finished Eliot.

"Everything's going to be all right, Perri," he said, and Dee snorted. No, it was not. Not this time. This time, Perri may have dug herself under too deep for Dee—or Eliot—to pull her out. No, please God, no. Dee knew about the kind of prisons that genemod offenders were sent to, and what happened to them there. In the current public climate, GMFA felons were the new pedophiles.

Perri said, "Well, it started when I went down to North Carolina. To the beaches. I heard that sometimes holo companies recruited actresses from there? It turned out not to be true, but by that time I'd met Carl and well, you know." She lowered her amazing eyes, but not before Dee saw the flicker of pain.

"Go on," Eliot said. "What's Carl's last name?"

"He said Hansen. But it might not be. Anyway, I got pregnant."

Dee exploded, "How—"

"Don't yell at me, Dee. I know it was my fault. The implant ran out and I forgot to go get another one. And then Carl disappeared, and I didn't have the money for an abortion, so I started sort of asking around about a cheap one."

Suddenly Dee noticed how pale Perri was. It wasn't just the lack of makeup. Lips nearly the same color as her skin, dark smudges under her eyes…"You fool! Are you bleeding?"

"Oh, no," Perri said. "Everything went fine, Dee, and anyway I'm strong as an ox. You know that."

Eliot said, "Who performed the operation, Perri?"

"Well, that's just it. I know him only as 'Mike.' This girl I know said he was safe, he'd done it for her friend, and he didn't charge anything at all. He did it out of idealism." Her lips curved in such a tender smile that Dee was instantly suspicious.

"Was this 'Mike' an actual licensed doctor?"

"He didn't do the operation. My girlfriend introduced us at this bar on the beach, and Mike took me on a powerboat out to where the big ship was with the doctor aboard."

And Perri had gone with him. Just like that. Un-fucking-believable.

Eliot said, "Names, Perri. The girlfriend, the doctor, anyone on the ship, the name of the ship itself."

"I don't know, except for my girlfriend. Betsy Jefferson."

"Do you think that's her real name?"

"Probably not," Perri said. "The beach is the kind of place you get to be somebody else if you want to, you know?"

"*I* know," Dee said grimly. "Perri, do you know how much crime and smuggling go through Hilton Head?"

"I do now."

Eliot said patiently, "Go on with your story, Perri. Our time isn't unlimited, unfortunately."

"The doctor did the abortion. When I came to, I rested a while. Everyone was kind to me. Then Mike said he couldn't take me back, the ship had to leave. But he would send me in a little 'remote boat.' That's a—"

"We know what it is," Dee said harshly. "Smugglers use them all the time. They're computer-guided to shore from out at sea, so if the feds are there to intercept the stuff, at least they don't get the perps, too. Did the damn thing dump you in the ocean?"

"Oh, no. It brought me right to a public dock in…Long Island? I guess so. The ship must have sailed a long way while I was knocked out. It was daylight. Mike said the remote boats aren't illegal. I would have been all right, except…"

"Except what?" Eliot said gently.

Perri didn't answer for a moment. When she spoke, her voice was low. "The ship was full of plants. Flowers, little trees, all sorts of stuff growing on the deck in the sunshine. Beautiful. I…I wanted something to remember Mike by. You don't know how good he was to me, Dee, how kind. I felt…anyway. I picked a flower when nobody was looking and put it under my shirt. I was wearing this loose man's shirt because since I got pregnant, nothing of mine fit right. Nobody saw me take the flower."

"One flower?" Dee said. "That's all?"

"The flower wasn't big. It had beautiful yellow petals that were the same color as Mike's hair. That's why I took it. Don't look like that, Dee! A cop saw the remote boat land and came over to the dock because even though they're so tiny I guess they're pretty expensive and he was checking it out. And I staggered a little getting out of the boat because it hadn't even been a day yet since the operation. I was feeling a little woozy. It was so hot, and it was a bad air day. The flower fell out from under my shirt. Below the petals along the stem were all these hard little balls, maybe two dozen of them. One burst apart when the flower fell, and the cop saw it and took me in. I don't even know what it was!"

"I do," Eliot said. "As your attorney, the charges were of course available to me and I downloaded them. The seed pods are awaiting complete analysis at the GFCA lab, but the prelim shows genetic modification for lethal insecticides. Airborne seeds, which makes it a class-two genemod felony."

"But I didn't know!" Perri cried. "And I never understood what's so bad about plants that kill insects, anyway! Don't look like that, Dee, I'm not stupid! I know the history of the Crisis as well as you do. But those genemod plants that almost wiped out all the wheat in the Midwest were only one kind of engineered plant, and if people like Mike believe that other genemods can be—"

Dee cut her off. "People like Mike are criminals in it for the profit. And it wasn't just the wheat-killing genemod that caused the Crisis. And you may not be stupid, Perri, but you surely have acted like it!"

Eliot held up his hand. "Ladies, the thing to focus on here is—"

"No, Dee's right," Perri said. She sat up straighter and her washed-out lovely face took on an odd dignity. "I've been a fool, and I know it. But I had no...what is it, Eliot? Criminal intent? Surely that counts for something."

Eliot said quietly, "Not very much, I'm afraid. I don't want to lie to you, Perri. The GMFA Act is intended to prosecute illegal genemod organizations working for profit and willing to do anything at all to protect that profit. The Act is wide-reaching and harsh because it's modeled on RICO, the old Racketeer Influenced and Corrupt Organization laws, and because genetic engineering represents such a danger to the entire planet since the Greenhouse Crisis. Or politicians think it does. Unfortunately, people like you fall under the Act as well, and I wouldn't be doing my duty by you if I didn't inform you honestly that your case isn't going to play well in front of a jury of the usual hysterical citizens whose grandmothers and babies are having trouble breathing."

"But the Greenhouse Crisis and the wheat kill-off were two separate things!" Perri cried, surprising Dee.

"But most people don't separate them because they happened concurrently," Eliot said. "All at once the air was ruined, there was no bread, prices for everything rocketed because the government made energy so expensive to try to control industrial emissions…all at once. In my experience, that's how juries see it. Perri, I think you're much better off pleading guilty and letting me plea bargain for you."

Perri was silent. Dee said thickly, already knowing the answer, "Where will she do time?"

"Probably Cotsworth. It's the usual place for the east coast."

Cotsworth. It was notorious. Dee had never been inside, but she didn't have to be. She'd seen other places like it. It wasn't as bad as the men's worst prisons—they never were—but a girl who looked like Perri…was like Perri….

Perri said, "All right, Eliot. If you think I should plead guilty, I will."

Trusting him completely, on a half-hour acquaintance. Exactly how she got into this in the first place with "Carl," with "Mike." She would never learn.

Eliot said, "I'll do everything I can for you, Perri."

A wan smile, but the astonishing blue-green eyes dazzled. "I know you will. I trust you."

Dee wasn't Perri. She probed, tested, cut. "What if the FBI finds 'Mike'?"

"They won't find Mike," Eliot said. They stood at the subway entrance before the hellish descent underground. Eliot was going to his office in Brooklyn, Dee to Queens. "God, you of all people know they won't find Mike. The Genetic Modification Crimes section of the FBI is overworked, there aren't enough of them, and Perri is such small potatoes they probably won't even look for Mike."

"The ship doesn't sound like small potatoes."

"They might not even believe the ship exists. Perri wouldn't be the first perp to falsify events."

"Do you think that's what she's doing?"

"No," Eliot said. "I think she's telling the absolute truth. I think she's that rare find, a person incapable of dishonesty. But I don't think the FBI or the federal attorney will think so. They're paid not to."

"But you think the ship exists," Dee persisted.

"Yes. There are dozens, maybe hundreds, of them out there, in international waters where it's much harder to do anything about them. They genemod everything from insect-killing supercrops for idealists who want to save the Earth, to insect-killing supercrops for profiteers who want to own it. And who don't care if they inadvertently kill off an entire Third World country's rice crop in the process. Oh, Perri's ship is out there, all right, with 'Mike' running it. Although why he's also performing abortions is a bit murky. But I'm going to downplay that aspect with the federal attorney. It makes Perri look irresponsible."

"She is irresponsible."

"Sometimes," Eliot said, "what looks like irresponsibility is really innocence."

*Here we go again*, Dee thought. But if a ridiculous infatuation would increase Eliot's work on Perri's behalf, let the poor sot be infatuated.

It was ironic. Raising Perri, she was always the one "mother" who wouldn't let Perri take the bus by herself, walk home from school alone, go downtown. Cops were like that. Unlike the other mothers, Dee had known what was waiting out there in the street. And then the grown-up Perri sought out more trouble than any of her childhood friends.

Dee said, "So you don't think the authorities will look for Mike. And even though it would help Perri's plea, you won't, either."

Eliot said bluntly, "I can't afford the resources to look. Can you?"

"No," Dee said.

"Also, the case will be heard in under a week, probably. They dispose of these small things as fast as they can, fair or not. *You* know that, Dee."

"Yes, I know that. But finding the ship would aid an appeal for Perri."

"Yes. But they're not going to find it, Dee."

"No," she said. "But I am."


THE COAST OF CAROLINA IS THE NEW FLORIDA! blared e-banners at the train station. Dee believed it. Ruin one area, making it so hot the ecology becomes frightening and the people leave, move on to another. Most of Florida was now genuine jungle, teeming with foreign plants and animals escaped from Miami International Airport, always the major import center for such things. Monkeys, caimans, lygodia, alligators, and insects carrying everything from dengue fever to new diseases without names. Some of them, of course, genemod. It was the diseases that had made West Palm retirees, South Beach fun seekers, and the Miami criminal underground all move north.

She took a cheap motel room far from the action and went shopping. To the experienced, cops were instantly identifiable. That included ex-cops. She bought a modest swimsuit which at least covered her nipples, added a loose sheer robe to veil her forty-four-year-old body, studied the locals and purchased something guaranteed to make her hair lie in flat sculptured loops along one side of her neck. She didn't overdo it, another classic mistake of undercover cops. Her lipstick wasn't too gold, her eye makeup not too blue. She bought her beach bag, sandals, and music cube at a used-stuff store. She would do.

The long stretch of white-sand beach, natural and artificial, turned out to be informally segregated: gay beach, retiree beach, kid beach, sex-and-criminal beach. "I'm looking for Betsy Jefferson," she told the bartender at the first bar on the right beach.

The bartender gathered up glasses. He looked like he'd been behind the bar for a very long time. "Why do you want Betsy?"

"I need to talk to her. Do you know where she is?"

"No. Last I heard, she's working someplace for her uncle."

Of course. It was the number one response cops heard. You ask anybody what they, or anyone else, did for a living, and they said, "Work for my uncle." The entire underworld was employed by uncles.

Dee said, "I'm really looking for Perri Burr. I'm her sister." Perri had used "Burr" as her "beach key."

The bartender squinted at Dee. "Yeah, you look a little like her," he said, which was either kindness or blindness. "Around the nose. All right. Betsy's working at the Adams. Out Surf Street."

"Thanks." *Adams. Burr. Jefferson.* Eighteenth-century WASP aliases for twenty-first-century punks. Dee wondered if they even knew who the originals had been.

The Adams was a sex-show-and-fizz club that wouldn't even open until midnight. Dee went back to her motel and shopped again, this time for a cheap e-dress that shimmered strategically on and off around her body. Then she slept.

At one in the morning Betsy Jefferson started to perform. She was older than Perri, and older than she looked, gyrating her aging flesh through stage sequences as repulsive as anything Dee had seen when she'd worked Vice. Dee, her dress on full coverage, tried to picture Perri in this setting. She failed. Eliot was right: Perri's fuck-ups had a quality of innocence foreign to the Adams, with its forced glitter and real sadism. Perri fucked up irresponsibly but not cruelly. When Betsy finished, blood from a dead monkey smeared the stage and her own naked body.

Dee sent a note backstage and the bouncer let her through. Betsy stood in a basin of water sluicing herself down. "Hi. I'll be done in a minute."

"Thanks for seeing me."

Off-stage and covered, Betsy Jefferson looked even older and much wearier. "Perri talked about you. She looked up to you. You still work with homeless babies?"

Actual discretion on Perri's part. Dee was grateful. "Yes. But it's Perri I'm here to talk about. You know she was arrested on GMFA."

"Yeah." Betsy didn't meet Dee's eyes. "I heard."

"She's disappeared. Got away from a federal marshal. Fucked her way free."

Betsy smiled. "Yeah? Good for her."

"I think so, too. But I'm worried, Betsy, because she's flatline broke. I want to give her money so she can go underground armed and flush."

Betsy nodded. "She said you always took care of her."

"And I always will. Do you know where I can find her? Has she turned up anywhere back on the beach?"

"Not that I heard."

"Then do you know where I can find 'Mike'? The guy that got her the abortion on the ship?"

"She told you about that, yeah?"

"Perri tells me everything," Dee said. "She knows I just want to take care of her."

"Yeah, she said. And you're fucking right about one thing. Without money, she won't last long here."

"That's what I figured."

Betsy studied Dee. Dee didn't have to fake concern. Abruptly Betsy said, "Perri never worked no place like this, you know."

Dee was silent.

"She didn't have to, with her looks. Wouldn't have done it anyway. I told her to go back to you and get a decent life."

"Thank you. Too bad she didn't listen," Dee said. For the first time, she saw why Perri had trusted Betsy, saw what wasn't totally extinguished in the older woman. Dee wondered if Betsy had ever had any kids of her own. Who was Perri substituting for?

"You won't find Mike, Dee. Not unless he wants to find you."

"Can you make it so he does?"

"Maybe."

"I really want Perri to have the money. It's a lot. All I've saved."

"Where you staying?"

Dee told her, and Betsy made a face. "Okay. Go back to Queens."

"Back to *Queens*?"

"Look," Betsy said, "You're new at this. Mike ain't here anymore, not after Perri's arrest. Perri ain't here, either, or I'd of heard about it. People know I sort of looked out for her. But I know Mike, Mike knows people, people get around. Give me your address in Queens and go home."

Dee had wacoed it. Her first contact on the beach and she'd exploded the possibility of more. If she didn't go back to Queens, Betsy would hear about it and question why. Word would get around much faster than Dee could. Nobody would talk to her. Nobody.

"Thanks," she said, smiling at Betsy.

\* \* \*

At her sentencing Perri stood ashen and dry-eyed. She wore a loose gray coverall so old and laundered that the tired cloth draped softly around her body. With her hair unstyled she looked incongruously virginal, a maiden in innocent distress. Dee, the only spectator in the court, grasped the ancient wooden railing so hard that its oily grime became embedded in the creases of her palms. The courtroom was on half AC; apparently somebody had decided that federal judges deserved some relief from New York air, despite the exorbitant cost of all emissions-creating energy. Even so, Dee couldn't breathe.

Eliot had made a deal with the feds. Dee suspected it had cost him all his markers. Perri pleaded guilty to class three genemod possession.

"The court has considered the federal prosecutor's recommendations in this case," the judge said in a bored voice, "and accepts them. Six months in prison, no time off for good behavior, followed by six years probation. Counselor, do you have anything to add?"

"No, your honor," Eliot said.

"Bailiff, remove the prisoner."

And that was all. Dee had seen it, participated in it, how many times? Dozens, maybe hundreds. But this was Perri.

"I love you, Dee!" she called as she was led away, and her attempt to smile for her sister's sake cauterized Dee's heart.

"You can visit next month," Eliot said somberly.

"If she's still alive by next month."

He was practical. "Did you put the maximum amount allowable in her prison account?"

"Of course," Dee snapped. "I know how the system works."

"Unfortunately," Eliot said. "Buy you lunch?"

"No. You stay inside—it's a bad air day," Dee said brutally. "I'm going home."

"Dee...I did the best I could."

He had. She was too enraged to give that to him.

At home she checked the non-traceable money chips hidden in her apartment, plus the legal surveillance equipment and illegal nerve gas. When Mike showed up, she would either buy her way to the ship, and to evidence for a legal appeal, or bring him down herself and let the authorities pursue it. Once they had a live body, they might actually do that. Maybe.

The money was safe. As she had done every night for a week, Dee swallowed the foul drink that would neutralize the nerve gas in her own lungs for twelve hours. Military stuff, it was highly illegal for her to have it. She no longer cared.

Then she tried to sleep.

The air was exceptionally bad today. Choked with greenhouse gases, $CO_2$ pushing maybe point seven-five, when had it gotten this bad? She was having trouble breathing, *she couldn't breathe....*

Dee awakened strangling. Cord bound her neck, her legs, her arms...no, one arm was still free. Desperately she worked a finger between her neck and the tightening cord; it gave slightly and she was able to pull it far enough away from her neck to gasp in a breath of fetid air. But that would only work for a moment, her assailant was sure to...

There was no assailant. She was alone in her apartment, strangled by tough green stems that had almost buried her in foliage. Dee screamed once, but then her cop reflexes kicked in. She flexed everything to see what was loose and found a frond not yet wrapped completely around both her body and her bed. She contorted her body so that her free hand, without removing the index finger from under the noose at her neck, brought the loose frond to her teeth, her only available weapon. She bit hard.

The stem parted and fell into two parts. She grabbed wildly with her limited reach for another stem. They were growing...she could actually *see* the stems growing around her in tiny, fatal increments. She bit through a second stem and filled her mouth with bitter leaf. What if it was poison? Don't think about it now. She bit another stem.

Writhing on the bed, half-pinned, Dee fought the mindless green with everything she had. At one point she thought she'd lost; there were too many tendrils. But the plant *was* mindless. By calculating where the worst danger was and working her way doggedly toward that point, by reason and strength and sheer luck, she got a hand free enough to break the glass of water by her bedside and attack with the broken glass. Blood streamed over sheets, leaves, herself.

She was free. She rolled off the bed, leapt away, and collapsed on the floor, panting.

From here, the plant looked to be growing much more slowly. No more than six inches an hour.

Six inches an hour. She didn't know that even the underground genemod labs had achieved that. Splice phototropism genes to growth ones, maybe? She didn't know. She didn't want to know. She had almost died.

The nutrient box sat under the bed, maybe two feet square, tilted toward the big south window that was the reason she'd taken the apartment. It hadn't been there when she'd gone to bed. Whoever had put it there had known how to disable the surveillance equipment and nerve gas. The plants had probably grown slowly, if at all, until dawn. Then the light had driven their super-efficient energy use to put everything into growth, a riotous deadly burst of it that had depleted them utterly. Already the oldest leaves were turning yellow at the edges. Live hard, grow fast, die young.

Dee looked for the patch. She found it on her ankle, peeled it off. Whatever had dripped into her bloodstream had kept her knocked out far into the light-rich morning. It was almost noon.

She crouched on the floor and watched the spent kamikaze plant die.

"And the money was still there," Eliot said.

"Not touched."

"So they just wanted to kill you."

"Head of the class, counselor," Dee snarled. She was still shaky. They sat in a coffee shop near Dee's building. The air was very bad today; some people wore masks even indoors. The room was stifling. Dee could remember when air conditioning didn't cost the Earth. Literally.

She continued, "I want to know what's best to do, Eliot. If I call the authorities and take them up to see the evidence of a murder attempt, will it help Perri's appeal?"

"I don't see how," Eliot said. He pulled his sticky shirt away from his chest for a moment. "You can't prove who did it, or even that the murder attempt was in any way connected to Perri's experiences. Yes, it was a genemod weapon, but that doesn't link it to any specific illegal organization."

"God, do you suppose I've got legions of people out to kill me? Who else could it be?"

"You're an ex-cop," Eliot said. "I don't have to tell you that ex-cops get deviled by people they arrested and sent to jail, sometimes years after the fact. There are a lot of crazies out there. Your 'evidence' is circumstantial, Dee, and barely that. There's no solid link."

"And what would be a 'solid link'? My actually turning up dead?"

"Not that, either. Dee, you're being stupid. You of all people ought to know that you can't play in this league. You just can't."

"And the FBI won't."

"Only if they just happen to stumble across it. Otherwise it's too small for them, and too big for you. *Give up, Dee.* Do you want to go with me to see Perri this afternoon?"

Dee grew still. "I thought she couldn't have visitors for the first month."

"Doesn't apply to me. I'm her attorney. I'll get you in as part of her legal team."

"Yes. Oh, yes."

Eliot opened his mouth as if to say more, closed it again. He finished his coffee.

Dee sat silent on the train to Cotsworth, preparing herself. Even so, it was a shock.

"Hello, Dee. Eliot," Perri said. She succeeded in smiling through her swollen lips. One eye was completely closed with bruises. Even in the prison coverall it was obvious she'd lost weight.

"Perri...Perri." Dee pulled herself together. "I told you not to fight back. With anybody."

Eliot said gently, "Guards or inmates?"

"Both. Eliot, don't file any complaints. It'll only make it worse on me."

He didn't answer. He knew she was right. So did Dee, but rage rose in her throat, tasting of acid.

Eliot said, "I've filed an appeal, Perri."

She brightened. Dee knew the appeal would be denied; there were no grounds. But anything to give her sister a little hope in this hell.

And Perri was magnificent. She chatted with Dee and Eliot. She asked after their lives. She did everything possible to pretend she was not in pain and despair. When the short visit was over, and all the checkpoints had been passed, Dee turned to Eliot.

"Don't ever tell me again to give up. Not ever."

She looked two places: the activists and the criminals. She was looking for the overlap.

The environmental activists were not as numerous or as angry as they'd been before the Crisis, for the simple reason that they'd won. Dee understood that. She also understood what had to be their next move: semi-underground activism.

It went like this: You spend your life driven by the desire to outlaw genetic engineering, and then it's outlawed, and you're spiritually unemployed. For a while you try other causes, but it's not the same. So you organize groups to attack suspected genemod violations, on the grounds the authorities are (pick one) lazy, corrupt, stupid, burdened by bureaucracy. You then can spend time ferreting out illegal labs and farms and destroying them. You're back in the game. Of course, you're also vigilantes and thus must fight the cops as well as the violators, but for a certain type of person, this only makes it more interesting.

Dee started with New Greenpeace. At her first meeting she met a woman angry enough to be a good candidate for "subversive projects." The woman, Paula Caradine, was suspicious of Dee, but Dee was used to suspicious informants.

"Why are you interested in subversion?" Paula asked. She was stocky, plain, very intense.

"My sister's in jail for a genemod offense she didn't commit. She was framed."

"Oh? What's her name?"

"Perri Stavros. I'm Demetria Stavros. I used to be a cop with the NYPD. Perri's conviction changed things for me. The FBI isn't getting the job done right, even though they've got the Act now, or Perri wouldn't be Inside and the polluters Outside."

Paula said, "Nothing's going on right now," which was probably a lie. Dee was used to being lied to. Everybody lied to cops: suspects, witnesses, victims. It was a fact of life on the street. Paula said no more, which was a good sign. She'd have Dee and Perri checked out, find out Dee's story was true. It was a start. Building informants was a slow process.

In Manhattan, they were already built, at least the ones that hadn't been killed or been jailed or died of "environmental conditions." Dee had only been retired a year. However, a week of networking and bribery turned up nothing but the usual empty lies. Then she turned up Gum.

Nobody knew how old he was, not even Gum himself. He had purplish melanomas on his bald head and exposed arms. Disease, or sunlight, or bad luck. He refused medical treatment, air masks, false teeth. Gum lived everywhere, and nowhere. He remembered life before the Crisis, before the business flight from Manhattan, maybe before the turn of the century. He was old, and stinking, and dying, and his sheer survival this long had earned him a sort of mythic dimension, like a god. There were punks and scars and hyenas in the Park who actually believed that killing Gum would bring horrible retribution. Although Dee had trouble imagining anything more horrible than the life they were already leading. The Park, along with several other sections of Manhattan, had slipped completely beyond police control. No cop would go there, ever, for any reason.

Dee caught Gum in a bar near the rotting East River docks, on a street unofficially declared a neutral zone. "Hey, Gum."

He peered at her blankly. Gum never recognized anybody overtly. Dee suspected he had an eidetic memory.

"It's Dee Stavros. With the NYPD."

"Hey."

"You want a soda?" Gum never drank alcohol.

"Hey." He hauled himself onto a stool next to her.

"Gum, I'm looking for somebody."

Gum said in his cranky, oldman voice, "I been looking for God for a hunnert years."

"Yeah, well, let me know if you find Him. Also a guy who could be calling himself 'Mike.' Or not. Runs a genemod illegal on a ship. Also does abortions there."

"Abortions?" Gum said doubtfully.

"Yeah, you know, rape-and-scrapes. Women's stuff. You hear anything about that?"

"A hunnert years," Gum said. "He went missing."

Gum meant God, not Mike. Gum only talked when he was ready.

"You hear anything, I'd like to know about it." She slipped him the money chips so unobtrusively not even the bouncer saw it.

"Just went missing, left us like this."

"Don't I know it, Gum."

"A hunnert years."

She went to another activist meeting, worked more on Paula Caradine. Before anything could happen, Eliot called her. His voice had the ultracontrolled monotone that a lot of lawyers used for something really serious.

"Dee, I want you to see something. Meet me at the genemod evidence center in an hour. You know where it is?"

"Of course I know where it is. Can you say—"

"No." He clicked off.

The Genetic Modification Felony Actions Evidence Center for Greater New York was in Brooklyn. It was another bad air day; Dee wore her mask for the entire trip plus the fifteen minutes she hung around outside. No admittance to the heavily guarded building without five million authorizations. Finally Eliot showed up ("Another breakdown on the subway"), got them inside, and was shown to an e-locked room. Dee recognized the negative-pressure signs in this whole wing. Nothing, not even spores, could drift out. She and Eliot had changed into paper coveralls. They would have to go through decontamination to get out again.

Eliot keyed the e-locked door and it opened.

Dee gasped. Years of training couldn't weigh against this. The single plant sat in the middle of the small room. A bush as tall as Dee's shoulders, it had broad, very pale green leaves on woody branches. In the center of each leaf was a closed human eye. Eliot turned up the light and the eyes opened.

Perri's eyes.

Each one was the startling blue-green that Dee had never seen on anyone else. Their pupils turned toward the light source. A hundred eyes, moving in unison, blind.

"The evidence biologist explained it to me," Eliot said. "The eyes are light-sensitive but they can't actually see. They're not wired up to any brain. There's a human eye gene, 'aniridia,' that can be introduced onto animals in weird places, insect wings or legs, and they'll grow extra eyes. Nobody knew you could put it into plants."

"*Why?* What is it?"

"It's an art object," Eliot said grimly. "A sculpture. Apparently the artist is well-known in the underground circles that traffic in these things. He's in custody."

"Mike—"

"Was the supplier, of course. The eyes were grown from the stem cells from Perri's aborted fetus. Stem cells are easiest to grow into any organ. But the so-called artist is refusing to talk. On advice of attorney."

"Will he deal? If you offer enough?"

"I can't offer anything, Dee. It's not my case. But no, I don't think he'll talk. More and more of these genemod illegals are being acquired by organized crime. The FBI and NYPD have just established a joint task force on illegals. The artist would rather face the court than face the mob."

"But it's obvious these are Perri's genes! They can do a DNA match!"

"Why bother? You can't prove she didn't give Mike the tissue, or sell it to him. It doesn't clear her at all. I just thought you ought to see that the chances of getting Mike on other charges have gone way up. He's connected to the artist who's connected to the mob, so Mike is going to get serious attention. They'll get him if they can."

Dee faced him. "I don't want revenge. I want Perri freed."

"Are you sure you don't want revenge? Perri's told me a bit about her childhood. You overprotected her, Dee. You made her feel the entire world is dangerous."

"It is."

"But you also taught her she can't cope with it without you. That without you, she's bound to screw up. And like a good daughter, she's been proving you right ever since."

"She's not my daughter, and—"

"She might as well be. You were the only mother she had."

"You don't know jack shit about it!"

"I know what Perri's told me."

Dee demanded, "You see her? A lot?"

"Every chance I can. Don't look like that, Dee. She's not a child anymore, and as you just pointed out, you're not her mother."

"Fuck you, Eliot. You're fired. You're not Perri's attorney any more."

"That's not your decision," Eliot said.

"I pay her bills!"

"Not this one." His gaze was steady.

Dee strode toward the door. Going through it, she slapped off the light. The blue-green eyes on the pale leaves, Perri's eyes, blinked and closed.

"We're hitting a farm tonight," Paula said abruptly. "You can come along."

"I checked out, huh?" Dee said.

"Why didn't you mention that the bastards tried to kill you with a bio-weapon?"

"I thought I'd give you something to research," Dee said. She hid her surprise that "the group"—pretentiously, they had no other name—had turned up the attack in her apartment. They were better connected than she'd thought. No official police report had been filed.

"We meet here at two A.M." Paula said. "Wear dark clothing that covers your arms and legs with at least three layers of cloth, and good boots. We'll supply gloves and mask."

"Got it. Paula…thanks."

"I know how it is," Paula said cryptically. Dee didn't ask what she meant.

Sixteen people, packed into two vans with blackened windows and an opaque shield between driver and passengers. No names, faces behind masks; Dee wouldn't be able to identify anyone except Paula. They rode for at least forty minutes at variable speeds. When the van stopped, they could have been anywhere.

"Stay in single file," their "group leader" said. He led them through the darkness, one flashlight in the front of the line, off the road through a small woods, then across at least three open fields divided by strips of underbrush. Finally the line halted.

The genemod farm was an acre lot of saplings. Sold as transplants, Dee guessed. Genemod illegals had learned not to fence or firewall their farms; it attracted too much aerial-surveillance attention. To Dee these saplings looked like any other stand of young trees. What were they genemod for? It didn't matter. Their creation was the kind of irresponsible activity that had caused the Crisis, when one food crop after another had been wiped out by fast-growing, herbicide-resistant, genetically created "super-plants" with no natural enemies. The kind of irresponsible activity that had, in the end, caused most of the Midwest to endure the controlled burn. The kind of irresponsible activity that had ruined agribusinesses, spurred hoarding, and weakened an already staggering economy.

The kind of activity that had jailed Perri.

"Chop each tree clean through at the base," the leader instructed. "Don't work on adjacent trees or you risk cutting each other. Be quiet and quick. The acid team is right behind you."

Dee took the row of trees he gave her. She buzzed her saw through its base, surprised at the savage pleasure it gave her. The air filled with muted buzz (much of the sound was white-noised somehow) and with the sharp smell of the acid poured over the fallen limbs and rooted stumps. Dee felt energy flow into her as she destroyed the crop. Over the havoc she listened for the sound of defending copters or guns, but no one came. She laughed aloud.

"What's so funny?" Paula said, on the next row.

"I just remembered something. An old poem. 'Only God can make a tree.'"

"Huh," Paula said. "Forget poetry and just saw."

Dee sawed, every vibration a vicious joy. When they were done, the activists slipped over the fields to the vans. Behind them, the carefully created grove lay in acrid burned waste.

"I found him," Gum said.

Dee tensed. It had taken a long time to locate Gum again. She'd finally found him inside the base of the Brooklyn Bridge, living with a group of people armed with shoulder-launched missiles of some type. Where the hell had they gotten them? The things looked military. The whole setup was one Dee would never have approached at all if two different informants hadn't said Gum was there. One, heavily bribed, had had the email address. An electric cable snaked across the ground and into the bridge, undoubtedly stealing very expensive energy until the power company discovered it. No longer Dee's problem. She emailed Gum, and at the appointed hour he emerged from the Bridge looking as dirty and demented as ever.

They sat on packing crates set a hundred yards from the Bridge in an empty lot strewn with broken glass, rags, unidentifiable chunks of metal. Dee counted six rats in two minutes.

"Where is he?" she asked Gum.

"Everywheres. Nowheres. Gone and back. A hunnert years."

"Not God, Gum! I thought you found Mike!"

"Gone and back. A hunnert years."

Dee held on to her temper. This visit was too important, and too dangerous, to ruin. She waited.

Finally Gum said, "He watches Mike. He watches me. He watches you. He knows."

"What does He know, Gum? Will you tell me so I can know, too?"

"He knows Mike din't do it. The plants."

"Mike didn't take my sister to a ship illegal with genemod plants?"

"Oh, yeah. Praise the Lord."

"Mike did take Perri to a genemod illegal?"

"Oh, yeah," Gum said. Rheum oozed from his filmy eyes. "Gone and back."

"He took her to the ship and he sent her back. But where is Mike now?"

"God sees."

Dee put her hands on her knees and leaned forward. Another rat ran across the lot. Closer to the Bridge a man stood holding a rifle and looking right at her. "Gum, what are you doing with these people who live in the Bridge?"

"A hunnert years. Straight to God."

"You're their priest," Dee said. It seemed unlikely, but not impossible. Since the Crisis, a hundred weird religions had sprung up to explain the Earth's new harshness, atone for the Earth's new harshness, find hope in the Earth's new harshness, all kinds of shit. Even criminals, it seemed, could believe in God. Some sort of God. And it might explain what Gum, old and mumbling and shambling, was doing with these well-equipped felons who frankly scared the fuck out of Dee. Priesthood might explain it. Or it might not.

Gum said, "He din't do it."

"God?"

"Mike."

"What didn't Mike do, Gum?" They were going in circles.

"He din't send that plant to kill you in your apartment."

Dee's breath stopped. "Do you know who did?"

"T'other side. A hunnert years."

"Gum, what other side? Who sent the plant to kill me?"

"Look to God," Gum said, and lurched to his feet.

Dee stood and grabbed at him. "You can't go now! You have to tell me the rest!"

The old man tried to pull free. The guard raised his rifle. Hastily Dee released Gum. As he shuffled away, she called after him, "What other side, Gum? Who sent the plant?"

"It was in all the newspapers," Gum said over his shoulder. "You was dead."

"Gum…"

He was gone.

* * *

She kept at her informants, getting the word out, spending her savings on sweeteners. She went on another raid with Paula's group, destroying another open farm in Jersey. She visited Perri at Cotsworth, and each time Perri was thinner and quieter and walked with more difficulty. Dee papered the Correctional System with complaints and charges and anger, and none of it brought any changes whatsoever.

Paula's group hit an arboretum in Connecticut. Under thick plastic grew bed after bed of lush foliage genemod for...what? It didn't matter. By now, Dee wasn't even curious. To get into the arboretum they had to blow open the glass with semtex. Instantly alarms wailed. They tossed in the flamers and scattered. Dee, following her instructions, circled widely to the left and ran through an underroad culvert full to her knees with stinking water. Spider webs tore from the roof onto her face. Lights raked the area from a tower she hadn't known was there, and she could hear a copter roaring closer. But she made it to the van and back onto the highway and all the way to her apartment.

Only later did she hear that two activists died in the raid. One of them was Paula.

The next evening Eliot called. "Jesus Christ, Dee, what the fuck are you *doing*?"

He knew about the raid. No, impossible, how could he know? Then he'd heard about her working the street. Dee said nothing.

"How could you go down to see Perri and then gouge into her about what a screw-up she is? 'You made bad choices, you've messed up your life, this prison time will follow you around forever'...how *could* you, Dee?"

"It's all true."

"So what? She's barely hanging on in that hell-hole and she doesn't need you to go in there and—"

"How the fuck do you know what she needs? I've taken care of her since she was two years old!"

"And you've made her believe she can't take care of herself without you. *You* screwed up her life if anyone did. So stop this—"

Dee slammed her fist into the OFF key. She raged around the one-room apartment until her own fury scared her. Then she tried to calm down: deep breathing, lifting weights, a cup of hot tea. At midnight she finally slept.

At three she jerked awake. Someone was in the apartment.

Her hand slid under the blanket for her gun. Before she could grasp it, both arms were jerked above her head and cuffed. The light went on.

He took off his night-vision hood and pulled a chair beside her bed. Silently he studied her. He was medium height and build, late thirties, brown eyes. Hair the color of a yellow flower. Dee stared back, refusing to show fear. She said, "You're Mike."

"Yes. Although the name is Victor."

She snorted and he smiled. "No, really. You don't look much like Perri, Dee. Come on, we're going out."

She began to scream. The walls were thin; someone would hear. Immediately Victor slapped a gag strip over her mouth. He pulled off her blankets and cuffed her ankles, ignoring her kicks. Wrapping her in the blanket as if she were sick, he lifted her easily and carried her, a dead weight, down three flights of stairs. He was much stronger than he looked.

A car waited at the curb. Dee thought, incongruously, *how long since I rode in a car?* Years. Cars were emission-producing demons. People destroyed them like cockroaches. Only emergency vehicles were exempt, and this powerful sleek car was no emergency vehicle.

They drove through the empty, pot-holed streets, Victor and Dee in the back and the unseen driver behind a shield in the front. Victor removed her gag.

"Dee, no one is going to hurt you." Oh, right, as if she believed that. "There's something I want you to see."

"Why?"

"Good question. I guess because I hate waste. You've wasted a lot of time raiding genemod illegals and harassing ineffective authorities and putting out the word on me throughout Manhattan. Is that ankle cuff too tight for comfort?"

"No. It's Perri whose time is being wasted."

"I'm sorry about that. There was never any intention that she be charged with anything. I had no idea she'd take a genemod plant."

"You merely took her fetal tissue," Dee said.

"Yes. It's the best tissue for human genetic engineering, you know. Stem cells are malleable, the amniotic sac grows organs well, the placenta…but I don't think you're interested in scientific details. It should have been a mutual gain. Perri wanted to abort, I wanted the tissue."

"To create plant 'art' that has her eyes."

"No," Victor said. He shifted on the back seat of the car. "I don't dabble in decorative perversity. I sell the girls' fetal tissue to whoever can pay well for it. Our real work requires money. No, don't ask questions now. I want to show you." And, incredibly, he leaned into a corner of the car and went to sleep.

Dee tested the door, her bonds, the seat belt. Nothing gave. Victor snored softly. She could probably kick him with both feet, but belted in like this, it would be a kick so feeble as to be pointless. Slack, his face looked oddly older. Forties, maybe. Even through her fear and outrage, he puzzled her. Something was off about him. He didn't seem like any criminal she'd ever seen, not even the smooth-talking, easy-sleeping sociopaths.

The car stopped. Victor woke and carried Dee along a deserted dock. A remote boat waited, barely big enough for the two of them. Victor untied the mooring lines and pressed a hand-held, and the boat took off silently across the dark water.

The night was cloudy. Dee could see various lights, but she had no idea what they were. Ships? Land? Buoys? A wind blew and the sea became choppy. Water sloshed into the boat. Dee felt herself growing seasick.

Victor must have known the signs. Expertly he held her head over the side while she vomited. "Almost there!" he called over the rising wind. Dee threw up again.

The storm looked ready to break in earnest by the time they drew up alongside what seemed to her a huge ship, completely dark. A metal basket was lowered and Victor dumped her into it. Dee hated feeling helpless. Almost she would rather be knocked out than trussed up and hauled in like mackerel or cod.

She got her wish. Someone on deck leaned into the metal basket and slapped a patch onto her neck. No way to dislodge it, and in ten seconds everything disappeared.

She woke in a narrow cabin as steady as if on land. Victor, looking much more rested, sat in a chair beside her bunk. Dee struggled for the dignity of sitting upright. "Where are we?"

"At sea. The storm passed while you were out. It's a lovely day." He lifted her and carried her into a narrow corridor where a wheelchair waited. The blanket slipped off her. Her pajamas smelled, but at least she'd been wearing them. What if she'd been naked when he kidnapped her? And what about her expensive, carefully installed nerve gas? This was the second time it had been disabled. Apparently all of underground New York had become security experts.

"I need to go to the bathroom."

"Yes. Just a minute." He wheeled her to another door, pushed the whole chair in, and closed the door.

Cursing, Dee stood up, still bound at wrists and ankles. She managed to get her pjs down and everything accomplished, after which there was no choice except to kick at the door.

"It's less stuffy on deck," Victor said cheerfully. Dee scowled at him.

It was less stuffy on deck. Also painfully bright. Sunlight glared off a blue ocean. If there hadn't been a breeze, the heat would have been unbearable. Dee said, "I can't stay out here long. I assume that you have on sunblock."

"So do you. Put on before you woke up. Anyway, we're almost there."

Where? Nothing but water in every direction. Dee folded her arms and said nothing. She wasn't going to cooperate in his elaborate games. If he killed her, he killed her.

She knew she wasn't really indifferent to death.

No one else appeared on this section of deck. Nor were the abundant plants that Perri had described anywhere in evidence. Maybe Victor thought that Dee, too, would steal one.

The ship moved over the ocean, although without reference points Dee had no idea how fast it was traveling. After about twenty minutes, Victor, who'd been lounging at the railing, straightened. "There. Four o'clock."

At first Dee saw nothing. Then she did. The sea was changing color, from blue to a dense, oily black. She said, "An oil spill?"

"I wish."

They drew closer. The blackness grew, until Dee could see it was actually a deep purple. It seemed to extend to the horizon. The ship moved a short way into the purple and stopped.

Victor lowered a grapple-looking thing over the side. "We can't go in any farther without risk to the screws. But aerial surveillance shows that the bloom already covers sixty thousand square miles. Do you have any idea how big that is, Dee? Half the size of New Mexico. Here, look."

He pulled up the grappler and held it toward her. It dripped what looked to Dee like seaweed; she was no marine expert.

"It's not ordinary seaweed," Victor said. "It's genemod. Made from altered bacteria. It replicates at ideal bacterial rate, which is to say it doubles every twenty minutes. It has no natural enemies. Nothing eats it. But it blocks sunlight almost totally, and so everything underneath it dies. Do you understand about the food chain, Dee? Do you know what happens if the oceans die?"

"Who made it?"

"Unknown. Best guess is that it was an accident, a mistake. It might have been designed to blanket Third World estuary breeding grounds of malaria-carrying mosquitoes. Or not. Anyway, it's out." Victor studied the dripping purple mass and Dee studied Victor. His expression was sad and thoughtful, not at all what she'd expected. How good an actor was he?

She said, "Did you put a genemod plant in my apartment to kill me?"

"No."

"Do you know who did?"

"No. But I can guess."

"Who?"

He laid the seaweed on the deck. "What would have happened if that genemod plant had succeeded in killing you, Dee?"

She snapped, "Don't play games with me. If it had killed me, I'd be dead."

"Right. Then what? Eventually somebody would have broken into your apartment, if only because your corpse would have begun to smell. A friend, your landlord, a neighbor…somebody. They'd have called the cops. The media monitor police reports, and genemod hysteria grows worse all the time. You'd have been a news sensation: 'Ex-Cop Murdered In Bed By Killer Engineered Plant!' Full re-creation sims on every channel."

*"Mike din't send that plant to kill you in your apartment,"* Gum had said. *"T'other side did. It was in all the newspapers. You was dead."*

Victor pulled a vial from his pocket. "The publicity would have aided anti-genemod funding as well as antigenemod feeling. It could have been GMFA supporters, it could have been one of the more fanatic of those activist groups you've gotten so fond of, it could have been a corporation that gains from public hysteria by keeping genemod products illegal."

"The government wouldn't—"

"I don't think so, either. Watch, Dee." Victor unstoppered the vial and poured it over the purple seaweed on the deck.

"I don't see anything." She was still shaken over Victor's casual list of people who might have murdered her.

"Wait a bit."

The purple seaweed began to dissolve. Only one corner of the mass, and then the reaction stopped.

"It's a genemod bacteria," Victor said. "It eats the bloom. Unfortunately, the toxins emitted by the dying bloom cells kill the eaters. But it's a start. Now that we have the right organism, we can go on tailoring it until it can successfully eliminate the entire bloom."

Dee stared at the seaweed. "And you created that? Here?"

"Yes. We did. Because we're not allowed to create it onshore."

"Victor, that doesn't make sense. Something like this, that could help clean up the ocean."

"And that will in turn replicate and, maybe, create its own crisis. Who knows the effect of releasing this unknown bacteria into the sea? That's what the activists say, and they're right. Only I happen to think that once the pomegranate seeds are eaten, the only cure is more genetically engineered pomegranate seeds."

"What? 'Pomegranates'?"

"Forget it. The point is, this is vital work that can't go forward if I, and people like me, have to spend half our time evading tracking by people like you. And like the FBI, of course."

She shifted in her wheelchair. The deadly sunlight was growing hotter. Victor noticed and took the handles of her chair, pushing it along the deck. "But, Victor, even if the United States won't or can't let you do this genemod work, then surely other countries— the oceans affect everybody!"

"True. And so does international trade. The Keller Pact forbids any trade with any country trafficking in genetically modified organisms…remember? A very popular piece of legislation in an election year. Even so, we get some surreptitious funding from a few foreign companies. Not much."

"But it isn't going to stop you."

"I can't let it stop me. Here you are."

They'd reached a section of deck with a remote boat winched up level with the railing. Victor dumped Dee into the tiny boat and pressed a button. The boat began to lower.

"Wait!" Dee called, panicked. "I can't take that much sunlight all the way back—the ultraviolet—"

"Yes, you can," Victor called down over the railing. "Your sunblock is genetically engineered. Good-bye, Demetria Stavros. Stop destroying the abundance that mankind creates in its new gardens and fields."

The boat detached itself from the winch, turned itself around, and took off. On this flat sea Dee wasn't sick. She noted the position of the sun; with that and the time elapsed before landing, maybe she could estimate where the ship had been. Although by that time, it would have already moved.

The involuntary boat ride was a long one. Dee had plenty of time to think.

* * *

When she entered the Cotsworth visitors' room, Eliot was already seated with Perri.

Dee scowled; this was supposed to be her time with her sister, not that self-righteous prick Eliot's. But then Dee looked again at Perri. Still thin, still sunken-eyed, but now Perri's amazing blue-green eyes glowed. Something had happened.

"Dee!" Perri said from her side of the table. "Eliot and I are engaged!"

Dee froze.

"Aren't you going to congratulate us?" Eliot said. She recognized the battle call in his voice.

"On what? Another screw-up for Perri, this time dragging you along with it? Or are you the one leading? You two can never make it work, Eliot, and you at least should have the experience and intelligence to know that."

"And why can't we make it?" Eliot asked in his attorney voice. Calm. Seeking information. Deceptive.

"You're too different! God, you're an upcoming defense lawyer and Perri is—"

"A criminal?" Eliot said. "A screw-up? That's what you just called her. Your own sister. What are you afraid of, Dee?"

" 'Afraid' my ass! Don't try any lawyer rhetoric on me!"

"You are afraid. You're terrified. You think you'll lose her, and then whose life will you periodically and heroically rescue from ruin to justify your own life?"

"You don't know anything about—"

"I know you've done it to Perri all her life."

"You think you—"

"Stop!" Perri shouted, loud enough that nearby inmates and their visitors stopped talking and turned to stare. The guard started toward them.

"Stop," Perri repeated, more calmly. "Dee, this isn't your decision. It's mine. Eliot, be quiet. I can justify my own decisions to my sister."

The guard said, "Problem here, counselor?"

"No," Eliot said. "Thank you."

Perri said, "Dee, I wrote you something. Take it. And I'm going to marry Eliot." She held out a small, tightly folded piece of paper toward Dee. On her left hand sparkled a diamond ring.

"Don't tell me I can't wear the ring in here without somebody stealing it," Perri said. "I know that. Eliot will take it with him. But in another three months I'll be out, if I keep my nose clean. I can last that long. I can do this, Dee."

*But I can't*, Dee thought, and was suddenly afraid to know what she meant. She turned away. "I'm going, Perri. I'll see you next time."

"All right," Perri said softly. Not panicking at Dee's anger, not pleading with her to stay. Not needing her.

Dee passed through the tedious series of prison gates, checkpoints, locked areas. Outside, she walked toward the train. The air wasn't too bad today, but it was very hot. She thought of Victor, out on the open sea, working to engineer an organism to stop the death of the oceans. To bring more changes, but different ones, known in purpose but not in consequence. How long would it take? *A hunnert years*, Gum had rambled. But even Dee, no scientist, knew that a hundred years would be far too long.

She unfolded Perri's note. To Dee's surprise, it was a poem:

> *Another love. I am weary of*
> *The starts of things. Too many springs,*
> *Too little winter make a bitter*
> *Everlasting yellow-green.*
> *Stop. Enough. Let harvest come.*

She hadn't even known that Perri wrote poetry.

Waiting for the train, Dee put her hands over her face. She didn't know who was right. Victor, changing whole ecologies like some sort of god. Paula's friends, preserving through destruction. The FBI, blindly enforcing a popular, vindictive law. Which one was bitter spring, which one healing winter? Dee couldn't tell. No more than she could tell if Eliot's terrible accusations about her were true. When was love actually destruction? Could he be so sure that his love for Perri was not?

There was a raid tonight, a hit on a farm in Pennsylvania that engineered biomodified trees to increase photosynthesis capacity. Some of the trees, Dee's group leader had said, incorporated human genes as well as plant genes. Dee didn't know if that was true, either. She knew only one thing for sure.

She wasn't going on the raid. Not tonight, not ever.

Let harvest come.